This hunk was her *bodyguard*?

She'd expected a middle-aged, burly, balding fatherly type with a gut. Instead, this handsome devil with jet-black hair, dressed in a suit and tie and speaking with a light Italian accent, arrived like some kind of gift. And he'd loosened his tie at some point, which was like foreplay to Zoey.

"Archer," he said, following her to the counter of the store. He pulled on the lapels of his jacket. "Archer Rossi."

Of course he had to have a cool name like *Archer*. What kind of name was Archer? Then she thought of her favorite archer, the mythical winged cupid, based on the Greek god Eros, who shot arrows of love at intended targets. Surely this was some kind of cosmic joke...

AF796470

Dear Reader,

Welcome back to Charming, Texas! It's autumn in south Texas, and though the leaves are barely falling and fireplaces are only lit when the air conditioner is on too, the feeling of fall is in the air. And if there's atmosphere missing, just visit Zoey's boutique, where she has pumpkins, apples, leaves, and orange fairy lights twinkling in her window.

Zoey is that pumpkin-spice-latte-wielding, autumn-embracing friend you love! She lived a different life as a younger person, though, and now that past is sliding into her present. Enter Archer Rossi, her bodyguard.

For the first time, I've written a physically disabled hero. Archer is a below-the-knee amputee and wears a prosthetic. He's done the tough work of accepting his new reality, but entering into an emotional and physical intimacy was not on his bingo card.

I hope you enjoy their story!

Heatherly

A TEXAS HERO

HEATHERLY BELL

Harlequin
SPECIAL EDITION

If you purchased this book without a cover you should be aware that this book is stolen property. It was reported as "unsold and destroyed" to the publisher, and neither the author nor the publisher has received any payment for this "stripped book."

MIX
Paper | Supporting responsible forestry
FSC® C021394
FSC www.fsc.org

Harlequin® SPECIAL EDITION™

PLEASE RECYCLE THIS PRODUCT IS RECYCLABLE
Recycling programs for this product may not exist in your area.

ISBN-13: 978-1-335-47275-5

A Texas Hero

Copyright © 2026 by Heatherly Bell

All rights reserved. No part of this book may be used or reproduced in any manner whatsoever without written permission.

Without limiting the exclusive rights of any author, contributor or the publisher of this publication, any unauthorized use of this publication to train generative artificial intelligence (AI) technologies is expressly prohibited. Harlequin also exercises their rights under Article 4(3) of the Digital Single Market Directive 2019/790 and expressly reserves this publication from the text and data mining exception.

This is a work of fiction. Names, characters, places and incidents are either the product of the author's imagination or are used fictitiously. Any resemblance to actual persons, living or dead, businesses, companies, events or locales is entirely coincidental.

For questions and comments about the quality of this book, please contact us at CustomerService@Harlequin.com.

TM and ® are trademarks of Harlequin Enterprises ULC.

Harlequin Enterprises ULC
22 Adelaide St. West, 41st Floor
Toronto, Ontario M5H 4E3, Canada
www.Harlequin.com

HarperCollins Publishers
Macken House, 39/40 Mayor Street Upper,
Dublin 1, D01 C9W8, Ireland
www.HarperCollins.com

Printed in Lithuania

1 2 3 4 5 6 7 8 9 10 LIT 28 27 26 25

Bestselling author **Heatherly Bell** was born in Tuscaloosa, Alabama, but lost her accent by the time she was two. After leaving Alabama, Heatherly lived with her family in Puerto Rico and Maryland before being transplanted kicking and screaming to the California Bay Area. She now loves it here, she swears. Except the traffic.

Books by Heatherly Bell

Harlequin Special Edition

Charming, Texas

Overboard for the Holidays
The Ex Next Door
Her Fake Boyfriend
Once Upon a Charming Bookshop
A Charming Doorstep Baby
A Charming Single Dad
A Charming Christmas Arrangement
The Charming Checklist
Winning Mr. Charming
A Texas Hero

The Fortunes of Texas: Fortune's Family Secrets

Wedded to a Fortune

Montana Mavericks: The Trail to Tenacity

The Maverick's Christmas Countdown

Visit the Author Profile page
at Harlequin.com for more titles.

For Tyler, a California hero

Chapter One

Zoey Lambert was a true-blue romantic down to the seat of her soul. Valentine's Day only happened once a year, so naturally it wasn't enough. When she was twelve, she'd declared to her mother that September 14 would be called Sweetheart Day. Why September? Well, Zoey was also in love with autumn leaves, pumpkin spice and cozy fires. Autumn basically started on the first of September for her and fit almost precisely six months between one Valentine's Day and the next. She didn't have to wait an entire year to celebrate love.

Her friends laughingly called February through September Zoey's "Sweetheart Season."

More important to Zoey in many ways, it was also the rainy season. September was the time of year when rain started to fall in South Texas, and Zoey looked forward to this year-round. Out came her sweaters and boots. But as this year's September 14 approached, she had an ex who couldn't accept that she'd broken off her relationship with him. And to top it off, her ridiculously overprotective father had just hired her a *bodyguard*. Even for her father, this was going above and beyond.

"No!" Zoey whined over the phone. "I do *not* need a bodyguard."

"Don't you tell me what you need," her father said.

This was what she got for confiding in her father. She liked it best when he kept his nose out of her love life, and she kept hers out of his. But she'd visited him in Amarillo last month on his sprawling ranch and in a moment of weakness spilled the truth. Once more, she'd dated a man more obsessed with her father, NFL Hall of Famer Patrick "Patch" Lambert, than her. She'd had men want introductions to her father in the past, sure, but Scott had taken it to a whole other level.

Now her father had launched into uber-protective mode. He'd hired bodyguards since she was a small child and the media was all over him, after he'd been traded from the Cowboys to the 49ers for a short time. Everyone in her family had to have a bodyguard with them at all times, as Dallas Cowboy fans were incensed at his perceived lack of loyalty and he was worried for his family's safety.

"It's nothing I can't handle," she told him now.

"I know you think I'm an old man, but I know what happens to young ladies. I watch the documentaries. Violence from an intimate partner is the number one cause of death in young women."

Number *one*? That couldn't be right. Besides, she hadn't even been intimate with the man! It wasn't her fault he was delusional. She didn't want to give up her privacy just when she might meet someone new. On Sweetheart Day, hope always sprang eternal.

"Listen, I don't have anything to worry about. He'll get over me soon enough. I'm seriously not in any danger. Honestly, Daddy, I'm serious. I could take him."

He snorted. "Sorry, baby girl, but all the stats back me up. You're getting a bodyguard and that's final. He'll be there in a couple of days, so be nice to the man."

When her father started spewing stats, she knew for sure it was too late.

"I'll give you an out," he said, and Zoey's ears perked up. "Cancel your Sweetheart Day party and I'll cancel the bodyguard."

She'd cancel her annual event when South Texas got some natural autumn color, or when she could start a fire in her fireplace hearth without first having to turn on the air-conditioning. Which was to say never.

"I can't cancel! We do it every year and Scott isn't even invited."

"Doesn't mean he won't show up. Well, you think about canceling this year and let me know. All I care about is your safety."

Her father had to know he had Zoey dead to rights. She wouldn't give up Sweetheart Day.

"But where's he supposed to stay?"

"Give him the guest room in the other wing of the house."

"In my house?"

How was she supposed to get a date to come to her party with a bodyguard breathing down her neck?

"That's usually how this works. You remember the drill. Besides, you told me once that the house is too big for you… this is the perfect situation! Don't worry, it's just temporary. This year, you need the extra security because of Scott." He hung up with a quick "Love you. Bye."

Great. Zoey could look forward to an old man in a suit guarding her 24/7. Probably questioning her fashion and life choices, too, just like her father did. That ought to be fun. At times like these, she desperately missed her mother, who with her wit and courage would have talked Zoey's father off the ledge. She would have explained to him that

Zoey, at five feet ten inches, could take care of herself. "Conchita" Fernandez-Lambert, at five feet nothing, had ruled over their home when she had been alive, and Zoey's six-foot-five father had kowtowed to her. But she'd been gone four years now after a long battle with breast cancer. Zoey missed her all the time, but never so much as in September. For years, they were the only two people who celebrated September 14. Even her daddy thought it was dumb.

Zoey's phone buzzed and there was yet another message from Scott, who still hadn't bought himself the first clue:

Hey there beautiful, any chance you could meet me for drinks at the Salty Dog tonight? I'm starting to feel ignored.

Was he completely delusional? She had clearly told him, "*No thanks, Scott... I don't know you well enough to accept your marriage proposal but have a good day. I think it's best if we don't see each other again.*" Scott told Zoey he thought he loved her during their second week of dating. When Zoey told a man she loved him for the first time, it would be after an appropriate amount of time—say after several months of seeing each other, followed by introductions to her father. With Scott, she never got there.

After she broke up with him, he had continued to behave like nothing happened, sending emails and texts describing his increasing frustration that she'd "ghosted" him. But her dad didn't understand there was nothing even remotely dangerous about Scott. He was simply desperate and sad, and Zoey felt bad for him.

She responded now:

No thanks. I'm super busy with work and the upcoming holidays.

Then she did what she should have done weeks ago, before her father hired her a bodyguard. She blocked his number. Maybe that would work. Life was tough with a big heart, and some people tended to ramrod right over her. But the right man wouldn't. She just had to find him. He'd be at least as tall as her, handsome and preferably Italian. She had a thing for Italians, especially those with sexy accents. Around here, all she ever heard was a slow Southern drawl. Incredibly sexy to many women, but mostly those who hadn't grown up in Texas.

Moving to her back storage room in Glamtique, the boutique she'd owned for the past few years, Zoey grabbed a box from the top shelf. It was marked, like all the others, with yellow, red and orange hearts and leaves. At home, she'd already decorated, but some folks got a little funny about starting seasons too early. And she had to face the fact that not everyone was in love with love. She'd patiently waited until after September 1 to decorate the store, and the day had finally arrived.

The chime over her shop door rang and Zoey rushed to the front. Ever since wealthy ad executive Lauren Montez had started shopping there almost a year ago, her sales had gone up. Even Tippy, the town's mayor, had been in last month for something to wear to the inaugural gala in November.

"Zoey, you here?"

The voice was that of her best friend, Twyla Cavell, who owned the bookstore, Once Upon a Bookshop. Years ago, Zoey's friends were other runway models but she was proud to say that most of her friends now were fellow business owners in their small town. She and Twyla went way back. They'd met during Zoey's first visit to Charming, when she'd stopped by the bookstore looking for the latest Harlequin romance novel. They'd bonded over books, and later, the quest for true love. Twyla was married to Noah now and had offered to help plan Zoey's annual Sweetheart Day party this year. Well, actually, she had begged. Zoey was a bit worried that Twyla didn't take this event as seriously as she did, because no one did. But it meant a lot to her to be able to help, so Zoey caved.

"I've got the invitations!" Twyla waved one in the air.

"You haven't sent them yet?" Something had *already* gone wrong. "It's September first!"

Twyla blinked. "This is just a formality. I sent a save-the-date out last month, remember?"

"Oh, right. Are they engraved?"

"From the same printer you use." Twyla set them on the counter near the register. "What do you think?"

They were orange and yellow, decorated beautifully with gold foil edges. They were nice enough to be wedding invitations.

You are cordially invited to celebrate a night filled with love.

Saturday, September 14, 2026
Sweetheart Day
A Night of Romance
6pm–midnight
At the home of Zoey Lambert

RSVP

"Oh. They're beautiful." Zoey sighed.

"Yay!" Twyla jumped up and down.

Zoey had to smile at her friend's enthusiasm. "I couldn't have done any better myself."

Christmas was Twyla's favorite holiday, but she had come around to appreciating the fall. Zoey had convinced her the season just needed a little help. Now it wasn't just about spiced pumpkin lattes and golden leaves, but also about love in its many forms.

Today, Twyla wore a gold-and-orange sweatshirt emblazoned with the punny saying, Fall I Want, and gold earrings in the shapes of leaves. She had officially come over to the autumn side. Zoey's work was done.

"And don't worry, I'm inviting a few singles, too."

Zoey always did the same. No better place to meet "the one" than a Sweetheart Day celebration. It was the kind of story you could tell your grandchildren. Zoey wouldn't be the only singleton. However, she wasn't feeling particularly optimistic about meeting someone new. Charming was a relatively small bedroom community along the Gulf Coast, not far from Galveston, Texas. Zoey loved almost everything about the quaint town with its renovated lighthouse, boardwalk, jetties, bay and beaches. She *didn't* love that all the best men her age were already taken.

"Love your dress," Twyla said, admiring the sleek gold-and-brown dress Zoey was wearing. "It must be rough to be so gorgeous you have to beat men off with a stick."

When Zoey made a face, Twyla backpedaled.

"Oh, no. He's not still bothering you, is he?"

"Nothing I can't handle. Unfortunately, my father doesn't believe me. He hired a *bodyguard* to watch me."

Twyla gaped. "You're kidding."

"My father has never met a statistic he can't use to his

advantage." Zoey grabbed Twyla's hands. "The stupid bodyguard is moving into my house and might still be here on Sweetheart Day! What am I going to do with a bodyguard at my party?"

"Don't worry, we'll figure something out." Then, Twyla pointed at her as if she had the answer. "Maybe we can make him the official doorman."

"Oh, yeah. That won't look weird at all." Zoey rolled her eyes.

"Well, maybe by Sweetheart Day Scott will have given up on you."

But if he hadn't given up by now, a couple of weeks probably wouldn't make much of a difference.

Chapter Two

Archer Rossi's foot hurt like hell, but he was still here at the appointed day and time of his ass-chewing. He'd sensed it coming like any alert soldier would. All the signs were there. Ian, his boss at Texas Executive Protection Management and head of the Houston Texas EP branch, wanted to see him. *In his office.* Yeah, maybe Archer had gone a little over-the-top on his first assignment, but he'd wanted to make a good impression. Instead, they'd pulled him off the job. With any luck, he wouldn't be fired today. He needed this job, his first one since arriving stateside after retiring from the U.S. Army. It was important to prove he could still do the work required of him.

"You can go inside, Mr. Rossi." The young assistant indicated the double solid oak doors. "He's ready for you."

Ian Jacobs, Regional Vice President read the nameplate on the door.

He was on the phone when Archer walked in, and waved for him to take a seat.

"Yes, sir. We're on it. I'll put my best man on the assignment."

Two more seconds and Ian hung up and gazed at Archer with a disappointed look, which said it all: He was not Ian's best man.

Archer cringed internally but told himself that was fine. He'd known he would have some adjusting to do when it came to the civilian world, but he hadn't expected it to be this difficult. He'd dealt with his foot, but he'd also been mentally cleared and regularly attended private therapy sessions to deal with some minor PTSD. His job involved danger and protecting others from it. Archer had a heightened sense of danger due to his training, so the job seemed perfect. Executive management protection was high-level security usually reserved for heads of state, celebrities and other high-profile individuals. But in his desire to show he was as capable as the others, he'd been too zealous and made a mistake.

"Why do you think I called you in here, soldier?"

"To chew me out, sir," Archer responded, and after a brief pause added, "But I am hoping you will not let me go."

"I'm not going to let you go." Ian shook his head. "You're a good man and I meant what I said. You have a career here if you want it, but we're going to have to find the best assignment to ease you into this."

"Sir, please do not put me behind a desk."

Part of the company focused on cybersecurity and assessing those threats; that wasn't what he'd signed up to do. Archer wasn't cut out for life behind a desk. He'd always been an adrenaline junkie and wanted to be on the front lines of any assignment. What's more, he was still perfectly capable, even after the accident. Being put behind the desk, to Archer, meant he was finished. Useless. He didn't see himself that way.

"No, that's *my* job." Ian said. "But you're going to need to calm the hell down. You can't do your job well if you view everything as a damn threat."

Good point. Archer wasn't sure how to respond to it. He

took a second to compose himself before he spoke. Every once in a while, particularly when under duress, Archer found himself slipping back into a slight Italian accent. He'd speak haltingly, too formally, sounding as if English was his second language. Which it was, of course, but he'd been in this country since age twelve. He rarely spoke Italian anymore, and if not for his mother, he would have forgotten the little Italian he still remembered.

"In my defense, I did not know the man was her brother."

"Yeah." Ian closed his eyes, leaned back in his chair and pinched the bridge of his nose. "I gathered that."

Archer had been part of a team involved with transporting a well-known reality TV celebrity who had received death threats, when a bulky man broke protocol and came at Archer's client, hand in the jacket of his pocket.

It all happened so fast.

"Gun!" Archer had shouted, before throwing his body over the man, knocking him to the ground.

There were screams, ensuing chaos, the client was whisked away in a car and in due order Archer found out the man was pulling out a *phone* not a gun. Not only that, he was the client's *brother*. Archer had imagined the gun; he'd preemptively acted and had done absolutely nothing to secure his client. If anything, he'd put her in danger by creating a huge distraction. Fortunately for him, the celebrity liked Archer. She'd convinced her brother not to sue him or the company and asked Ian to please not punish Archer, by pointing out that her brother could definitely be perceived as a threat. And though she'd wanted Archer back, the assignment was given to someone else.

"I get it," Ian said. "It makes sense. You're still adjusting. I think we might have put you in the middle of high-stakes action too soon. We'd just been raised to code orange, and the brother *is* huge, and he was coming at her suddenly. I spoke to the others and they all agreed. What I think you need is a little warm-up assignment. Something to show you where the real threats exist and *don't* exist in the civilian world. I've got just the thing for you."

"I appreciate this."

"Are you familiar with the town of Charming? It's a little beach town just south of Houston. About a thirty-minute drive or so, depending on traffic. I got a call from Patch Lambert."

"The NFL player?"

Archer wasn't much into football, more of a soccer guy himself, but he'd seen the player providing commentary on a postgame wrap-up show a few nights ago. Still sharp as they came, the former Dallas Cowboy player knew the game better than most.

"Yeah, that's the one."

"Problem with an obsessive fan?"

"Well, not exactly." Ian picked up a piece of paper and handed it over to Archer. "More like a new onslaught of hate mail, phone calls, and threats seemingly from someone upset about a statement he recently made on ESPN. Years ago, when Patch defected from the Cowboys to the Niners, he made a few enemies. Then he returned, and not long after, retired at the height of his game. Things were fine for a while, but now this. Somebody's sending death threats to Patch because he complimented the Niners defense and criticized the Chiefs."

Dio mio. American football fans were ridiculous.

"Sounds serious," Archer lied. "I'm on it."

"Hang on. The thing is, Patch already has a security detail. He wants a bodyguard for his only child, a daughter." Ian's finger traced a paper on his desk. "Zoey Lambert."

"Okay," Archer said slowly. "I understand. Sometimes you need a bodyguard for family members. Has she also received threats?"

"Not exactly." Ian winced. "There's an overzealous boyfriend involved, but none of us are taking that very seriously. Not even Patch. We've looked into it and the dude is harmless."

"I don't understand." Archer shook his head.

"Patch is being a rather sly father and using that as an excuse to hire a bodyguard for her. He's very protective of his daughter, and Zoey isn't exactly low profile. She throws a big party every September, apparently, which once got a mention in the local society papers. It has her father worried due to the timing of these threats. It would be easy to make the connection, and even if the threats are only directed at Patch for now, he's worried they might target her to get at him. And…he doesn't want her to know he's received death threats because it will only cause her distress."

"So what's my approach?"

"You'll be on-site security detail in her home. Stay on until Patch's security detail is satisfied there's no longer a threat."

This sounded like Archer's nightmare. He would be a glorified security guard for an entitled rich girl.

"I appreciate this, sir, but doesn't Ronan Sheridan live in Charming? Or have a fiancée or cousin who lives there? He might appreciate this one."

"Yeah, well, he's in Greece right now."

Damn. Ronan had been given the coveted assignment of being part of an elite team guarding a head of state. Archer understood he was too green for that one, but it was exactly what he wanted to do someday. Archer missed the feeling of being on edge, alert, feeling alive every moment—this job wouldn't give him that. But he had to swallow his pride and appreciate that at least he wasn't being let go.

"She owns a boutique called...um, Glamtique." Ian grimaced, reading over his notes. "You'll transport her to and from work."

A boutique? Was he going to have to stand like a *doorman* at a shop? Archer couldn't help but feel he was being punished. Probably because he was.

"Is there nothing else for me?"

Ian shook his head. "Do well on this one, and I'll graduate you to something better. I'm assuming this won't go on for long. The father already has his own security team in place. This is mostly just covering all the bases—a temporary thing."

"When she has a wealthy father?" Archer gave Ian a doubtful look. What were the odds it would be temporary?

Ian steepled his fingers. "His daughter, if I haven't mentioned, is *thirty.* How long do you think she'll tolerate a bodyguard spying on her every move?"

"So, this is not her idea." Archer smiled with relief.

"Not even a little bit. He had a difficult time talking her into it." Ian stood. "Whether she likes it or not, that's not our problem. We have a job to do. And I'm counting on you to do it well."

Archer didn't see a way out of this. He'd take the job, prove himself and go on to bigger and better things.

He reached across the desk to shake Ian's hand. "Sir, I will not let you down."

The next day, Archer packed a bag and drove from the condo where he'd been staying in Houston, to Charming, Texas. When he got off the highway, he took a scenic road along the seawall that drove him past the bay. He spotted a lighthouse in the distance and a boardwalk. If nothing else, the scenery lived up to the town's name. It might not be the worst thing in the world to hang out here for a while.

Last night, he'd given himself a pep talk. He just had to get through this big party of hers. He figured in about two weeks or less, the daughter would be so sick of his interference—or her boyfriend would be so jealous—that she'd beg her father to call off the dogs. She'd be tired of him in a week, and he would have shown himself to be a team player.

Archer arrived as scheduled to meet his client, who he expected would not be happy to see him. When he opened the door to the shop, the door chime rang in a tune that sounded like angels on high. A woman immediately greeted him with a smile, and Archer nearly swallowed his tongue. What were the odds this woman was his assignment? He couldn't *possibly* get that lucky.

This woman had long legs and wore a yellow shirt and matching skirt that accentuated every curve. Her dark brown hair fell around her gorgeous face in ringlet curls, and she had a smile that could stop time.

It could also stop the power of speech, apparently.

"Hi," she said. "I'm Zoey, the owner. Can I help you find something?"

Dio mio. He'd reached a new level of anxiety because now his *thoughts* were in Italian.

This had to be Zoey Lambert. He loosened his tie because suddenly it was way too hot in here.

When he didn't reply right away, she must have felt compelled to fill the silence. " I don't have very many male customers..." She looked behind him. "Are you alone?"

"Yes," he said, with a dry throat, tamping down his accent. "I work alone."

She laughed. "That's cute. Well, shopping can be considered *work* if you think of it that way. But I'm here to make it fun. I can direct you to a few one-of-a-kind items I carry. What size does she wear?"

"Size?"

She seemed to be…saying words…indicating she thought he was a customer. He should correct her, but he was too busy watching her glide across the floor like a dream.

"Yes. Dress size, or shoe size? You don't know?" She cocked her head and stared at him as if he was a simpleton. "Is she about my size?"

"Oh, um…uh…"

Why couldn't he just tell her the truth? *Speak, Archer!* Speak!

"She's probably shorter than me. I'm pretty tall for a woman. I've got some gorgeous vintage boots that just came in. Do you happen to know her shoe size at least?"

Archer was still staring at her. Any minute now, he'd think of something to say so she'd stop mistaking him for a customer.

He shook his head.

"Oh, well, you're not much help at all, are you?" She laughed and tossed her hair. "How about some jewelry? You can never go wrong with that, but unfortunately my pieces, while vintage, are costume. If you want something spendy like a diamond, you'll have to go to the jeweler."

She began to sort through necklaces, pulling out one with blue and greens stones set in gold, holding it up for him to inspect. Then she put it down and held up a sapphire ring. She quirked a brow, those chocolate brown eyes devouring his soul.

Archer held up a palm. "No, no. You do not understand. I am not here to buy anything."

"Then, what?" Understanding seemed to dawn in her eyes and she put the ring down and slowly backed up.

"Nice to meet you." He held out his hand. "I am Archer Rossi, your new bodyguard."

Zoey dropped the ring. "Oh, hell, no."

Chapter Three

Did the universe mean to tell Zoey that this hunk was her *bodyguard*? She'd expected a middle-aged, burly, balding fatherly type with a gut. Instead, this handsome devil with jet-black hair, dressed in a suit and tie and speaking with a light Italian accent had arrived like some kind of early Sweetheart Day gift.

She couldn't stop chatting, which was her fallback when nervous. *Mami, are you messing with me from heaven?* She'd been envying the lucky lady he'd come in to shop for, wondering why she had never met a man like this. But he was here for her. Well, not here for *her*. Here to perform a job for her father. Like most men she met, he was already indebted to her father. This time through actual employment and not hero worship, but either way. *Indebted.*

"There's been a mistake," Zoey said.

"I do not think so." He clasped his hands in front of him and slowly shook his head. "No mistake."

She held up a finger. "Let me make a call. I'll be right with you."

Her father answered on the first ring. "How are you, my baby gir—"

"Don't you 'baby girl' me! This man just showed up to my boutique saying he's my bodyguard. Arthur—"

"Archer," Archer said, having followed her to the counter. He pulled on the lapels of his jacket. "Archer Rossi."

Of course, he'd said that, but she forgot because her brain tended to go on hiatus when her hormones went into overdrive. And of course he had to have a cool name like *Archer*. What kind of name was that? Then she thought of her favorite archer, the mythical winged cupid, based on the Greek god Eros, who shot arrows of love at intended targets. Surely this was some kind of cosmic joke.

"That's who they assigned to your case. I didn't have a choice. It was whomever had availability." Her father paused. "Why? Are you worried about him? Should we ask him to be reassigned? Is he leering at you? Is that dirty old man *checking you out*?"

She wished…

"No! He is definitely not either one of those."

Archer's eyebrow arched…well, maybe it quirked.

"Because if you feel unsafe for one *instant*, I'll find someone else. All it takes is a phone call. But this agency comes highly recommended. It's run by former military men. I didn't think they'd send some old creep over."

No, indeed. And Zoey couldn't be responsible for this man being reassigned simply because she found him good-looking, and hence, a little intimidating.

Then there was that accent…

"Of course, not. That's not what I'm saying. He's definitely not a…"

Archer cocked his head.

"Okay, then, if I'm hearing you right, you're still not happy I hired a bodyguard. Well, too bad." She heard someone yell "Fore!" and her father cursed. "Time to tee up. Love you."

Zoey was still holding the phone when her father hung up.

"Is there a problem?" Archer said.

"Not really." Zoey put the phone away. "You're in the right place."

"But?"

"I just…to be honest, my father is overprotective. Simply put, I don't need a bodyguard but he got me one anyway."

"He sounds like my father," Archer said. "I have four sisters and he is very protective."

"Four sisters? *Four?*"

"We are Italian." He shrugged. "I am an American citizen, but my family came to this country when I was twelve. I was not born here, but three of my four sisters were. They act like they are better than the rest of us."

"Oh, no," Zoey said.

"That is a joke," Archer said with a slow, easy smile.

"Ah…hahaha." Zoey laughed while thinking, *God, I hope you're single.*

"Maybe you don't mind me here for a couple of weeks?" he said, and he adjusted his tie. "By then your father will feel more comfortable with your safety."

"Actually," Zoey said, a bit shamelessly. "I'm worried, too. A little. This guy I dated, for like a month, won't give up on me. But it's just texts and emails. Flowers. How can you arrest someone for being nice?"

"He is not being *nice*. It is about control. I can make sure this man gets the message," Archer said, and of this, she had no doubt.

"You're going to ask him to stop sending me flowers?"

"If that is what you want. But my main job is to make sure he does not come anywhere near you."

"I guess this is going to work after all." Time to go on a fishing expedition. "Where is your wife staying while you're in town with me? It must be hard for her when you go away on these assignments."

"What wife?" He shook his head, put up a palm. "No, I do not have a wife, so do not worry."

"Oh, I'm not worried." Zoey smiled.

"Good. I am not, either."

He smiled back, and this time his eyes crinkled. It was almost as if he knew. Zoey hoped not to make it so obvious she was crushing hard on this man.

She'd work on that.

For the rest of the afternoon, Archer stood like a sentry at the entrance to the shop. And, she realized, he was going to be great for business. Women had been coming in and out all day, mostly to browse, but they left with smiles on their faces.

"Oh, helloooo!" said Debbie, the head waitress at the Salty Dog Bar and Grill. "Are you new here?"

"Yes, I am." Archer nodded. "Archer Rossi, at your service."

The only thing lacking from the scenario was for him to bend at the waist and kiss her hand, but Debbie melted anyway.

"Hi, Debbie. Can I help you find something?" Zoey came around from behind the counter where she'd been counting receipts.

Debbie leaned over and whispered, "I had to come see for myself what all the fuss was about. I know you're a wiz at marketing, but this is genius. How much did it set you back to hire a model?"

If Zoey had been drinking anything, she would have spewed it out of her mouth.

"He's not a model."

"Oh, an actor looking for employment? He looks like that guy who was in the *Housemaid* movie and he has an accent. Oh, swoon!" Debbie fanned herself.

"Calm down," Zoey whispered. "And please, don't tell anybody, but…he's my bodyguard."

Debbie's eyes widened. "You have a bodyguard?"

"Unfortunately, yes. For now, anyway. You know my father?"

"That's like asking if I know who the Dallas Cowboys are," Debbie said. "Yes, I know Patch Lambert."

"He thinks I need a bodyguard because of Scott, and *of course* he's overreacting. But what can you do?"

Debbie took another scan of Archer and sighed. "Just grin and bear it, I guess."

"Exactly."

She and Debbie both turned at once and stared at Archer's backside. He stood, ramrod straight, as if he was guarding the president of the United States. Zoey admired a man who didn't think any job was too small to take seriously.

"Christmas came early," Debbie said.

"Preach." Zoey held out her fist to bump Debbie's.

When it was time to close up shop, Archer walked Zoey to her sedan so he could follow her home. Her car was a royal blue BMW, a gift from her father, of course. If Archer was impressed, he didn't say anything, which she appreciated.

From time to time Zoey felt embarrassed about all the nice things she owned because of her father. Throughout his football career, Patch had endured several concussions, back and shoulder surgery, knee surgery three times, and now had a permanently bad back. But he never complained, because in the process of wrecking his body he'd made millions in endorsement deals. As a proud Black man, he was far too aware that many men who looked like him weren't as lucky. But he'd had a gift and love for the game from the time he was a kid and honed it with hours and years on the field. She was extremely proud of her father and his legacy.

But it wasn't *her* legacy.

She wanted her own. Like her father, Zoey had used her attributes to the best of her ability and worked them. She'd been gifted with a tall, svelte body and flawless skin. Her hair was a mix of her mother's thick waves and her father's kinky curls. Zoey had dark brown ringlets everyone thought she paid to have. She'd accidentally fallen into modeling at sixteen when a fashion agent attended one of her father's Super Bowl parties. It helped that, like her mother, she loved clothes. Before her mother got sick, she accompanied Zoey all over the world as she modeled for Donna Karan and others. They'd had some of the best times of their lives drinking espresso in Rome and eating pastries in Paris. Plenty of memories.

But once her mother died, Zoey lost the heart for modeling and the travel involved. Her father, too, was despondent and didn't want Zoey going anywhere. They both went into a deep depression born from grief and retreated to his ranch on the outskirts of Amarillo. A dear friend of her mother's pulled Zoey out of her depression when she suggested she find her own dream. If it would no longer be high fashion and modeling, it could be something adjacent. And it was on a yacht trip along the Gulf Coast of Mexico with her father a couple of years later that she took a day to go off on her own. She drove along the coastal road in Texas and discovered the town of Charming.

Though she'd been all over the world, Zoey found Charming unique. She found a spirit of friendship and comradery in this small town, as well as a beautiful bay and beach, a renovated lighthouse and quaint little shops. There was a family-owned bookstore like the one in *You've Got Mail*, and an art gallery. She wandered into a boutique on that auspicious day and met a woman who wanted to retire. This became the seed of a dream; this would be her legacy. She renamed the boutique Glamtique and envisioned a place where haute couture met affordable fashion and was available to women from all economic walks of life.

Soon, Zoey had a business plan even her father's financial manager approved. She moved to Charming, obtaining her father's blessing only when he could buy a "suitable" home for his only child. A safe place where he wouldn't have to worry. She wound up on the outskirts of town, where many doctors and lawyers had vacation homes. The house was beautiful, one glass window from top to bottom, facing the view of the bay. She had four bathrooms and five bedrooms. Zoey was a little embarrassed by it all, since she hadn't worked to earn any of it. Again, she was benefiting from her father's legacy. But legacies took time to build, she could almost hear her mother say, and it wasn't wrong to please her father.

Scouring estate sales and using her contacts in the fashion world, Zoey found one-of-a-kind clothing. Many of these items would have wound up at an auction were it not for her network of buyers. The boutique initially succeeded mostly by word of mouth and her contacts with the other small-town shopkeepers, like her best friend, Twyla. But a year ago, when local advertising executive Lauren Montez became a rabid fan, the boutique's sales tripled. Women discovered they could look like Lauren and not spend the month's grocery bill to do it.

Zoey hoped that her mami would be proud of her. So

much of what she did was in honor of her mother. Conchita Lambert had always found haute couture overpriced. In those early years with Patch, when he was a college player, her mother had to make do with what she could piece together, and nothing pleased her more than finding a bargain. Last year, Zoey found an underserved market in secondhand designer wedding dresses. She wanted to carry more of them, but needed more room, so last year she'd bought the storefront next door and created an annex.

She'd started her own legacy, one to complement the one established by her father.

Chapter Four

Archer hadn't struggled with his English this much in months. When he was under stress, he tended to fumble words, sounding like someone fresh off the boat instead of someone who'd been a US citizen for twenty years. At least he hadn't reverted to speaking in Italian, which he still spoke fluently.

But this was the least of his problems.

The first was an intense and fiery attraction to his principal, the woman he'd been assigned to protect. Considering what had happened on his last assignment, he'd have to be careful not to let his personal feelings get in the way. She was the kind of woman who inspired double takes—or triple takes. He wouldn't be surprised if she literally stopped traffic sometimes. He'd always had a thing for tall women with long legs, gorgeous hair and dark brown eyes. She could have been a model.

At the end of the day, she locked up the shop and headed to her luxury sedan. He followed her past the coastal highway to the outskirts of the town and into an exclusive gated neighborhood. The homes here were more like estates, with spacious front lawns that led to circular driveways and porches with Greek columns. Zoey's was a slightly less ostentatious, sprawling ranch style home—although it did have a circular driveway.

Archer parked behind her near the front, grabbed his bag from the trunk and followed her up the flagstone patio steps.

"Nice place."

"Thank you," she said, lowering her head. "And don't worry, I have a state-of-the-art alarm system."

He would expect nothing less in a luxurious home like this, which probably housed plenty of valuables besides Zoey. She reached for the keypad lock and punched in a code. When she left the door open, he followed her inside, shutting it.

"I'll give you your own code, if you'd like."

"No need, the firm gave it to me. Plus, I will always be right behind you."

His first reaction was to admire the cathedral ceilings in the front entryway. For a short time as a teenager, he'd worked in his father's painting business, and he knew the challenge of keeping those walls spotless. His second reaction was to realize Zoey's home—just like her shop—was an explosion of color everywhere. There were decorative artificial trees with orange and red leaves, blinking orange lights strung across in strategic places, and garlands of orange and yellow leaves. On the left side of the house was an open-plan room with a stone fireplace, whose hearth was decorated with a million pumpkins and scattered leaves.

"I decorate every fall. Kind of like Christmas, you know?" She shrugged.

"Uh-huh."

"I have the guest room ready for you."

"Thanks, I don't need much."

"It's this way." She pointed in the other direction. "My bedroom is on the other side."

He followed her to a separate wing of the home, past the spacious kitchen and down a hallway lined with family photos.

She opened the door to a room with double French doors leading outside. "If you go out these doors, there's a shortcut to my bedroom—it's on the other side, with doors leading to the patio. Not that you'll ever need to go there but just so you know, you're not actually *that* far away from me. You know, in case this mortal danger I'm in ever materializes."

He walked to the doors and spotted a deck and kidney-shaped swimming pool outside. The lawn was the size of a small park and the landscaping was impeccable.

"You've done well for yourself, Zoey."

"Oh, it's not me who's done well," she said with a shake of her head. "Daddy bought me this house. I'd have been fine sharing a house downtown with a friend, but he didn't think any of those places were safe enough."

It didn't surprise Archer that the daughter of a wealthy athlete would live in a home like this; what did surprise him was that way Zoey made excuses for her good fortune. In a way, he understood. If it were his property, he'd have wanted to earn it himself, but then he'd been called obstinate more than once.

"What time will we leave tomorrow morning?" he asked.

"I open at ten."

"I will be ready. Remember, for now, you are not to leave your house without me. You let me know if you need anything and I will be there in an instant."

She rolled her eyes. "How about if I scream?"

"Scream," he said slowly as if this was a new word in

his vocabulary. Sometimes he still missed American nuances. Surely, she didn't mean it literally.

She held her hand to her neck and made exaggerated motions with wide eyes.

"Help!" she screamed. "Help me!"

She sounded like an actress in an old-school horror movie. The sound was loud enough for Archer to take a step back, and then she dissolved into laughter.

Honestly, it pissed him off. "Is this funny to you?"

"Yes, kind of," she said, one hand on her hip. "And it would be to you, too, if you saw Scott. I could seriously take him in a fight, not that my daddy would ever believe me."

Of course. Archer reminded himself she did not know about the other, far more credible threat to her and her father's safety. He had to tread cautiously here, but, she had a point. She looked more than capable of defending herself, but there were many other factors involved. No use elaborating; civilians never understood how real threats could be. They were used to living in their stable worlds where destruction and bombings were an aberration and not the norm.

He quirked a brow and crossed his arms. "Describe for me how you would 'take him.'"

"Actually, I would demonstrate, but you, on the other hand, look like you might take *me*."

"Thank you for that."

"I took kickboxing lessons for a while." She held her hands up like fists and swung once. "And I know how to pack a punch, believe me."

He bit back a chuckle because she'd left herself completely open to attack with that stance. But no use belaboring the point. Suffice it to say, his job was secure.

She reached for his shoulders, her knee inches from his

crotch. "If you really want to know, I would grab Scott like this. And then I'd raise my knee like so and hit him *right in the family jewels*."

"I see. Thank you for not testing that on me." He cleared his throat.

Her delicious scent was thankfully not pumpkin spice, but a flowery smell that hinted at springtime and fresh sunshine.

She stepped back, lowering her hands to her sides, no longer smiling. "So, you see my point."

"But, nevertheless, fathers worry about these things, which is good for me, as now I have a job."

She nodded. "I wouldn't want to take away your livelihood."

They stared at each other for what felt like an interminably long time before Zoey said, "I'll let you get settled, then," and left him alone in the guest bedroom.

Archer threw off his jacket, sat on the bed, pulled off his tie and rolled up his shirtsleeves. He wanted to take another look at his client's background and get to know her better. He kicked off his boot, removed his prosthesis and rubbed his stub. Relief poured through him, and for the first time all day the phantom pain he occasionally felt subsided. The human body was amazing. His left leg still protested that something was missing. He wanted to remind his leg that plenty of his *friends* were missing, never to return. Forget the damn foot. Both he and his left leg were lucky.

His amputation was below the knee, and meant the healing time and adjustment had been faster than one took above the knee. Even so, it had been over a year since the training accident that took part of Archer's leg. He recuperated in Germany and got his prosthetic and physical therapy at the VA in Houston. According to his therapist, he healed faster than most of his patients, thanks to his youth and a fit body otherwise. Of course, his mind was another story. It took months and plenty of therapy before he'd stopped reliving the day.

He found himself in a good place when he heard a former Marine was hiring returning military personnel at his security firm. It meant staying in Texas, an affront to his mother, who wanted him home in Connecticut with the rest of the family. But he'd been stationed out of Texas for over a decade. Going home would consist of a 24/7 pity party, with his mother and sisters praising him for his service and tending to him like an invalid. That was the last thing Archer wanted. No one he loved had ever seen him with part of his leg gone, and he'd like to keep it that way. It was his job to show the rest of the world that nothing had changed.

When he transitioned to executive protection, he'd envisioned elite assignments to celebrities or politicians but he could now see he wasn't ready for that. It was a good thing he'd been sidelined to something small, because occasionally the prosthesis bothered him. The doctors explained that the tissue would swell and shrink during the day and could cause occasional pain. Archer didn't like taking meds for pain so he endured it, making himself lift weights to the point where another part of his body hurt instead.

He'd scheduled an appointment on Monday at the local hospital to confirm his new prosthesis model fit adequately and nothing had gone wrong. He might have to cancel since he was a team of one on this job, but he'd check in with Ian on threat levels and see if he could get away for a few minutes.

Archer leaned back on the bed and opened the folder he had, which included the full background on Ms. Zoey

Lambert. He'd only been briefed on the particulars: recent credible death threats to father.

As he read, he chuckled when he discovered Zoey had previously worked as a runway model. That fact did not surprise him. The man with the deep pockets was a former professional football player, legend and two-time Super Bowl champ with the Cowboys. Mr. Patrick "Patch" Lambert had quite a résumé, and even Archer was impressed. He was more of a soccer and basketball fan but appreciated the determination it took to be a success in any sport. And having witnessed many a soccer match that went wildly out of hand, he understood the fanaticism behind sports. Fans could be dangerous, and if this one ever came near Zoey, he'd live to regret it.

The whole thing was a strange situation, when he couldn't even let his principal know the very real threat, which wasn't her ex at all.

But he'd been specifically instructed not to let Zoey know of the real threat her father faced. It might be difficult at times, but Archer would do as ordered.

Chapter Five

Zoey quickly grew a little tired of Archer standing near the doorway like a soldier. Sure, this was his job, but did he have to make it so obvious? Every now and then when things got slow, she'd go up to him and make a funny face, sticking out her tongue.

He blinked. "Why are you doing that?"

"Well, you're acting like you're in the King's Guard, so I thought I'd make a face and see if I can get you to smile the way the tourists do."

He lowered his aviator shades and peered at her over them. "I will smile when something is funny."

Twyla stopped in at lunch, bringing Zoey a turkey sandwich from the Salty Dog. Archer nodded to Twyla as she walked by, and when his back was to her, she mouthed to Zoey, "Wow."

Yes, "wow," and too bad he didn't seem the slightest bit interested in Zoey. She supposed it would be too much to ask to get both a handsome bodyguard and a date for Sweetheart Day.

"My new bodyguard, courtesy of my father."

"That's the best shop decoration *ever*," Twyla said, speaking softly. "When we joked about making him a doorman, well, I didn't seriously think he'd look like a super-hot bouncer."

"You thought he'd be a middle-aged man? Balding, with a paunch?"

"Exactly," Twyla said, then studied the ceiling. "On the other hand, I just remembered Ronan Sheridan is a bodyguard and he's incredibly hot. Maybe it's a job qualification."

"They're calling it executive protection now." Zoey made air quotes. "But technically he is a bodyguard. I read up on it last night."

"Hey, maybe he'll still be here for Sweetheart Day." Twyla took a sip of her Cheerwine. "And he could be your plus one."

"If he's still here by then, it's because my daddy has money to burn."

"He wouldn't call protecting his only child burning money."

"You know what I mean."

"Yes, and I also know your daddy *does* have money to burn."

Zoey sighed. "I wish he wouldn't waste his money on me. There are other people he could help."

It was still top secret, but a while ago when Twyla's bookstore was in trouble, Zoey arranged on the down-low for her father to come in as an "angel" investor. To this day, Twyla had no idea whom the money had come from, but it didn't have to be repaid, and it had saved her third-generation family bookstore. Maybe someday Zoey would tell her best friend, but for now, she privately enjoyed the fact that her father had the means to help her friends, too. And who knew? Maybe someday Zoey would also have a multigenerational family business with Glamtique. She already felt her mother's presence here—a silent business partner, if you will—but if she were so blessed as to someday have a little girl, or a boy who loved fashion, and they had a child…it could happen.

"You don't have the decorations up yet," Twyla said with a pout.

"I've got all the boxes down. I'll take care of that this afternoon."

Twyla hooked a thumb toward Archer. "He's even taller than you are. Have him help you."

Zoey shook her head then reconsidered. "You know what, my friend? You are an evil genius."

She was going to have such fun, watching her sulky and way-too-serious bodyguard, as he helped her tape yellow and orange hearts, pumpkins and leaves in the window.

Twyla took off, greeting Lois Finch as she passed her walking into the shop.

"Weren't you in that men's cologne commercial? Dolce & Gabbana?" Lois asked Archer, as she looked him up and down.

"I think it was Giorgio Armani," said a pretty redhead behind Lois. She was holding a baby in a front pack.

"No, ma'am," Archer said. "It was not me."

Zoey smothered a laugh and walked over to greet Lois, who was not a regular customer. She wanted her to feel welcome so that she'd return more often. The holidays were coming up—a chance to make more money in three months than she'd made so far that year.

"How can I help you?"

"Zoey, meet my dear friend Ruby." Lois gestured to the redhead next to her. "She just had a baby girl a few weeks ago and nothing fits like it used to."

"Sweet baby." Zoey peeked at the little face framed with

red curls, bundled inside the baby carrier. "Are you shopping for a special occasion?"

"A nice dinner with my husband. We were in town a little over a year ago, so we're making it a yearly tradition."

"Nothing too fancy, then?" Zoey led them toward the section of the store that carried day dresses and other casual wear.

"Well," Ruby said, "it *is* special. We reunited that day, and he dressed up and bought me a dress, too, to wear to dinner at the fancy hotel where we stayed. We're staying there again, so—"

Zoey slapped a hand over her mouth and lowered it. "Was he the cowboy who came in looking for some 'fancy duds'? Did he buy you a beautiful pink cocktail dress?"

"Yes, that's Wyatt. It's hard to forget him, that's for sure." Ruby grinned. "But the dress just doesn't fit anymore."

"Say no more!" Zoey led Ruby and Lois to her rack of extra special dresses, from which she'd picked out the pink dress for Ruby a year ago.

"Needs to be kinda fancy," he'd drawled. *"I have to talk her into coming back home with me."*

Now the three of them flipped through Zoey's designer collection until she came up with three dresses she thought might fit Ruby. Lois helped her unstrap the precious little baby from her chest and held him, while Ruby tried on all three dresses, eventually deciding on the perfect one, in Zoey's opinion: a powder blue dress with an A-line waist and a flowing skirt.

After they paid and were on their way, the day began to slow. There was always a quiet time in the late afternoon until it picked up again in the early evening. Zoey usually closed at seven, but she had longer hours closer to the holidays. Archer had been standing for hours, the poor man, with nothing better to do than answer questions as to whether or not he'd been in some Giorgio Armani commercial or not. Zoey felt bad for him.

"Sorry," she said. "Not much excitement around here for you."

"That is the way I like it."

"But you must be bored. Actually, I could use your help, since it seems I'm not in mortal danger at the moment."

He turned. "What can I do for you?"

The boxes of fall decor were all open by the time nine o'clock rolled around, and Zoey had tasked Archer with taping yellow and orange hearts to the storefront window. The shop had a box window, making it perfect for displays and a mannequin or two. Every holiday she went all out.

"Why orange hearts and not red ones?" Archer reached up to stick a paper heart to the upper part of the window. Despite being so tall, he still required a small stool.

Zoey climbed up on the ledge beside him. She had kicked off her heels and was barefoot. "It's fall now, and that's the color scheme."

"Yes, but it is usually leaves and pumpkins for fall, no?"

"True, and I do have those, too, but I need hearts for Sweetheart Day." Zoey dug through another box, pulling out some pumpkins, trees and leaves.

"Sweetheart Day?"

Whenever Archer looked perplexed, a deep crease formed between his eyebrows.

"Look." Zoey cleared her throat. "December has Christmas, November has Thanksgiving, and October has Halloween. What does September have? Nothing. And you don't know me, but I'm a big fan of love. In all its many forms. That is agape, philia, storge and eros."

The four types of love: sacrificial, friendship, familial and romantic.

"You are a fan of *love*?" Archer gave her a look as if she'd just said something incomprehensible.

She sincerely hoped this guy wasn't one of those "down with love" types. So retro. So overdone.

"What? Is something wrong with that?" Zoey plunked her hands on her hips.

"It's like saying you're a fan of oxygen."

"Oh." That wasn't the response she'd expected.

"You can't live without oxygen, you can't live without love." He shrugged.

"It's good you agree! And so, what I've done as a champion of love, is give it another special day. September was just crying out to be known for something other than pumpkin spice lattes. Which are great, of course, but c'mon! So, when I was a little girl, I created Sweetheart Day on September 14. And now I celebrate it every year."

"Like Valentine's Day on February 14." Archer nodded. "I like it. It is not a national holiday, so no one is forced to buy flowers or a card."

"Right. It's something I celebrate with family and friends."

"And that special someone?"

"Well, when there is someone. This year, there isn't."

"Yes, I'm sorry. There *is* someone but the feeling isn't mutual."

She nodded and handed Archer the string of orange lights that would go from one end of the window to the other. "The thing is, like so many of the men I date, he was more interested in getting to know my father than me."

"The NFL legend?"

"He's kind of a big deal." Zoey sighed. "Especially if you're from Texas."

At this, he nearly smiled. "No offense but I much prefer what Europeans call football."

"No offense taken, but it's *soccer*," Zoey said, reaching to pin a section of the string lights.

"If you say so."

She snorted, but it was pretty amazing to find someone who wasn't a huge fan of Patch Lambert.

"Where are you from?"

"Connecticut is where my mother, father and sisters still live," he said. "But I've been living in Texas since I first signed up for the service. Texas is home."

"I've always wanted to live somewhere where the leaves change colors in autumn. We don't have that in this part of South Texas."

Once, when she was younger, her family had taken a trip to New England in the fall. Zoey had always wanted to go back, but shortly after that vacation, her mother got ill for the first time. Suddenly, there had been far more pressing matters.

By the time they were finished decorating, the window display was magic. A splash of color, with orange twinkle lights, pumpkins and hearts, decorated in trademark Glamtique style. On each step of a small rustic ladder sat a pumpkin.

"Something's missing." Zoey tapped her chin while judging the display from outside.

Archer shook his head. "No…nothing."

Zoey held up her finger. "I know! Ophelia."

"Nothing is missing!" But Archer followed her into the storage room in the back.

She heard him curse and she whipped around, prepared to tell him she didn't need his opinion on this matter and he could leave if he wished, but then she noticed his face had become a mask of pain. He bent to touch his left boot.

"Are you okay?"

With all her experience with injuries, Zoey could be overzealous at times. Once, Twyla had fallen off a ladder in her bookstore and was knocked out cold. Zoey had been terrified she'd lost her best friend. And then, of course, there was her father: she and her mother would dote on him after an injury, taking him to doctor's appointments and physical therapy. Zoey was well acquainted with the inside of a hospital well before her mother got sick. Suffice it to say, she could tell when someone was hurting. And she had no doubt that Archer was hurt.

"I am fine," he said through gritted teeth, straightening to his full height.

Seems Archer was one of those people who preferred to let everyone think he was indestructible. Very much like her father. The only times she ever heard her parents bicker was when her father had taken another hard hit on the field.

"*Think of your family. Your daughter. One more hit to the head and you might not make it*," her mother would plead. *"We need you more than the fans do."*

"*I can't quit the game. My players need me and I made a commitment to the team*," her father had said every time.

The arguments would go on for a while, and they would inevitably end with her mother giving in to her dad because she had no choice. She loved a man obsessed with the game and she had to take everything that came with it.

"I feel bad if you injured yourself helping me," Zoey said.

"No, I didn't. It's fine."

She didn't know Archer well enough to press further, so she let it go. Maybe he didn't want her to worry that she had a second-rate bodyguard, but for the love of God, had he looked in the mirror recently?

Zoey reached for her naked, headless mannequin and carried her to the front of the store. Time to dress Ophelia again. She began grabbing clothes off the rack. Slacks, a sweater, a colorful scarf. She'd complete the outfit with a kickass pair of knee-high boots. This mannequin would be placed next to the barrel of apples Zoey would pick up tomorrow. Perfect.

"I'm going to dress Ophelia in a new season-appropriate outfit. It's the only thing missing from the window. Well, that and a barrel of apples. I'll get the apples fresh from the market."

"You *named* her?" Archer narrowed his eyes.

"Yes, Ophelia and I are old friends. I found her for a bargain."

"Yeah, that's not weird at all."

Zoey shook a finger at him. "No judging, please. Here, help me pull her pants on. As long as you're here."

Like her, Archer did not have a light complexion, so if he blushed, she couldn't see it. But he did hesitate a moment before he pulled the sweater over Ophelia's torso.

"This is strange."

"What? Not in your usual job description?" Zoey teased while she pulled on Ophelia's pants one leg at a time.

He snorted his answer.

When they were done, Zoey locked up and went outside, Archer following her. That's when they both noticed, sitting just outside the storefront, a bouquet of red roses lying on the ground.

Archer picked them up and handed them to Zoey. “Read the card.”

Zoey did and couldn’t believe her eyes. “They’re from Scott.”

Chapter Six

"'Why did you block me? Stop ignoring me.'" Zoey read the card out loud. "'I'm not mad. I still love you. Nothing will ever ruin my love for you.'"

Archer took the card from her. The crease between his eyebrows deepened.

"I finally blocked him so he couldn't send me any more text messages," Zoey explained, fumbling in her bag and removing her phone. "His feelings are hurt. Maybe I shouldn't have done that."

Gently, Archer removed the phone from her hands. "You did the right thing. This is *his* problem."

He sounded like her father now, but the funny thing was she didn't actually mind the advice coming from Archer. He wasn't an overprotective father getting into her business from hundreds of miles away. He was her bodyguard, a professional, and he'd now witnessed the situation firsthand. Obviously, Scott must have noticed her inside after shop hours, with another man inside, and just left the flowers for her. Maybe he didn't realize this was creepier than simply knocking on the door.

"So… I should just ignore these flowers?"

"Yes, certainly do *not* call or text him." Archer handed the phone back.

"Not even to say thanks?"

Archer quirked a brow. "It isn't the roses that are concerning but the note."

"He doesn't want to give up on me."

"It's straight out of the stalking playbook. Unwanted gifts and phone calls. But he will have to accept 'no' eventually. If he does not understand no in English, I will speak to him in my language."

"Italian?"

He didn't answer. Zoey didn't think Scott spoke Italian and almost said this out loud, but then she noticed Archer's smoldering look—well, she would call it smoldering but others might call it intimidating. Threatening. *Extremely* serious. If he spoke to Scott with that body language, he'd probably pee his pants.

"Oh, I see," she said. "That's not necessary."

"*I'll* decide what's necessary and what is not."

It took everything in her not to stick out her tongue again. He made her feel five years old again as he led her to his car.

"Do I have to sit in the back seat again, or may I sit in the front with you like a normal person?"

"Sit in the front if you like," Archer said, opening the door like an actual chauffeur.

She asked Archer to stop by the market on the way home so she could get a bag of fresh apples. Not surprisingly, he walked inside with her, two steps back like her shadow.

"Again, do you have to be so obvious?" she hissed in the produce section.

"What's an acceptable amount of distance? Six feet?"

"Pretend you're my friend, at least." She held up an apple and smiled. "Do you think this looks juicy?"

He blinked. "How can I answer that question honestly?"

"With the truth." She put the apple back. "Never mind. It's better it be red than juicy."

He picked up a basket of his own and stayed several steps behind her.

Zoey tried to remember what life had been like back when she'd lived at home and her family had a bodyguard. She didn't remember this awkwardness. Their bodyguards had been friends, not like the Secret Service detail for the president. If she recalled, Alec had three adult children he'd put through school on his own after his wife left him. Harry had married an old friend of her mother's. They were present at birthdays, anniversaries and vacations. She only now realized how odd this was, but she hadn't had a normal childhood.

She and Archer wandered through the aisles, grabbing a few things here and there. She grabbed more pumpkin spice, stopping to admire the fall-themed display of cookies, cupcakes and candy.

In the checkout line, she saw Archer's basket filled with cookies and doughnuts and bit her lower lip to keep from smiling. He looked like he ate ammo and grenades for breakfast, lunch and dinner, but he was just a regular human being with a sweet tooth. She could work with that.

Back at the house, he insisted on unloading all the groceries for her. It wasn't much, but she'd purchased the ingredients for a couple of meals. She would hate to eat popcorn every night while she had company. Her mother, even after she could afford a live-in cook, always made dinner for the family.

"I'll make a quick frittata for dinner," Zoey said. "If that's okay."

"You don't have to cook for me."

"Well, we both have to eat, don't we?" She eyed his bag of treats. "You don't plan on subsisting on *sweets*, do you?"

"I'll order myself some food." Archer waved a palm dismissively. "You don't need to feed me."

"Excuse me?" She put her hand on her hip. "You don't think I'm going to let you sit here and starve while I eat, do you? My mother would come down from heaven to slap me for being a terrible hostess. She used to cook for our family's bodyguards, and I don't mind doing the same."

She gathered eggs, cheese, tomatoes, peppers and cilantro. This was her mother's recipe.

"Sorry. Sometimes I forget that you've been in this situation before," Archer said.

She nodded. "Yes, but we had those bodyguards because there were serious death threats against my father. Texans take their football *very* seriously."

He cleared his throat. "I am sorry you have to go through this again. I apologize for my gender. There are too many men who do not understand the word 'no.' For that, I am very sorry."

"Archer, you are not the representative for the male species," Zoey said, taking out her cutting board. "Either way, I accept your apology on behalf of all mankind."

When she opened a cabinet door to reach for a bowl to crack the eggs into, he grabbed it for her. "I've been thinking. Maybe I can make this easier on you."

"How so?"

"You did not want me to be obvious about guarding you."

"It just makes people curious as to why I need a bodyguard. And I'd prefer the whole town not know that I've got an obsessive ex. Twyla knows…and probably her husband, Noah, but that's about it. I'd like to keep it that way." She cracked an egg and then another and started whisking.

"Maybe I could pretend to be visiting from out of town."

"Like a friend?"

"A cousin, or a friend of a friend?" He coughed. "Or a boyfriend."

She whisked harder. "A *boyfriend*?"

Her heart pounded against her rib cage. She liked the idea far too much. "Like a fake relationship kind of thing?"

"It's an idea. But I don't want you to feel uncomfortable in any way."

"There's one big problem. A boyfriend wouldn't hang around me at the store all day. And if he did, that would *definitely* draw some attention."

"Right. Not what we want, either."

"But..." Zoey said. "How about I hire you to work for the store?"

"Like a security guard?"

"Or...a salesclerk."

"A salesclerk at a boutique. Me."

"You could sell the men's clothing and I'll sell the women's."

His lip quirked in a hint of a smile. "You're not trying to take advantage of me, are you?"

"If you're going to be with me all day..."

"The proposition is intriguing, but I still think you're better off if men *know* you have a bodyguard."

"I don't want to scare all the men off! You seem to think I want to keep all men away, and that's not the case."

"It's not?" He wore the hint of a smile on his lips.

"No, Archer. I would like a date for the Sweetheart Day party on the fourteenth."

"About this party, will there be many people there?"

"Yes, quite a few. It's my annual event." She chopped harder.

"Can you cancel it this year? Just because of the, you know, situation with, um… What's his name? Scott, is it?"

How interesting. He'd almost forgotten the name of the person he was supposedly protecting her from. Who was supposedly this huge threat…

"You have got to be kidding me, dude." Zoey pointed her knife at him. "I am not going to let him win. This party is happening. That's why you're here."

"Right. It's a higher-level alert. Anytime you're going to be around a lot of people, the threat level rises."

"Then you're going to have to really try and be less obvious there. Or we're not going to have any fun *at all*."

"*Fun* is for when the threat is gone."

This time, she really did stick her tongue out at him and he laughed, which while not her desired reaction, made her heart thrum pleasantly.

After dinner, he thanked her and cleaned up the dishes, then they made their way to opposite corners of the house. Hours later, Zoey lay in bed curled under the covers, feeling somehow less lonely. She'd always felt like this house was too big for one person but every time she'd been close to having a roommate, they wound up getting engaged. It was lovely to know there was another heartbeat in her house besides her own.

Her faux roommate was a hunky bodyguard on the other side of those double French doors, and she couldn't stop thinking about him.

Chapter Seven

The next morning, Archer grabbed a cookie from his stash and set up his laptop to check in with Ian and the rest of the team in Houston, as they did every Monday. Their agents were scattered in other parts of the country, and even abroad, like Ronan was, currently. The call began like all the others, with brief introductions and updates. Another new hire, former special ops officer Jax Townsend, reported on his assignment with a Texas oil tycoon. He'd been working with the agency longer, so he had his pick of high-level clients.

But at this point, Archer had zero complaints. He was going to enjoy every minute of sticking close to Zoey. A tough job but someone had to do it.

Finally, Ian updated them on Patch Lambert's situation.

"I'm in touch with his security and they seem to have it under control. The police are giving him the usual runaround that there isn't much they can do until there's contact, and it's true their hands are tied. The threat keeps resurfacing, however, so we're not in the clear yet. We're monitoring all electronic activity. Archer, how's it going there?"

He told the group about the flowers and his overall lack of concern about the ex-boyfriend. He had never noticed anyone tailing Zoey—looking at her, checking her out, sure. Every single male with a pulse did that, but he couldn't blame them.

"Can you see if you can get her to give up this big party she's having on the fourteenth. What's it called... *Sweetheart* Day?" Ian winced. "That will greatly reduce any of our concerns. With the size of that party, I would almost have to assign someone else to help you. What do you think? Can you talk her into it?"

"I will continue to try, but she resisted the idea when I brought it up. She seems excited about this day. Not sure I understand why since she already thinks I'm going to ruin it by being there."

Ian sighed. "All right. We'll see what the threat levels are at that time and reassess."

After everyone else had logged off the call, Archer stayed on with Ian.

"I have an appointment today for an adjustment, but I can cancel it. Zoey said the store's closed today, so I assume she will just stay in."

"Go ahead and take the appointment, and I'll alert you of any changes here in real time. As long as she's in the house, alarm set, we should be good for a short time."

With a new prosthesis, Archer had been advised adjustments might need to be made. His left foot had been killing him by the end of the first day with Zoey, such that he couldn't even hide it from her. She'd noticed, but then again she didn't miss much.

After logging off the call, he was thinking about making some coffee, when he heard a splash from outside. Alarmed, he went to the double French doors and saw Zoey emerge from under the water at the opposite end of the pool, a swimming cap on her head. Nice to know the pool wasn't merely decoration; she actually used it. The water looked inviting, and the woman swimming laps from one end of the pool to the other even more so. He watched her, mesmerized by her easy form, as her long arms pulled out of the water and back under.

He hadn't been in a pool since he'd done his initial therapy, but he couldn't see himself in there with her. If she did this on a regular basis, he'd make it a plan to watch from the sidelines.

After a quick shower, he found Zoey in the kitchen. She was still wearing the rubber cap and had tied a wrap around her swimsuit. She was reaching for a mug from the cupboard.

"Good morning. Coffee's ready." She rubbed an eye.

Damn, she looked even younger without makeup.

"Thanks," Archer said, taking a mug. "No work today, right? You said the store is closed on Mondays."

"That's right." Holding the mug close to her lips with both hands, she peered at him from under hooded eyes. "It's my 'me' day."

"You make it a habit to swim in the morning?"

She nodded. "On my day off, yes. I was on my high school's swim team for a while, before all the modeling gigs. Imagine the daughter of an NFL player being on the team. They thought I was going to be their ringer, but my swimming was barely passable."

"You looked pretty good to me." He cleared his throat. "I heard the splash."

She nodded. "It's not like my father didn't encourage me, but I don't think competition is my thing."

"No, I can see how it wouldn't be." He pressed back a smile.

She canted her head. "Really? How can you see *that*?"

"First, swimming isn't a team sport."

"That's why I do it. I'm in competition with myself."

"And second of all, I can't see you pushing anybody out of your way. Instead, you'd probably get out of the way so they can get ahead of you and have a chance at winning."

She quirked a brow. "Don't sign me up for sainthood yet."

"You're too nice. Way too nice."

"That better not be another word for *doormat*." She narrowed her eyes.

He snorted. "Not even close."

"You make it sound like being kind to people is a bad thing. And it's not. Kindness matters. It counts in even the smallest of ways. You never know when your attitude is going to change the trajectory of somebody's entire day."

He nodded, because though he didn't quite see things the way she did, this wasn't the time for an argument.

"I have an appointment in town. I won't be long. You will stay here, with the alarm on, corporate monitoring the house from Houston. That way there's no lapse. If there are any threats, I will be alerted in real time."

She blinked. "Really? Corporate is monitoring the house? Because of *Scott*?"

Yeah, she didn't appear to be buying it and Archer didn't blame her. Regardless, this was the cover. A lovesick boyfriend, who so far hadn't even made an appearance.

"We take our work seriously," Archer said.

"Yes, I guess you do."

Within minutes, he was on the road to the local hospital, where he'd been advised the staff there were prepared to make any necessary adjustments to his prosthetic. Unfortunately, he wound up waiting far longer than he had hoped.

He didn't like being away from his principal for this long. Yes, it was a low-level risk, but the hours were passing by. He kept checking the app on his phone that would alert him to any breaches to Zoey's security system. Nothing.

Finally, the medical assistant, Tammy, called his name and led him to the unit for prosthetics. Passing other offices, he caught sight of a little boy getting a new leg.

"Mom, check this out… I got a robot leg! This is so cool."

Archer chuckled. The kid had the right idea. Children were the best. Attitude was everything. No use in regretting what might have been or picturing life with his old intact leg. In decades past, he might have spent the rest of his life in a wheelchair or hobbling along on crutches. But modern medicine had brought about amazing advances, and Archer—just like that little boy—was one of the lucky recipients.

He could give himself a pep talk all day long and believe it, but nights were another thing altogether. More like 3:00 a.m., when he'd wake in a cold sweat without fail, questioning all his life choices. Suddenly every mistake he'd ever made was put under a microscope. He had no mercy on himself, either. His father hadn't wanted Archer to join the service, worried about the escalating conflicts overseas in the wake of 9/11 and the seemingly endless war.

"*This is not your war*," Enzo Rossi had said in his broken English. *"Do not go and die. You are my only son."*

"*I won't die.* They're *going to die*," he'd said to his poor father, filled with a nineteen-year-old's hubris.

His father couldn't understand Archer's beliefs, maybe because he was an immigrant. Archer was an immigrant, too, but he was a first-generation Italian American filled with a patriotic spirit that had gripped him after 9/11. Archer was in fifth grade when the twin towers fell. New to the United States, he'd found inspiration in the national pride that swept the country. He and his new classmates wished they were old enough to enlist, because they would go over there and kick some ass. He had never let go of that dream.

"How's the new foot?" the male specialist asked now. "Need some adjusting?"

"My position requires me to be on my feet all day. Yesterday the foot bothered me a lot. It's radiating pain, but I can take it. I just want to make sure nothing's wrong, or that it doesn't need to be readjusted."

"No need to take the pain. Let me take a look."

Archer's new foot was removed in front of the only kind of people who'd ever seen him without one. Medical professionals. Sad and pathetic though it sounded even to himself, Archer preferred a male attendant. He would prefer no woman saw him in this condition. Yes, he'd had someone waiting for him when he'd left the country, but he'd come back a different man. Even if she denied it, he'd seen it in her eyes. He wasn't the same man.

The transition to intimacy was rough for some men, and in the end his relationship wasn't strong enough to withstand the changes. He wanted to believe he was confident enough not to care, but unfortunately he did. If he ever wanted to have a relationship with a woman again…well, he'd cross that bridge when he got to it.

Archer waited as both of what was left of his foot and ankle were briefly examined, and then the prosthesis. A surreal feeling once again enveloped him. Not many people could understand the feeling of having an essential part of their body removed. It was odd to watch his foot wander away without him.

The attendant came back after a few minutes, having taken a look at the prosthesis.

"As you know, the swelling and contracting of tissue on your residual limb can cause pain. The socket seems fine. It may be that you're still getting used to it. But we'll check again at your regular exam. Meanwhile, do you need the doctor to prescribe any pain meds?"

He'd been offered OxyContin after the amputation but Archer liked it a bit too much. Since then, he'd medicated with nothing stronger than Tylenol. Sometimes he thought the problem might be that he didn't spend enough time with the foot off at home. He only took it off before bed. Even *he* had a difficult time looking at his stub; he couldn't imagine how anyone but a medical professional used to his condition might feel seeing it.

On his way out, the little boy and his parents were also leaving. An attendant stopped Archer and pulled him aside.

"Do you think you could say a few words to our young amputee, Joey, about your prosthesis?" The attendant lowered his voice. "Whatever you feel comfortable with, of course. It's actually more for the parents than him."

Archer couldn't imagine how he'd feel if his child had lost a foot. Especially one so young. The kid looked to be about seven or eight. Archer only had to look as far as his own parents to see the classic parent response. They'd reacted far worse about his injury than Archer had. It had become his job to convince them he wasn't going to die and would simply need to learn to walk with a prosthetic foot. Certainly not in any way a death sentence, even if it wasn't ideal.

The attendant introduced Archer to Joey and his parents.

"I'm also a patient here." Archer smiled, and patted his lower left leg. "Just coming in for a checkup."

Joey's eyes widened. "You have a bionic foot, too?"

"It's been about a year for me. How about you?"

"He just got it today," the boy's mother, Darcy, said, and Archer noticed her eyes were a little bloodshot; no doubt she had been crying while trying to hide it from her son. "He loves it."

"I love mine, too," Archer said, even if he'd prefer the foot he had been born with. "And there's nothing I can't do with this. It's a part of me now."

"How did you hurt your foot?" The young kid's eyes were wide and brimming with curiosity.

"Joey," his father said, hand on the boy's shoulder. "That's not polite."

Archer waved a hand dismissively. "I was in an accident when I was overseas."

Every once in a while, Archer woke up from a nightmare, sweating. The memory of metal and bone crunching together lingering in his mind. But the strongest and most painful memories were beginning to fade with time.

"I want to play soccer again with my new foot," Joey said.

"You will," Archer said.

They parted with a fist bump. Archer strolled out of the orthopedics wing of the hospital feeling much better, as he always did when he could help someone. As he turned toward the lobby, Archer recognized someone familiar. He couldn't believe his eyes; she was not supposed to be here. His heart raced, knowing there would be only one reason why she would not listen to him and stay at home. It seemed as if she hadn't told him everything; maybe the agency didn't even have all the current information.

Because Zoey Lambert was walking out of the cancer ward.

Chapter Eight

Even after an awful day, Zoey always felt better after visiting the Conchita Lambert Cancer Ward. There was one in every major hospital in the state of Texas and a few across the country. Some might think it strange to feel better after visiting cancer patients, but Zoey believed it was her purpose to bring sunshine into the lives of those fighting the good fight. She'd done it for her mother, and she could do it for these people, who were at first strangers and in some cases became friends. They wrote and emailed her, thanking both her and her father for all they'd done. She liked to come at least once a month, but she came more often in the fall.

Today, she had with her a bouquet of a dozen fresh red roses that she handed out to all the nurses on the ward. Scott's efforts at getting her back with flowers wouldn't completely go to waste. A single long-stemmed rose for every hardworking nurse. And to make the day extra special, she was able to watch a breast cancer survivor ring the bell at the end of her treatment.

"This is Patch and Conchita Lambert's daughter, Zoey," a nurse said. "How about a photo op?"

"Yes, please!" The young woman, who couldn't be much older than Zoey, beamed.

Zoey posed for a photo with the patient and wished the woman many years ahead of being cancer-free. She heard survival rates were improving every day and was delighted. Early screening was so high-tech now that they could often catch cancer *before* it ever happened. Mami would be so proud of what they'd done here, in her name.

But all her joy swiftly left her when she saw Archer standing near the front of the lobby. She'd planned to be back well in time for him to return from his appointment. He looked shocked more than angry to see her. But her main concern was that he'd somehow hurt his foot while helping her decorate the store. She had a feeling that had happened, but he'd been too much of an alpha male to complain.

"Look. I know what you're going to say," Zoey said. "I shouldn't have come here alone. But this is a regular appointment for me, and as you know this is my only day off."

Archer stepped forward, his eyes soft. "I am so sorry, Zoey."

"What? Why? I'm the one who's sorry I didn't listen to you. But I had to be here today."

"I…didn't know."

"Yes, well, that's the point. You had your appointment, and I didn't tell you because I knew you'd try to stop me. I knew how you'd react."

"Why would you worry about *my* reaction? You should have told me that you're ill."

"I'm…what? *Me?* Oh, no. I didn't come here for…" And then it hit her. "You saw me coming out of the cancer ward, didn't you?"

He held up a palm. "No need to explain, please. I am just…sorry."

Zoey bit on her lower lip to keep from laughing. "I'm not sick."

"You don't have to tell me anything. I understand."

"No, you *don't* understand. I was just here visiting. This is one of my father's biggest charities. The Conchita Lambert Cancer Ward. It's named after my mother."

"Dio Mio." His dark eyes were sorrowful.

Zoey reached out and took his arm. "Come with me. We need to talk."

She led him to the outdoor tables in the gardens near the campus café. At this time of the year, even the hospital was decorated. They had pumpkins strewn about and fairy lights strung on the shrubs. Zoey loved it.

"Have a seat." She pointed.

Archer scanned the area first. This guy was never relaxed, not even in a healing garden. He slowly took the bench seat opposite hers, folded his hands and raised his head to meet her eyes.

"Archer," she said. "My mom passed away from cancer. But you don't need to worry—I don't have cancer, nor have I *ever* had cancer."

"I'm glad of that, and sorry I assumed." The crease in his brow deepened. "I thought it was the only reason you'd leave the house without letting me know was not wanting to skip your treatment."

"Honestly, I thought I'd get back before you did. I visit the cancer ward often to offer my support in any way I can. Almost every Monday. It's my dad's charity in my mother's memory."

Archer slumped. "I am so sorry for your loss."

"It's okay," she said. "Well, it's *not* okay and it never will be, you know? But I've learned to live with the grief, and every time I'm here, I feel her here with me." She paused, and then said, "Why would you think I wasn't just here visiting someone?"

He quirked a brow. “I assumed you wouldn’t ignore my orders for any other reason than if you were getting treatment.”

“Fair. And why were *you* here today? I suspected you hurt your foot yesterday but you wouldn’t say anything. How bad is it?”

Archer rose. “Why don’t I get us some coffee?”

“Sure. I’ll have a pumpkin spice latte, please.”

Either he was avoiding the subject or trying to be kind in view of his big mistake. Still, she appreciated the sincerity she’d seen in those amber eyes of his. He was definitely not someone who lacked compassion. A good sign. She watched him walk toward the café counter without a hitch in his step, no longer leaning to the right. Maybe she’d been imagining that she’d detected a limp.

He set her latte down. “Tell me more about your mother.”

There was no surer way to get Zoey to talk for hours. She’d cut it short for him.

“Well, she was a force to be reckoned with.”

“Like you.”

“Definitely more so than me. She could stand up to my father, even though she was all of five foot three and he’s a solid six five.”

“You got your father’s height.”

“It helped with my modeling career. My mother was my biggest champion and protector. When I was sixteen, we started traveling the world together so I could model. She accompanied me everywhere as my chaperone. My father, of course, would not have allowed it without her. I’m so grateful now. So many girls didn’t have that kind of support. Because of my mother, I stayed out of trouble. Anyway, that’s how I got involved in the world of fashion.”

“When did you stop modeling?”

A stone formed in Zoey's throat. "When she got sick."

"How old were you?"

"Twenty, plenty old enough to stop modeling—I was almost aging out of the industry. The modeling world is pretty crazy. I was ready to do something different anyway, but I gave it up to be with her. She fought the good fight for years, and my father and I had time to get used to the idea. She was my best friend."

"Your mother sounds wonderful."

Zoey nodded and took a deep breath. "Archer, why are *you* here?"

"Same as you, to visit patients and support the hardworking medical professionals." He winced and drank from his coffee cup.

Zoey made a face. "Okay, don't tell me then. I just thought you'd hurt your foot helping me yesterday and I felt bad about it."

Archer shook his head. "No, that had nothing to do with it."

He wasn't going to tell her, and since it was a medical issue, she couldn't push it. Not everybody was as open as Zoey. She'd accepted this long ago.

Archer walked Zoey back to her car. He couldn't bring himself to scold her about ignoring his orders to stay home. She was pretty much a saint and probably got her orders from the big guy upstairs. He wasn't messing with that. Fortunately, Archer was well acquainted with women like Zoey. He'd grown up with them: his mother, his four sisters. Still, they were going to have to put some parameters in place. He had a job to do. To do it well, he'd have to outsmart her.

"Next time you want to come to the hospital, let me come with you."

He had long ago learned that the best way to get a woman to do as he bid was to ask nicely. Better yet, let her think it was her idea.

Zoey hesitated, reaching for the door handle of her sedan. "Well, you would certainly cheer up many of the patients."

"That would be my goal."

He wasn't above offering a harmless lie, if required.

"You really want to help?" She blinked.

"Of course."

Another lie.

He didn't love the idea of watching people suffer, having seen enough of that to last him a lifetime. But this was different than what he'd experienced overseas. It might even be uplifting, if he could somehow boost their spirits. Either way, he was going to call his family tonight and make sure they were all getting their regular cancer screenings.

"Okay, that's fine. I'll let you know next time I go."

"And where are we going next? Would you mind if I tag along?"

"I was going to drop in at the bookstore and see Twyla."

"I've been thinking of buying a book," Archer said. "I didn't bring any with me."

This wasn't technically a lie. He liked to read, but the bookcase in Zoey's guest room was filled with romance novels. Not his cup of java.

"Then you'll have to check out the only bookstore in town." She climbed behind the wheel of her vehicle, and when she did, her skirt shifted and showed off her long legs. "Today is book delivery day and also books-go-away day."

"Books-go-away day? What is *that*?" He leaned into her open door, his hand on the door frame.

"It's when Twyla gets a new shipment of books, which is so exciting, but then because of shelf space, she has to return books that haven't sold. It's always a difficult time. Occasionally, we'll go out for drinks at the Salty Dog afterward to commiserate over all the good books that just wouldn't sell."

She seemed serious about this, no hint of teasing in her voice. It wasn't a joke. Her friend was sad when books were returned. Every now and again, Archer couldn't quite grasp the nuances of American humor. But then again, no civilian understood gallows military-style humor. Especially not his mother.

"It sounds like fun," Archer lied. "I wouldn't mind following you there."

Again, this was a skill. He could be grumpy that she wouldn't fall in line, or he could try outsmarting her. Of course, he sensed he'd only get so far with this game. Zoey was as bright as they came.

"It's downtown. Just follow me."

Once they'd arrived and parked, Zoey waited for him. He reached for the shop door of a store similar to Zoey's boutique, except it apparently sold nothing but books. Stacks of books were displayed in the window, along with cutouts of famous literary characters, like Sherlock Holmes.

"Twyla!" Zoey called out. "You here?"

A pretty brunette wearing fashionable glasses appeared.

"Aw, you remembered. It's book-go-away day." Twyla lowered her head.

Zoey stepped forward and embraced the petite woman.

"But it's also book delivery day! Let's focus on the positive. And guess what? I brought you a new customer!" She stepped aside and pointed to him. "You haven't been officially introduced. Twyla Cavell, meet Archer Rossi."

He noted that she hadn't introduced him as her bodyguard, which was just fine with him.

Twyla smiled. "Are you looking for a book?"

"I prefer mysteries. Lots of action—at least a couple of dead bodies, but preferably more. Plenty of suspense."

"Well, too bad you're too late for copies of a debut thriller I already packed up to send back today. But, lucky for you, I received more copies of the latest blockbuster thriller by a *New York Times* best-selling author. It's a book everyone's going to buy, so you may as well, too."

"Oooh, that sounds good, even to me," Zoey said, following Twyla as they walked farther into the store. "I'm usually a romance fan," she said over her shoulder. "Especially Westerns."

"Like we don't get enough of that around here." Twyla scoffed, smiling.

"It's the whole ranch-lifestyle aesthetic and a simpler kind of life. There's nothing better than a good cowboy romance."

"You just keep telling yourself that," Twyla said, and handed Archer a book. "If you're to go by all of the reviews, you'll like this one. I've read it even if it's not what I typically enjoy. But there's lots of suspense and three dead bodies. One explosion, if I recall."

Archer found it hard not to smile. He was kidding about the dead bodies. Only his buddies understood his sense of humor.

Turning it over in his hands, he read the back cover. "I'm sure I will enjoy this."

"Now, direct me to the latest Beverly Jenkins book," Zoey said.

"Sure, but you know it's not a Western." Twyla smirked.

Zoey elbowed her. "I make exceptions for great authors."

"Big of you." Twyla chuckled.

They moved to another area of the store and Archer didn't immediately follow. This was a small place. He could watch her from here and still have a great view of the front door. Also, there weren't any men in here but him. He'd seen a photo of the man suspected of sending death threats to Patch Lambert: Tall, thin and gangly, with a full dark beard and long scraggly hair, at least at the time of a booking photo for another arrest unrelated to Patch.

Before getting this assignment, Archer had come down to Charming a couple of times and hung out at the Salty Dog Bar and Grill. There, he'd run into Ronan Sheridan at least once. Archer had a photographic memory for faces, which served him well in this line of work, and he didn't remember ever seeing the man then, either. Then again, he lived hundreds of miles away and hadn't made any direct threats to Patch's daughter. Archer was fully aware the assignment might end soon. The only issue that remained was this party she wanted to host. He'd be here until he talked her out of it, which might involve a little too much honesty. It wasn't his place to explain to her that her father was once again receiving death threats and the party might draw too much attention. But he'd tell her as a last resort.

After Zoey browsed what seemed like the entire romance section, she was finally ready to go. They each paid for their purchases, and he held the door open for her, following closely behind.

Zoey suddenly stopped and turned, almost running into him. "Again, do you have to make it so obvious that you're my bodyguard?"

"This is not top secret work. It's good to be obvious. That keeps bad men away."

She quirked a brow. "Well, it keeps *all* men away. Didn't we already talk about this?"

"Maybe that's best for now."

After a long moment, she sighed. "It's just…can you please *try* not to be so obvious? I hate people knowing my business."

"No one has to know but us."

He followed her to her vehicle and waited until she buckled in.

Window lowered, she stared at the book in his hands. "You'll have to tell me how it is. Apparently, I like mysteries."

Archer wasn't sure what she meant by that because she gave him a long look, as if *he* was the mystery.

Chapter Nine

Color Zoey not surprised that Archer was in the kitchen bright and early on Tuesday morning when she staggered out of her room wanting coffee. All of this reminded her of the old days, when her family never went anywhere without a chauffeur and a bodyguard. Even now, her dad still employed two regular bodyguards, but it was nothing like it was back when he was getting death threats.

In a throwback to her childhood, she now had her own chauffeur—her handsome, brooding, very Italian chauffeur. If life were a romance novel, she'd quickly fall into bed with said man, immediately fall in love and, after a few obstacles, live happily ever after with him. Or, if her life was a cozy mystery novel, she'd find him dead in the kitchen, a knife sticking out of his back. Then she'd have to solve the mystery with the help of her gardener.

Neither of those scenarios was going to happen, but sooner or later she would solve the mystery of Archer Rossi. Last night, he'd watched TV with her and had not once complained about her choices. They hadn't discussed the hospital situation again, and she thought it best that way. For now.

This morning, she found him dressed in his usual uniform of black slacks that fit him like a glove, a white button-down with the sleeves rolled up to his elbows and a tie.

"I made a coffee run," he said, and handed her a cup from Ava Del Toro's café, The Bean. "Here's your pumpkin spice latte."

Zoey rubbed her eyes and accepted it. "Thank you."

He pointed to her Styrofoam cup. "I don't know how you and my sisters can drink that stuff."

"Because it's divine and it only happens once a year, and we need to celebrate the little things."

Honestly, Zoey would bathe in pumpkin spice if she could. It was a crime that it was only available once a year, but then again, it made her appreciate it that much more.

"I don't suppose you thought of breakfast while you were out," Zoey said. "The most important meal of the day."

"I never eat breakfast." He shook his head.

"You never…you never eat breakfast?" She stuck her hand on her hip. "Did you mother let you get away with that?"

"I got away with a lot, being the only son."

Zoey snorted. "No doubt."

She could not imagine what her father would have done with a son. Zoey's mother could not have any more children, but at one time, she had confided in Zoey that she'd worried about a son having to live up to his father's legacy. No thoughts as to how a daughter would do the same. Kind of old-school, her parents.

"Well, we are not leaving until we both have some protein in our system." She reached for her blender and some protein powder. "The only way I used to get away without breakfast was with a power shake."

Zoey would take care of this man or die trying. She scooped in the powder, almond milk, frozen strawberries and a handful of kale. After blending the ingredients together, she poured the beverage into two travel mugs and handed one to him.

"We can drink breakfast on the way."

This morning, Archer had *kale* in his breakfast. He was working incognito at a *boutique*. If only his friends could see him now! He and Zoey had decided the other day that he would pretend to work at the shop. He'd rather have pretended to be her boyfriend, because pretending was as far as he'd ever get with someone like her. But no, here he was, faux consultant to fashion choices. He couldn't have been further out of his wheelhouse.

The woman in front of him held two dresses against her. "Be honest. Which do you think would look best on me? The blue or the black?"

"I don't feel qualified to say," Archer said. "Why not ask Zoey? I am here giving advice to men."

"And there are no men here now," she said, and pointed to Zoey. "She said you would help. I actually need a man's opinion."

He scowled and caught Zoey's eye. She simply grinned.

"C'mon, what do you think?" She held up and jiggled one dress in one hand and then the other.

"Well." He tugged on his tie, not having a clue. "I'd say the black one."

She took a better look at the dress, draped it against her body. "Here's a better look at the dress *on* me. Still think black is good for my complexion?"

"Black is always good," he insisted.

"Is that because it's all you ever wear?" She canted her head.

"It suits my mood," he said between clenched teeth.

"I don't know, I like *color*," she said.

"It sounds like you've already made up your mind."

This was taking him back to the good old days when he'd had girlfriends who would ask him for advice without really wanting it. All they ever wanted was for him to say, "Looks good." The eternal question was *why anyone would ask him and not want the truth*?

"Maybe you're right," she said, putting the black one back. "I have made up my mind."

"How about some jewelry with that?" Zoey appeared behind the counter. "You're going to need some bling." Zoey held up a sapphire blue necklace. "This piece I just got in and it's truly one of a kind."

"That's gorgeous!" The woman held a hand to her chest. "But what does *he* think?"

Both women turned to him expectantly and he felt his jaw tighten into crush mode.

"Yes, what do you think?" Zoey batted her eyelashes comically. "We need a man's opinion."

He wanted to say, "*You don't need a man's opinion... you're just having fun torturing me!*"

Instead, he nodded. "Very attractive."

"I'll take it!"

The woman grabbed the necklace, thankfully without asking him what he thought of it against her neck. Finally, she was off, carrying her purchases with a wave.

"Thank you! That was a good sale." Zoey appeared at his elbow. "You are turning out to be quite a gem, pun intended."

He was far more like a rock, but when she set her chocolate brown eyes on him, he did feel, if not shiny and bright, maybe a little bit less...broken.

He caught himself staring at her a little too long and

cleared his throat. "I notice you don't have many men coming in."

"That's true, but I do carry an assortment of men's ties and accessories, as well as some beautiful leather jackets, because women like to shop for their men." She walked toward a sumptuous brown leather jacket and slid her hand down the lapel. "Once in a while, I do get a male customer."

"It makes my job easier not to have random men in here, and I'll know to look out for the few brave souls that show up."

"You had better not chase any men out of here." She shook her finger. "I need the business."

Then she said something that struck fear in his heart.

"This jacket would look good on you. It looks like your size."

"No. It won't fit, and anyway, I don't do leather." He shrugged. "Well, not anymore."

"Then you're missing out because women love a man in leather. It's so sexy."

"What? *Why?*" This was a sincere question but she laughed.

"A man in leather is confident, self-assured. Sometimes, though not always, they drive a *motorcycle*."

She landed on the word *motorcycle* as if it was a simile for *orgasm*.

"I hope you don't have any plans to hop on a motorcycle anytime soon, because I will have to torpedo those plans."

"No, I don't, and you are starting to sound like my father." She took the leather jacket off its hanger. "Here, just try it on."

"Um, no. Thanks, but no." He straightened. Let her see he meant no.

"Please?"

He tugged on his tie, the lilt in her voice unnerving him. "Look, over there. I think you have a customer."

She didn't bother looking. "I do, and it's you. I'm going to get you to relax and unwind if it's the last thing I do."

"And you think *leather* is going to help?"

"It can't hurt." She now held the jacket in her hands by the shoulders, shaking it, threatening him with it.

"Fine," he said through clenched teeth. "I am *not* going to unwind on the job, but sure. Why not? Give me the stupid jacket if it will get you to stop talking about it."

He tried to take it from her but she held it out, and after rolling down his shirtsleeves, she slipped it on one arm and then the other. It went on easily so she'd guessed correctly on size. But as he expected, he didn't feel any differently because it was *leather*. The jacket had nothing to do with the way he felt. If he had relaxed at all, it had everything to do with Zoey. It had to do with the way she smiled, with a mix of acceptance and heated desire.

And, as if she'd seen exactly what she wanted…and it was him.

Or the jacket.

Archer whipped out of his trance when the doorbell chimed. A man had just walked into the shop. He didn't look much like a threat, wearing jeans and an unassuming polo shirt, but Archer knew far better than to judge a book by its cover. He turned to Zoey, to gauge her reaction, and a shot of alarm coursed through him. Her eyes had opened wide; she was clearly shocked to see this man. But this was not Scott—Archer had seen enough photos to know. He turned to block the strange man's approach.

"Can I help you?" Archer said putting his body between them.

Zoey came around him. "Peter? What are you *doing* here?"

Peter. Wait, who the hell was *Peter*? Archer had not been told of anyone named Peter.

“You know this man?” Archer asked, glad he hadn’t tackled him. That would be tough to excuse twice.

“Yes,” Zoey said. “I know him.”

There was no fear in her tone, but he thought he detected a hint of apprehension. He would need to know more about this man, and soon.

“It’s been a while,” Peter said. “A long while.”

Chapter Ten

Zoey hadn't seen Peter Connor in a couple of years. In some ways, she'd moved to Charming to get away from him.

"That still doesn't explain what you're doing here," Zoey said, her hand lightly touching Archer's arm so he'd stand down.

Peter, for all his many issues, wouldn't hurt Zoey. At least not physically.

"I was in Houston for a meeting and thought I'd stop in and say hello." He tipped back on his heels.

This was not a welcome development. Zoey didn't want to be rude but there was a reason she hadn't talked to Peter since their breakup. She didn't want her father encouraged in any way to think that she'd ever get back together with "his choice" for her. No way, no how. Her father had a weird way of screening men. In his opinion, they had to be financially well off, and not in a profession that was the least bit hazardous. No danger of concussions or knee injuries. He *really* liked accountants for her.

But one of the last times she'd seen Peter, she asked him whether he'd ever consider moving away from Amarillo and working for someone other than her father.

"Why would I do that? Your father is the best man I know."

"Yes, but…it's weird, you working for my father. Don't you think?"

She'd always believed that his allegiance was to her father, and not her. Peter claimed that wasn't true. But when pushed, he'd always choose her father. Whether it was the chance to attend a football game in the box or any sporting event in conjunction with her dad, he chose that over Zoey every time. And she couldn't fault him completely since he'd been her father's accountant first.

"If you're feeling safe here," Archer said, removing the leather jacket that made him resemble James Dean—if James Dean were Italian, "I will be right over there if you need me."

He strode toward the front of the store, where one of her customers, a woman, accosted him, holding up a glittery gold party dress with a plunging neckline.

"What do you think of this?" she asked. "Would you date me if you saw me wearing this?"

Archer scowled.

"Who is that guy?" Peter said.

"Don't act like you don't know," Zoey said, moving behind the counter.

"I'm not acting!"

Zoey wondered if there was any way in hell Peter could not know her father—his boss—had hired a bodyguard for her. Surely, he'd been the one to send the payment.

"Daddy hired him." She crossed her arms. "Through an agency."

"That's him?" Peter stage-whispered. "The *bodyguard*?"

"So, you do know. Did you suggest the idea to him?"

"No," Peter said. "And I sure wouldn't have suggested someone like him."

Zoey snorted. "Of course not."

"Zoey, that man is someone who's going to try to get close to you, for reasons that have nothing to do with his job."

"Oh, really." Zoey cocked her head. "You probably didn't notice, but he's the consummate professional."

"Sure, of course, that's how it's going to look at first. But before you know it—"

"I'm sorry you came all the way out here for nothing," Zoey interrupted. "Because I don't have the time to hang out or catch up."

"Does your father know what he looks like? Or does he think your bodyguard is some grizzled old man?"

"I have no idea, nor do I care. *He's* the one who insisted I have a bodyguard." Zoey threw her hands up.

"Well, now I think I've got to stick around for a while. Make sure you're safe."

"Safe from my *bodyguard*?"

"From your bodyguard taking liberties."

Zoey pointed. "I swear, if you say anything to my father about this—"

Peter held up his palm. "I won't, if you don't want me to. But that just means I'll have to keep a close eye on him and his intentions."

"No, it doesn't. Really, you don't have to—" But Zoey knew she was losing this argument.

If there was one thing Peter hated more than disorder, it was a man much better looking than him. And, at least in Zoey's eyes, Peter had quickly been downgraded from his usual nine to a seven in Archer's presence. Archer, on the other hand, was a *twelve*.

"It's not a problem. And if this Scott guy is still bothering you, let me take care of that for you, too."

"He's not bothering me anymore. Just sending little gifts and not taking no for an answer."

Peter patted his chest. "I'll have a little talk with him, get him to see reason."

"Good luck. I've tried already, and I don't think anything you say will change things. He's another big fan of Daddy's." She said this slowly and hoped Peter would catch her meaning.

Peter shook his head. "But it isn't Scott who's dangerous. He's not the main problem."

"What do you mean?"

Peter blinked as if he'd just walked into a brightly lit room after being in the dark for hours. "Um, I mean…isn't there someone else stalking you?"

"No," Zoey said. "And I would rather you leave. I'm trying not to hurt your feelings, but surely you remember we're done."

"That was a mistake."

"Was it, really? Because I recall you bounced back pretty quickly with Miss Texas, was it?"

Peter waved a hand dismissively. "Ancient history."

"Not to me."

"We had a good thing going, didn't we?"

Zoey sighed. In her mind, they did not. She'd tried with Peter, especially because it meant so much to her father. He thought of Peter like a son and trusted him with his daughter in addition to managing his financials. But love didn't just need to be a part of a relationship, it had to be everything. She wanted the kind of love and attraction which made it difficult to be apart for even a few hours. Like her mother and father. And she'd never once felt that intensity with Peter. He was like an old, reliable piece of furniture. Convenient, comfortable, but definitely not someone she couldn't do without. A marriage to him would have fizzled out after the first year. There had to be passion, fire, chemistry. Peter felt like a brother and always had.

"Thanks for dropping by," Zoey said. "When you see my father, be sure to tell him I'm doing fine."

Finally, Peter took the cue and left, giving Archer the side-eye as he walked past him.

Archer rejoined Zoey. "Everything okay?"

"I'm fine."

"Was he bothering you? Because unless I misread the signals, he wasn't any danger to you."

"No, he's definitely not any danger."

Archer cleared his throat. "And it seemed like you wanted to talk to him."

"Not really," Zoey said. "But I figured I should. Anyway, he shouldn't be bothering me anymore."

"If he does, I will be here."

"He's… I used to date him for a while."

"I assumed that."

"It didn't work out. He's always worked for my father. It just always seems that men are interested in me because they want to get close to my father."

"I'm sure that's not true."

"That's how it was with Scott, and well, Peter…he's like a son to my father. He never put me first."

"You deserve someone who will."

"Thanks," she said.

"You're welcome."

A curl of heat slid up her neck and she turned away. She'd known this for a long while but hearing it acknowledged and said out loud by Archer affirmed it.

Later that night, Archer had retired to his bedroom, and Zoey was sitting on her living room couch in her bathrobe, her hair already in her bonnet, a bowl of popcorn on her lap. She was video chatting with Twyla.

"I have a problem."

"What's the problem?"

"It's official. I have a raging crush on my bodyguard," she whispered.

"Well, who can blame you? But you've had crushes before. It will work itself out."

"A crush on my favorite musician who stopped in town and gave me an autograph and a selfie is not the same thing. Naturally, that worked itself out. Archer is with me every day, all day. *That* is hard to resist."

"Do you have to resist?"

Zoey had been considering this logically. Yes, technically, he worked for her father, but in another way, a more *important* way, he worked for her. And the problem with all that workplace attraction was that she did not want to be one of those women who took advantage of the situation. For instance, she'd never ask her gardener out on a date. Of course, he was a fifty-something-year-old man, but still. She would never.

"Honestly, this is going to be tough. But I don't want to get sued for workplace harassment." Zoey popped a kernel in her mouth.

"The workplace being *everywhere you go*?"

Twyla had a good point. Their association was the real issue. He had a job to do, and lord only knew, he took it seriously. She'd have to be patient and wait until he'd finished the job and then tell him how she felt. If only she knew whether he felt the same way. He was a mystery to her.

"You haven't told anyone but Noah that I have a bodyguard, have you?"

"No. Why?"

"I don't want people to know. That's my business. And having a bodyguard makes it sound like the whole thing with Scott is far more serious than it is."

"What do people think now? That you hired security for the boutique?"

"Some thought I'd hired a model, which wasn't a bad idea. He drew quite a few customers just standing there. But eventually we agreed that I'd pretend he's my new employee. All he's done so far is give women advice."

Twyla snorted. "I bet he loved that."

"Oh, he was irritated as hell. You should have been there. It was *great*!"

"You are so evil."

"It isn't just his looks that attract me, though. He's just… he told me about his family, and he loves his mother and his sisters. You can just tell by the way his eyes light up when he talks about them. I love a man who respects the women in his life."

"It's a good sign."

"I saw him at the hospital yesterday," Zoey said. "And he saw me coming out of the cancer ward. He was worried about me, but I explained everything. Then he wouldn't tell me why *he* was there."

"Did he follow you there?"

"No, he thought I was staying home all day and he'd been cleared to go to an appointment. He was pretty surprised to see me there. There's something mysterious about him, Twyla. He's got a secret, and I can tell it's a big one."

"He's not married, is he?"

"Girl, you know I asked that first thing. There's no one missing him while he's in town. I'm telling you, *how* is a man like that single? It's a mystery!"

"Mysteries are intriguing."

"Yes, and that's the word for him. Intriguing."

"And hot." Twyla giggled. "Like, Noah-level hot."

"What?" Noah's voice could be heard in the distance. "I'm in the kitchen!"

Twyla giggled. "Nothing, baby. I'm just talking to Zoey!"

Zoey heard a sound like that of a growling tiger and realized it was Twyla's evil cat. Only Twyla would keep a mean cat.

"What is that sound? It sounded like he just hissed, 'Feed me or die.'"

"I already fed him." Twyla turned away from the phone. "He must not have liked it."

"You need a baby. When are you and Noah going to get busy and give me a little niece or nephew?"

"Pretty soon, I think." Twyla smiled and moved with her phone into the kitchen.

There was Noah, his back to the video, cooking something on the stove. *Sigh.* To have a man cooking dinner for her. And here Zoey sat, eating popcorn because Archer had insisted he wasn't hungry.

"What's for dinner?" Zoey asked.

"It smells delish," Twyla said, pointing the camera to Noah.

He turned and flashed his dimpled smile. "Tuscan salmon with penne pasta."

Damn, did he have to be cooking *Italian* tonight? She thought of Archer again and how amazing he'd looked in that leather jacket. Dark and sexy. Brooding. Like an expensive cologne commercial.

"Same me some leftovers."

She hung up with Twyla, and loneliness settled in her bones. She'd always pictured a life with a husband, a couple of children. It wasn't supposed to be taking this long. Dating wasn't actually the problem; Twyla used to joke about how easy it was for Zoey to get a boyfriend. She'd signed up for kickboxing classes once and started dating the instructor.

The issue of finding a good man, however, was entirely different. Every single time she got close, something went wrong. Either he had a fear of commitment, a lack of ambition, a reluctance to have children, or his idolizing of her father got to be too much. Zoey always saw this last one as a big red flag.

Zoey didn't believe in settling. That attitude was probably why she was thirty and still single, but there was no way her mother would be proud if Zoey accepted less than everything she deserved.

Chapter Eleven

The next morning, Zoey checked on her chilled pumpkin bars. After refrigerating overnight, they were perfect. She'd felt notably better the prior evening after taking out her sorrows baking. Something about measuring ingredients, mixing and taste testing soothed her soul. The exacting nature of baking left nothing to the imagination and seemed to be the only way Zoey could cook. When it came to food, she wasn't terribly creative. Give her fashion and makeup any day of the week, but cooking remained a challenge.

Last night, in the middle of mixing batter, Zoey came to a decision: she had to know if Archer would be interested in her, if not for their unique situation. She didn't believe that every man could possibly be attracted to her, even if she didn't downplay her looks. Looks were important to some men—the wrong kind of men. Last night, she'd devised a plan.

Her phone pinged and she picked it up from the kitchen counter. There was no caller ID.

Did you get my flowers?

How was it Scott again? She'd blocked him. Had she screwed that up somehow? She wasn't the techiest person.

Then she noticed it was a different number. He had a new phone, or a burner. Had it come to this? Using burners? Didn't only drug dealers use those?

Yes, got them, and while that was nice of you, it wasn't necessary.

At least you had something to give the nurses at the hospital.

Zoey sucked in a breath. Had he seen her going to the hospital? Had he been there too? For the first time since this all started, Zoey felt a pulse of alarm sweep through her.

Are you following me?!!

Don't be crazy. I know you go there almost every Monday. Did you actually give them to the nurses?

He inserted an eye roll emoji. Of course, he knew that she went to the hospital regularly. They'd dated so he knew her schedule. Wait: He *knew her schedule.* But no, her father was wrong. A bodyguard *was* overkill. She simply had to stop engaging with Scott, as Archer had suggested.

Archer waltzed in from the patio, aviator shades on, moving like a panther.

"We need to talk. Why was the alarm disarmed when I woke up this morning?"

"Well, good morning to you, too, Archer!" Zoey met him halfway. "The gardener is coming this morning and I disarm it so it doesn't accidentally go off and send the cops over."

"No."

"No, I didn't disarm it? Or no, my gardener isn't coming?"

He lowered his shades. "No, do not ever disarm the alarm again. You can only do that when there are no threats."

"And when would that be? When there's peace on Earth?" Zoey put a hand on her hip.

"Let's not argue today." He waved a hand dismissively. "Are you ready to go to work?"

"No." She loved arguing with him. "I'm not ready."

He lifted his wristwatch and glanced at it. "But it's time."

"Yes, but I had a fashion emergency," Zoey lied.

"Please don't tell me you need a man's opinion." He scowled.

Zoey laughed. "As if. I never ask a man's opinion when it comes to my fashion choices. I'm the one who has to wear the thing."

"Finally, something that makes sense." He uncrossed his arms. "Then why do you keep asking for my advice when it comes to your customers?"

"To give you something to *do* besides standing around and looking pretty."

He harrumphed. "Okay, if you don't need my opinion, how can I help you now?"

"I didn't say you could help," Zoey said, pointing to the couch. "Just relax while I try to fix this issue."

"Fine." He plopped down on the sofa.

"Help yourself to the remote."

Stupidly, she'd placed a screen in the guest room so they didn't even have to watch TV together in the evenings. She suspected he did it from time to time just so he could keep an eye on her. He'd study his phone, glancing up at her every few minutes as if worried she wouldn't still be there. Every once in a while, when the laugh track went off on her comfort show, *Frasier*, he'd look up, the crease between his brow deeper. She'd be laughing so hard she wanted to pee, but he just didn't get it.

"Why is this so funny?"

"Because Frasier can't remember the words to the song! He's on live TV, a marathon for charity, and he's just faking it. *'And bum da bum da, buttons and bows!'*"

God, it was hilarious. She and Mami used to watch *Frasier* reruns. Zoey would lay her head in Mami's lap sometimes, and other times she used the opportunity to braid Zoey's hair.

Now she left the room before Archer could growl at her again.

Zoey wandered into her bedroom. Now the real work began. She didn't think she'd behaved like such a schoolgirl since she was…wait. She'd *never* done this before. Usually men were after her, chasing, flirting, until *she* noticed them. But those had been all the *wrong* men, hadn't they? Peter. Mick. Scott… It occurred to her that if she wanted to change things, maybe she had to make the first move. She had to be the one to initiate the chase and go after a man who *wasn't* so obviously interested, to see where it might lead.

In her bedroom, she heard the sounds of ESPN drifting from the living room. Archer was watching soccer.

Flipping through her work-appropriate dresses, she found one that zipped up in the back. *Perfect.* Now, all she had to do was act like one of those helpless women who couldn't zip themselves up. After years as a runway model, Zoey practically had double-jointed arms and could reach firmly behind her without any issues. But she'd seen plenty of girls need help. Girls with shorter arms, for instance. For a few minutes, she could pretend to be one of them. Then she'd see if there was even a hint of interest from Archer. She'd found the perfect knee-length dress, a silky white one that complemented her skin. She purposely zipped the dress only three-quarters of the way up.

She strode toward him, a firm plan in her mind, but chickened out halfway down the hallway. Luckily, he was engrossed in the game and didn't notice. Was she really going to do this? *Pretend she couldn't zip up her dress by herself?* What was she, five? But no. She reminded herself of all the girls she'd helped during fashion week. This was a common-enough occurrence. Sure. Of course! *Just do it.*

"Thank you for waiting," Zoey said. "Just one last thing. Could you help me with my, uh, zipper?"

He stood, and she didn't imagine the double take she saw flit across his eyes. Score! This dress always drew attention from men. Twyla said it showed off her legs in the best way.

She turned so he could better access the zipper and lifted her hair out of the way.

"It probably seems silly, like I should be able to do this, because I have long arms, but you know how it is. Sometimes... um, you just can't reach? At least, that's what's happening right now."

Stop talking. She'd had no idea that having a crush on someone could be such torture. Years ago, she used to think if she could just meet Idris Elba in real life, her life would be set. But it might have gone something like this. Awkward. Her nerves on fire with the pull of her attraction.

"It is no problem," Archer said, but his voice was low, gruff, just a scrape of a deep sound.

His warm, strong fingers briefly touched her bare skin and she closed her eyes. She thought she might have heard a swift intake of breath as he pulled the zipper up. *Not* quickly. It was a slow slide and she enjoyed every second of it. His hands didn't leave her all at once. One callused hand slid down her bare arm before his touch stopped. When his hands were no longer on her, a cold snap filled her. She could get used to those hands. She turned ever so slowly to see whether this exercise had any effect on him.

Clearly, there *had* been an effect, because he looked at her as if he'd never seen her before. Or…wait. Oh. Just like he had that first time they met, when she'd been so preoccupied. When he'd let her go on and on about a gift for his girlfriend. His eyes were smoldering, pupils dilated, his lips slightly parted.

"I hope my hands weren't too rough on your skin," he said.

"Not at all."

"It has been a long time since I've had to perform that function."

It was difficult to believe that.

"Well, it's much appreciated." She made a point not to break eye contact.

He also didn't look away, a blazing heat in his gaze.

"Thank you." She took his hand in hers, a bold move. "And I'm sorry again about making you wait."

Archer slid the back of his hand down the curve of her jaw. "Now this is *soft*. You are so beautiful."

Zoey had heard those words for many years, from men, photographers, strangers, friends and family. But they had never in her life made her heart squeeze in such a powerful tug. Those words from him meant far more than they should. She wondered if he also felt the heat sliding between them, the sizzling chemistry.

"You think so?"

"There is nothing wrong with my eyesight," he said, and

for some odd reason she felt as though he was telling her that something else about him was defective.

And in that case, it had to be something she couldn't see.

Like his heart.

Chapter Twelve

Archer dropped his hand as quickly as he'd raised it to cup her face.

He couldn't have this. Couldn't have Zoey. It was inappropriate to zip her dress, to touch that luscious skin, but, damn, that dress paired with that *face*. He was a goner.

Missing pieces and all.

He cleared his throat and tugged at his tie. "Shall we go?"

"Yes, but..." She walked out of the room into the kitchen, giving him an amazing view of her behind. "I want to be honest with you, and I'm not going to downplay this anymore."

She swiped and unlocked her phone and handed it to him. "I blocked him, but this must be another number."

He read the text from someone without a caller ID. The freaking nerve of this guy! He'd like to meet up with him in a dark alley, though he doubted there were many of those in Charming.

"Is this the guy? The one who sent the flowers?"

"Well...who else could it be? It *sounded* like Scott." She pointed. "In the card, he asked why I'd blocked him."

"Right." He nodded, then started texting without her permission.

"What are you doing?" She leaned over his shoulder, and *Dio Mio*, she smelled as good as she looked.

He took a step back, for the sake of his sanity. "Don't worry, you'll get final approval."

In the end his text read:

Listen: do not contact me again. The unwanted gifts verge on stalker behavior. Cease and desist or I will go to the police if you continue.

He showed it to her and she blinked.

"That sounds *mean*."

"Good." He quickly hit Send.

"But it also doesn't sound like me at all," she said. "I don't use words like 'cease and desist.' He's going to wonder if it's actually me."

The phone pinged almost immediately:

Who is this? Zoey? Why are you talking all weird?

"See? I told you!" Zoey's palms went up.

"That is fine," Archer said. "We gave him the message. Now we hope he understands."

The phone was still in hands when it pinged again:

WTF. I just want to get together so you can tell me what I did wrong.

Interesting. Archer showed it to Zoey and her lower lip quivered.

"What *did* he do wrong?" Archer asked, curiosity getting the best of him.

"Nothing. I feel bad for him. He wanted to get married and I—"

"What did you say?" He couldn't have heard right. *"Married?"*

"Yes, he suggested we get married but…we're not a match." She shook her head.

Archer scratched his temple. "I'm sorry, I misunderstood. I thought you had dated this man a short time, but this was a long-term relationship?"

Zoey shook her head and her curls bounced. "Nope. I only dated him a month, which is why I was so shocked."

Archer cursed in Italian.

"We're going to have to find a better way to discourage him."

"Do you have any ideas?"

Archer's only idea was to make the man think Zoey was seeing someone else. But if he ramped up his stalker behavior, he'd discover there wasn't really anyone new in her life, other than her new employee.

"Wait," Archer said. "I've got it."

Zoey smiled. "Yeah?"

"It might help if he believed you were at least interested in someone else," he said. "Not that you necessarily need to be *dating* anyone, but simply make him think that there's interest. It might discourage him enough to realize you're not marriage material."

"Okay, yeah. I could do that. I don't have to give him a name."

He handed Zoey the phone and her thumbs flew across the screen.

"There!" She finished, then showed Archer the phone.

Archer read the text.

Listen, there's someone else. We're not dating or anything, but I just can't get married when I have these kinds of intense feelings for another man. I hope you understand. Also, he's Italian. I'm so sorry, but you need to move on.

"That's…that's good."

Archer swallowed around the golf ball in his throat. She'd gone ahead and decided to use him in a small way, just as they'd talked about before. The whole fake boyfriend angle.

"Except for apologizing. No need to apologize. Just be direct."

She held her arms out, stretching to the sky. "Thank you! This feels so…freeing. Telling the truth—there's nothing like it."

Normally, Archer would agree. But in this case, the truth gave him chest pains.

That night, alone in the guest room, Archer went down the rabbit hole. Several online searches later, he had sourced a lot of information about bodyguards crossing the line with their clients. It seemed Hollywood was particularly fond of this idea. He even found a series about a secret service agent who falls for his client. It seemed this situation was quite common, though possibly not as common as Hollywood would have people think. Perhaps it was because of how much time bodyguards and their clients spent together. There were obviously ethical issues involved, and Archer was certain he'd read something along those lines in the contract he'd signed with his agency. It was definitely not encouraged and fell decidedly into a morally gray area.

In the end, it came down to what he'd suspected all along, and Archer was unbending when it came to his morals. It came with the territory of the military code. He'd never violate an oath.

But he also hadn't counted on Zoey Lambert.

He hadn't expected how direct she'd been with him. This was a huge turn-on, too. He loved women who knew exactly what they wanted. Women who made the first move. Unfortunately, he wasn't in the position to return the favor, and the job wasn't the only problem.

It was time to make a phone call and he picked up his cell. The phone rang three times before Sally, his therapist, picked up.

"You said I should call," Archer said.

"I didn't mean like this. It's after hours."

"Sorry. Never mind."

He was about to press the End Call button when she said, "Wait! Let's talk."

"There's no point. I don't even know why I'm calling."

"You *know* why you're calling me," Sally said. "Something must have happened."

"Yes," Archer said.

"And…?" She hesitated. "It's your turn to say something."

Archer sighed and raked a hand down his face. "I'm out of town on an assignment. That's why I canceled my appointment."

"Archer, don't avoid the question. It's okay to tell me you got overzealous again. You're still adjusting to civilian life."

"No, that's not it. I…may have met someone."

"What did I tell you? I knew it wouldn't be long." Archer could hear the smile in her voice.

"I said *'may'* because it's impossible. We…"

Archer didn't know how much he wanted to tell her about Zoey. These calls were confidential unless he threatened to hurt himself or others, but he didn't like discussing such private matters. Still, he had worked hard on his mental and emotional health. Early on, he'd decided to work as hard on those aspects of himself as on his physical therapy.

"The timing is off," he said. "Let's leave it there."

"But this woman…you're attracted to her?"

"Yes," Archer groaned. "And she is attracted to me."

There was a long beat of silence. "And she doesn't know."

No need to ask what she meant. "No, and I'd like to keep it that way."

"I guess that means you don't have any thoughts of being intimate with this woman?"

Dio Mio, this was so uncomfortable.

"I…wouldn't say *that*."

"You've read the literature. Women are far more accepting of amputees than men realize."

"I doubt she would be the problem. It's me."

"I see. So, you're still stuck in the same pattern of thinking that ended your prior relationship."

"That was a different situation."

With Jenna, everything changed when he returned stateside. She wanted to immediately pick up where they'd left off, but Archer's feelings had changed. In many ways. He needed more out of a relationship than someone who was entirely focused on the physical. That wasn't an indictment of her; she had been kind and accepting in every way. She'd wanted to take care of him. But Archer couldn't accept the fact that their roles had changed. He always took care of people, not the other way around. And when their former intimacy didn't immediately resume as she would have liked, she was upset. He actually wasn't sure who'd pulled away first, but he'd been the one to tell her they were over.

"Do you think *you've* accepted your new body?"

How did a person simply accept missing a piece of his anatomy? It was easier said than done. Unless he was in pain, Archer kept his prosthesis on even when he was alone. He only removed it at appointments, and to sleep, because that was recommended. Even *he* didn't like looking at his stump. It reminded him of…everything.

He'd read about people who dated amputees, but the most disturbing thing he'd learned was that a condition existed called acrotomophilia, where some people were sexually aroused by amputations. This brought about a power imbalance in which the amputee could be exploited. Sally had told him about it in one of their sessions, because she'd been worried after seeing some of the mail Archer received when his photo was posted on the organization's Instagram account. He'd received a dozen marriage proposals from strangers after that.

You'd never have to work another day in your life.

Here's some money.

I'd take good care of you.

Humiliating stuff that pissed him off.

But on the other side of that uncomfortable obsession, there were women who Archer suspected might be completely turned off by a man missing his ankle and foot. Sally assured him that wouldn't be the case for most women, but he begged to differ.

She had encouraged him to go on a few dates, even if he wasn't particularly interested in the woman. It would be "good practice," she said. But Archer had not been on a single date since he'd moved to Houston, even if there had been opportunity. And now he saw Sally's point. Faced with someone who really mattered, he didn't know how he could tell the truth. All he wanted was for someone to appreciate him for who he was, and not what he'd lost.

Zoey was such a soft touch. If he told her what happened, and she started to cry, he wouldn't be able to handle it. He could not stand her pity. It would be for the best if she never had a reason to find out.

"I don't know," Archer said. "This woman…well, she's extremely compassionate. She's worried she'll hurt someone's feelings with the smallest of things."

"And you think she won't admit how she truly feels about the prosthesis because she would be too worried about hurting your feelings?"

"Well…yes. But it's a moot point. I can't see her, anyway. There's a conflict of interest."

"All right, then we're back to what I talked about before," Sally said. "You might not be able to be physically intimate with her, but what about friendship? If you trust her, and you're spending time together, share the truth with her. It will make it that much easier to do it with someone else in the future."

Practice…on *Zoey*? The idea held zero appeal. He didn't want to *practice* on Zoey, like she was some kind of placeholder. She deserved more. Even if he couldn't give it to her.

"If not her, then how about someone else as practice?"

It wasn't as if Archer hadn't been flirted with since he'd arrived in Texas. He simply hadn't had the desire to date anyone, but now he was motivated. Besides, a date didn't mean anything. It was just a chance to get to know each other.

"Take a direct, confident approach," Sally said. "For example, 'By the way, I have a prosthetic foot, but it's not a big deal. Just thought I'd mention it.'"

Seriously?

It felt like it should be more of a natural progression.

"Or, you could wait until intimacy is near," Sally said. "With the right person, someone you've connected with on every other level, they'll be accepting. After all, you forget that *everyone* has issues. No one is perfect."

She had a point. He didn't know everything about Zoey. She *couldn't* be perfect, could she?

Chapter Thirteen

On the good news front, Zoey had dropped a clue the size of Texas that she was attracted to Archer. Rules be damned! She wasn't much of a rule follower, anyway, never had been. On the bad news front, she wasn't sure he didn't think this was all a ruse, as he'd initially suggested pretending that he was her boyfriend. Not only had Archer ignored her comment about her crush being Italian—or pretended she couldn't mean *him*—Scott had texted back:

So, who is this guy?

She hadn't texted him back, considering the possibility that Archer—and her father, and well…pretty much everyone—could be right, and she might be a little *too* nice.

Over the next few days, Archer and Zoey were together from sunup to sundown, with her insisting on making him both breakfast and dinner. He retired to his guest bedroom at the end of the evening, and she went to hers, alone. On Saturday, after she'd closed up shop and they were home, Archer once more brought up the idea of canceling the party. He'd mentioned it every couple of days in an off-handed kind of way.

Like, "*Are you still having that event?*" To which she'd unfailingly respond, "*Are you out of your mind? Of course!*"

Now, when he asked her again, she turned to him, as he sat facing her on one of the stools in the kitchen. "It's a week away! I can't cancel now."

"But explain. What's so special about this event?" He picked up one of the shiny red apples in her fruit bowl and bit into it.

"I already told you," she said, reaching for a pan so she could start a quick dinner.

The main course was a pumpkin pasta recipe she'd looked up online, served with pumpkin spice tea and her pumpkin cupcakes. He didn't complain about her food, just raised a brow every time she said *pumpkin*. He'd told her once that he'd be drunk in two minutes if he took a shot every time she said *pumpkin*.

He wasn't wrong.

Every day, Archer insisted that she didn't have to feed him, but he also didn't hesitate to finish his plate. She'd explained over and over that this was what her mother used to do with their family bodyguards, and it just seemed natural to her. Besides, it was Saturday night and she'd invited Twyla over, too, so that the three of them could go over the logistics of the party. Twyla was in charge of the guest list and Archer had been asking for this meeting so he could get his hands on it. It shocked her to think he was actually going to do background checks on all of her guests.

"The party is my annual tradition and it means a lot to me." She chopped garlic and stirred in some olive oil as the base.

"You've said that, but why?"

"I've already told you that I am a champion of love."

"And there are a million people who feel the same, but they don't have a party to celebrate it every year."

She sighed. "I don't see why I should cancel. You know I could take Scott easy, and with you here, we truly have nothing to worry about. I don't even think he's going to show up."

When Twyla arrived on schedule, carrying with her a bottle of wine, Zoey hugged her tight and whispered, "He's a little on edge about the party."

Twyla got the message: Assure Archer the party guests would behave like relatives of Mother Teresa.

"It is nice to see you again." Archer nodded. "I am enjoying the book. So far only one dead body but I am hopeful."

Twyla chuckled. "Be patient, more are coming."

Zoey led them into the living room, where she'd laid out a spread on the coffee table: a charcuterie board piled with cheese, olives, grapes, crackers and rolled slices of deli meat formed in the shape of hearts. A pitcher of pumpkin spice tea sat nearby next to three iced tumblers.

"How sweet. You didn't have to do all this."

"Nonsense, you're my guest." She turned to Archer, standing by as always, like a soldier who needed to be ordered "at ease." "Twyla's husband owns Nacho Boat Adventures, and he had a big event of his own today. You'll meet him at the party."

"Here's the guest list of those who've RSVPed." Twyla pulled it out of her purse and handed it to Archer, who started to peruse it immediately.

"If you'll excuse me, I'm going to do a quick check on these guests." He took off down the hallway toward the guest room, and Zoey plopped down next to Twyla on the sofa, helping herself to an olive.

"I see what you mean," Twyla said. "He's very serious all the time, isn't he? Even when he jokes."

Zoey reached for Twyla's hands. "He's going to do a background check on each one of my guests, including you and Noah. I'm so sorry."

Twyla shrugged. "He's going to find out about that speeding ticket I got last year."

"Oh, you and Noah are fine, but good grief! Can anybody say they've had a perfect past?"

Twyla frowned. "I'm thinking he's looking for serious things like assault and battery. He is being paid a salary, so I can understand why he's doing it. I'm sure it's not much of a hardship to simply hang out with you every day."

Zoey smirked. "Except for when a customer comes in and I make him work. I love watching him sweat when the ladies ask him for his opinion."

"You're so mean." Twyla laughed. "I like seeing this side of you. How come you're not nice to him like you are to everybody else?"

"I'm not mean. I'm *flirting*."

"I've forgotten you angry-flirt." Twyla smiled and popped a grape in her mouth. "Well, he definitely notices you, if that helps."

"He does?"

"Yes, there's definitely an awareness going on there. I can sense it."

"Well, I'm not sure he's getting the message," Zoey said, and handed Twyla her phone. "Check out the last text I sent to Scott."

Twyla read and her eyes widened. "That's pretty direct. *And also, he's Italian?* Why did you feel the need to add that?"

"Why do you think? Archer has been advising me on

what to tell Scott so he'll stop texting me and sending me gifts. I thought he should see what I wrote. And I loaded it with a big clue."

Twyla laughed. "And…?"

Zoey shrugged. "Nothing."

"Well, you need to consider that this is his job and he doesn't want to be inappropriate."

"It's not inappropriate when he's given an invitation, is it?" Zoey said.

"How *many* have been given an invitation?" Archer's voice boomed from the hallway, making Zoey jump.

"Um, uh…" Zoey elbowed Twyla. "How many?"

"We sent out twenty with plus-ones, but so far only fifteen have RSVPed."

Archer nodded. "And Scott, he is not invited, right?"

"Oh, no," Twyla assured him. "He's definitely not."

Archer quirked a brow. "So, twenty guests and their plus-ones, which makes forty people."

"It's fine. We have plenty of room!" Zoey waved her hand dismissively.

"There's room, yes, but this whole plus-one thing…how do you know who is the plus-one?"

"He's got a point," Twyla said. "We *don't* know. I'm only assuming no one will bring Scott, but that's not out of the question. We have mutuals."

"Exactly." Archer nodded.

"Okay, so what do we do? Check people at the door? As in, *show me your papers*?" Zoey said facetiously.

"No," Archer said patiently. "It is a free country. But if Scott comes to the party, either we ask him to leave, or I'm afraid you will find yourself with a shadow all night."

"I told you I don't want people to *know* I have a bodyguard."

"I've got it!" Twyla stood. "You can pretend he's your date!"

"My…date?" Zoey said.

It was basically what Archer had suggested they tell people at her shop, but that wouldn't have made any sense at all. At a party, though, it was reasonable. It would also give her a chance to flirt more openly with him under the guise of plausible deniability.

"Just for the night!" Twyla said. "It makes sense. That way no one will wonder why this man is sticking so close to you."

"But what if Scott doesn't show up?"

"It still works," Twyla said.

Archer nodded. "I agree. It's the best way to handle it. Either you let everyone know I'm your bodyguard, or…"

"I know, I get it." Zoey held up her palms in an "I give up" gesture. "Fine."

Truthfully, she wasn't the least bit mad about it.

The next day, Zoey went for a morning swim before work. It was Sunday and not part of her regular routine, but the exercise had started to help with some of the stress she felt surrounding the party. She could meditate in the water. Something was not right about all of this. She could feel it in her bones.

Archer was keeping something from her, and she had no idea if it had something to do with her or if he had a secret of his own. But she hadn't heard from Scott again after his last direct message, and Scott had never been a violent person. She couldn't shake the thought that he wasn't the problem, that there was something else, and she wished she could get to the bottom of it.

She dived under the water, hoping to clear her head,

but when she came up at the other end, she saw the boots on the ledge. Her gaze slid up to look at the man who belonged to those boots. Archer, standing by to take her to work, at the ready.

"Only in South Texas can you swim outside in September," he said.

"And Florida and California," she reminded him.

"This is not your usual day for a swim. You're off schedule."

She pushed back and smiled. "Why don't you join me? It's good exercise."

He held up a hand. "No, I'm on duty."

"I guess you're always on duty," she said, doing the backstroke.

"When I'm with you, yes."

"It's like you don't have any downtime."

"When we're on assignments, we usually don't get much of that. Of course, with more serious situations, there is a team and we take shifts. Eight- to twelve-hour shifts, then time off."

"So, this is just one very long shift to you, is it?"

"Well, yes." He took a seat on one of her wicker chairs. "I have some good news and some bad news about your guest list."

She'd been wondering about the security checks but didn't want to sound like she was digging for dirt on her friends. Archer would tell her if something was important enough to pass on.

"And? Which one of my friends is wanted by the law?"

"No one," Archer said, tipping back on his heels. "A few of them have trouble obeying the speed limit, a few divorces, nothing unusual or remotely dangerous."

"I'm glad."

"But people are unpredictable. I still want you to consider canceling the party."

"No," she said, and swam away.

Zoey completed one last lap and then climbed out of the pool. Today, she'd taken pity on Archer—or given up on flirting—and worn her one-piece racer back suit that revealed nothing but a lot of leg. When she reached for her cover-up, she caught him purposefully not looking in her direction. His aviator shades were on, and he had a scowl firmly planted on his face. She toweled off, then sat on the chair across from his.

"How did you luck into this assignment? Are you the rookie? Or do you all draw straws to take the worst jobs?"

Archer didn't answer, but instead turned to her and lowered his shades to peer at her over them. "What do you think?"

"Oh, my God, you're being *punished*, aren't you?"

"What makes you think you're the worst job?"

"We're talking about Scott here! I mean the lowest level threat, right? Isn't that what you said?"

"Yes, true. But that's not the only way assignments are measured. There are other factors, like location and the type of client. Some are difficult and unpleasant. You're by far the best client. I was lucky to get this assignment."

"Aw, that's sweet. But I imagine no one wants these boring assignments. There's no action for you adrenaline junkies."

"What makes you say I'm an adrenaline junkie?"

"You seem like the type."

"Boring is good." He removed his shades and pocketed them. "But yes, I made a mistake on a past assignment. And I'm a new hire."

"What was the mistake? Did you get involved with your client?"

Hope sprang eternal.

He chuckled and shook his head. "No. I mistakenly thought that a man was reaching in his jacket for a gun, so I tackled him. It turned out he was the client's brother and he was just reaching for his cell phone. No threat to her at all."

Zoey bit her lower lip to keep from laughing out loud. "Oh, dear."

"It's okay, you can laugh." Archer's lips quirked in a smile. "It is funny now. Even to me."

"It seems like a mistake anyone could make."

"There you go, being too nice again."

"Is that a crime? I don't know why we can't all be kinder to each other. You never know what kind of battle someone is fighting. You don't know what kind of day they had when they cut you off in traffic and curse. Maybe they just got fired, or their spouse asked for a divorce. It could be the worst day of their life. We need to stop judging each other so much."

"More people should be like you, Zoey, but then I would be out of a job."

"Well, I don't want *that*."

They simply gazed at each other for a long moment. Then Zoey looked away because his intensity was almost too much for her. He was…simply smoldering. And that mouth of his, *so* generous and sexy.

"You would never consider getting involved with a client?" Zoey asked. "Just…out of curiosity."

"It's against the rules and unethical." His amber eyes were shimmering.

Damn, she hated rules that cost jobs.

"I wouldn't want you to lose your job."

She lowered her head, not meeting his eyes. This felt so impossible.

Archer rose. "I'll wait for you inside."

She watched him swing open the patio doors and disappear inside the house.

Why were the good ones always out of reach?

Chapter Fourteen

Zoey took off her cap, styled her hair and was getting dressed for work when her father called to check in.

"You still mad at me?"

She sighed. "No, I understand why you did it. You were in classic overprotective daddy mode and I should have seen it coming."

Daddy chuckled. "Are you not getting along with him?"

"I never said we weren't getting along."

"You wanted him to leave the day he arrived."

"That's because I thought it was too much and unnecessary."

"Do you still think so?"

Maybe, but this assignment was an easy transition for him, and that was the point. She wanted to help with that. The poor guy mistook someone's brother for a stalker, and his phone for a gun. Here in Charming, he was almost getting a paid vacation. But there was something else going on with Archer. Overall, he carried himself with confidence, but there was also something deeply vulnerable about him. Something he hid from the world.

"I don't know why, but he keeps asking me to cancel the party. He thinks it's too dangerous and even did background checks on all my guests. Is he overreacting?"

"I don't think so. You should trust his judgment on this. He's been properly trained."

"Yes, but…so Peter was in town and dropped in to say hello, and he said something interesting."

"Yeah?"

"Yeah. He said something to the effect that Scott wasn't the *real* danger, and then he corrected himself. Like somehow I'd heard him wrong, but I didn't. Daddy, please tell me the truth—is the real danger that I might actually meet someone else and you're still intent on us being together?"

Her father laughed like the idea was ridiculous. "No, I gave up on you two a long time ago."

She wanted to tell him that Peter didn't want to give up on them, but she didn't want the conversation to take another turn.

"Honestly, I don't need a bodyguard," she said. "But I appreciate the thought. Archer's a good guy."

"Yeah? I got close to my bodyguards. We're still friends to this day, even if they no longer work for me. What's yours like? Does he like football?"

Zoey rolled her eyes even if he couldn't see her. Her daddy thought the world revolved around football.

"He's young, about my age. And he likes *soccer* but calls it football."

He laughed hard enough to hack up a lung. "One of *those*."

"Having a bodyguard and a chauffeur has certainly brought back memories."

"I'm sorry about all that, baby girl. Football fans have been known to be unreasonable at times."

"It actually brings back good memories of you, me and Mami. It was sort of like we were the Three Musketeers and it was us against the world. Every time someone said something terrible about you on ESPN, I could literally see the fumes coming out of her ears. She was your biggest champion. But then she got sick, and everybody loved you again."

"God, I miss her. Every day." Her father's voice broke.

She hadn't meant to bring up painful memories. Thinking of her mother made Zoey happy, but with her father it was different. He only fixated on what he'd lost, not what he'd had.

"I want what you two had, Daddy. My person. The one who will always be there for me, who will be on my team. I need my *own* team."

"And I want that for you, baby."

"Then you're going to have to accept that you can't choose that man. I will need to date plenty of men to find the one, eventually."

"I don't have a problem with that. But maybe you need to screen them better. Maybe I should have them screened *for* you."

"No thanks, because no one is going to be perfect. He just has to be *my* kind of perfect, not yours. Only I can screen for that."

Her father chuckled. "You mean he might not appreciate American football?"

"What I'm saying is that's not a qualifier."

"Makes sense to me. All I want is for him to be someone who puts you first, who won't hurt you, who will never leave you and will always protect you."

Zoey rolled her eyes. "Interesting. You've just described a bodyguard."

"Well, he won't get *paid* to do it. How about that?"

"I can take care of myself. You're just going to have to accept that."

"Just make sure you leave room for the man you love to feel wanted, as if you *need* him to protect you, even if you don't."

"Is that romance advice from *my father*?"

"I think it's what your mother would say."

He was probably right.

"I have an appointment today," Zoey announced as she and Archer were opening the store.

"Where are we going?"

"Nowhere. She's coming to us."

Someone wanted a wedding dress! The timing could not be more perfect, as it was September, when to Zoey it seemed like everything was right and proper with the world.

Rachel, the bride-to-be, worked as a paralegal at the law firm belonging to Michelle LaCroix, now officially Michelle Sheridan, although she hadn't changed her last name for professional reasons. Rachel had booked the appointment six months ago, right after she'd been proposed to by her police officer boyfriend, Cameron.

"What should I do?" Archer asked, probably worried she'd want him to give his opinion on wedding dresses.

"Just stand down, if you don't mind. These bridal fittings are by appointment only, and Sundays are usually so slow that it's not a problem."

"How many wedding dresses do you usually sell in a month, say?"

"This is something new, and I'm still working on getting the word out. I've been working at building up my inventory. A few months ago, I scoured online estate sales looking for vintage gems."

Her business plan was very specific as to how much she could spend and she'd honored it, but that meant she had a ways to go before the wedding dress side of her boutique was what she'd like it to be. Nevertheless, she'd managed to collect dozens of beautiful gowns and was confident she had something here for Rachel.

Rachel showed up right on time, and Zoey greeted her client with open arms. Fortunately, Rachel, too, was a hugger. "I can't believe this day is finally here."

"Hello," Archer said from next to Zoey.

He, on the other hand, wasn't a hugger. Zoey made the introductions.

"So it's true that you hired help," Rachel said to Zoey.

"I help the men who come in and also the women at times, when they have questions," Archer supplied.

Damn, he was a good liar.

"It's been nice having someone else around when it gets really busy," Zoey said, feeling only a little bit bad about lying to a customer.

"That's great," Rachel said, her gaze pausing as she seemingly admired "the help."

"Archer, why don't you order us some lunch? We'll just be in the back."

Zoey led Rachel to the annex and the dressing area with a large mirror and pedestal that she'd bought from a store in Austin that was going out of business.

"I know I have something in here for you." Zoey had already chosen a few dresses to begin with. "I've set aside a few choices—sweetheart collar, long train, short train, strapless. All first-rate designers. But you tell me, what did you have in mind?"

Rachel set down her purse and turned in a circle. "Oh, my gosh! So much white!"

"I have some off-white, too, and maybe two that are a sort of beige. But yes, the designers do seem to be sticking to the tried and true." Zoey walked over to the dresses she'd picked out. "Were you thinking white or off-white?"

Rachel worried a fingernail between her teeth. "Oh, um… I've been looking through all the magazines and searching online for hours. I love so many of the styles, but what I want—all I really want—is a dress that will make him realize he's made the best decision of his life!"

"Okay, girl, I got you." Zoey had just the dress. She hadn't initially picked this one out, but now, seeing Rachel and her buxom hourglass figure, she had a great idea. "Try this one on and tell me what you think."

Archer couldn't get out of the shop fast enough. Zoey wouldn't approve, but he flipped the sign to Closed and locked it from the outside with the key she'd had made for him. He wouldn't be gone long, and Sunday was apparently a slow day. But even though he wasn't going far, leaving his post felt wrong.

He headed to the Salty Dog Bar and Grill owned by a trio of Navy SEALs, who'd retired and gone into business together. For that reason, a large number of veterans patronized the place. This was where he'd first run into Ronan Sheridan after his initial interview with Texas EP. His boss was the one who had told him about the bar in Charming, about a half hour's drive from Houston. There weren't many places he could go to commiserate with fellow soldiers and other military personnel. He felt safe here, wholly accepted. On the walls were photos of service members, emblems like Semper Fi and framed photos with sayings like, "The only easy day was yesterday." Only a soldier could relate.

He ordered a classic burger and fries and, while he waited, took an empty stool in the bar section. Max Del Toro was bartending tonight, one of the three former Navy

SEALs who bought this place. Archer liked his direct approach to customers. It wouldn't be to everyone's liking, but Max wasn't the type of person who put up with any funny business. Archer could relate. Max was a big guy, too, and Archer could picture him as a bodyguard himself. The last time he'd been here, he'd seen him "escort" a guy out of the bar who'd had a few too many and groped at their waitress. *Escort* was a kind word; he more or less threw him out on his ass.

He needed more friends like Max because his own former crew was scattered all over the country. Sally had told him that even if he didn't go to group counseling sessions for PTSD, he should surround himself with like-minded people. Which was the entire reason he was here, wondering how in the hell he could ever navigate an intimate relationship when he was not the same man he used to be. He should probably get on those online message boards for amputees, but Archer wanted the human connection. The comradery in this place relaxed him and put him at ease. His accent all but disappeared, and he imagined that most of the people didn't even know he was Italian.

"Hey, it's Archer, right?" Max said, coming over to his end of the bar. "Nice to see you again. What can I get for ya?"

"Get me a beer," Archer said. "Domestic, please."

Two minutes later, Max set a frothy mug of ice-cold beer in front of Archer.

"How've you been?" Max asked, throwing a dish towel over his shoulder. "Did you get the job you interviewed for? What was it, executive assistant?"

Archer fought a smile. "Executive protection. And yes, I got the job. I'm basically a glorified bodyguard."

Max nodded. "Good to know they're hiring vets. I've

put the word out, too. There's no one better to have your six than someone who has already laid their life on the line."

"Once or twice." Archer chuckled, taking a pull from his mug.

"Exactly." Max took the towel off his shoulder and gave the bar a wipe. "Where did you serve?"

"Iraq mostly, one of the few thousand soldiers left behind to train and advise Iraqi security. Probably still be there if it weren't for the accident. I survived two tours but it's training that sidelined me."

"No kidding." Max leaned in. "What happened?"

Archer got caught up in the memory, explaining how they'd been training a few of the soldiers to use the old MRAPs. They'd had a translator, of course, but apparently something had been lost in translation.

"It really was an accident, but one of them ran me over."

Max made a pained expression and groaned. "Man."

"Yeah," Archer sighed. "After all those years, I almost made it out intact."

Max quirked a brow. "What did you lose?"

This time, Max gave Archer a look, his eyes narrowed. But Archer wouldn't call it compassion, or pity. More like simple curiosity. Yeah, Archer definitely liked Max.

"Part of my leg." Archer downed the rest of his beer.

"Sorry," Max said, though without a hint of pity. "You know, I would've never guessed by looking at you walk in here."

"They've made some amazing advancements in prosthetics," Archer said. "Mine was the ankle and foot, and a below the knee amputation, is a faster recovery."

"It's tough to talk about this stuff, I know." Max reached under the bar and came up with a pen. Then he grabbed a napkin and wrote down a number and pushed it toward

Archer with his finger. "Don't undermine what you lost. My buddy has a group, if you're interested. You've probably noticed we've got a lot of veterans around here. It's not just me, Cole and Adam. But Adam started this group not long ago. A lot of our regulars attend."

Archer wasn't sure he'd be around long enough to participate, but because Max had offered, he took the piece of paper.

"I'll think about it."

Chapter Fifteen

When he got back to the shop, the sign was flipped back to Open, the door unlocked. Zoey still wasn't in the front, but there were plenty of customers flitting about, checking out shoes and dresses. No doubt one of them had literally knocked on the door to be let inside, and naturally Zoey had obliged. He set the burgers and fries down behind the counter, but before anyone tried to approach him with a fashion question, he hightailed it to the annex to find Zoey.

"Oh, yes! Yes! This is the one."

He heard Zoey's voice carry from the annex room in the back, and when he peeked his head into the wedding dress section of the store, his eyes immediately went to Rachel, standing on the raised podium in front of the mirror, wearing a white dress with a long train he'd be afraid to step on. He'd been to his sisters' weddings and his thoughts ran something along the lines of *Don't wear a long train if you have a brother you want in the wedding.* It would also be difficult to dance in… Should he say something? No, for God's sake, this was just a cover. *He wasn't a fashion consultant!*

"Gorgeous," Rachel said. "I like it so much better than the first one."

"Yes, the slit up the leg wasn't really your style," Zoey said, shaking her head. "But, oh, this sweetheart collar!"

Archer wished he could get Zoey to model that one with the slit for him.

"Archer, what do you think?" Zoey turned as if she'd just noticed him standing in the doorway.

Rachel turned, too, and both looked at him expectantly. This was where he could share his fashion expertise. But maybe instead he should say something profound, like *the wedding day doesn't matter, it's the marriage that counts.*

Instead, he found himself saying, "I think your fiancé won't actually care about the dress. He's going to see the woman he loves, and you could be wearing a potato sack and he'd still have a stupid grin on his face. Men are simple creatures. If we love you, we love you, and we don't care what you wear."

He expected Zoey to give him a dirty look for not helping her with the sale, but instead she smiled. "So, basically, get what makes *you* feel like a princess, because he's going to show up in a rented tux."

"Ouch," Archer said. "For my wedding, I'd *buy* the tux."

"You don't know how expensive they are," Zoey shot back. "It doesn't make sense to buy it for just a day."

"And it makes sense to buy a dress for *one day*?"

"A woman dreams about this day for years, and the dress is hugely sentimental."

Now she gave him the first look he'd expected to see: the glare. They hadn't indulged in an argument like this for a couple of days. Rachel's head bobbed between the two of them, as if observing a tennis match.

Archer held up his palms. "Sorry, I stand corrected."

"But…do *you* like the dress?" Rachel asked, her finger trailing along all the lace and fluffy stuff at the train.

Archer stepped closer, avoiding the train. He tried to take in the dress, the sequins, the buttons, the…whatever. Then he made his pronouncement with all the assuredness of a soldier on his first day of boot camp.

"Do either of you have brothers who will be in the wedding?"

"Um, no," Rachel said, looking perplexed.

"Then it's perfect."

"I agree," Zoey said. "But why not think about it since you still have time. I also might be getting in a new shipment next week."

"Will you hold the dress for me? I wouldn't want to lose it by waiting."

"Absolutely," Zoey said. "No one sees this dress until you decide. And be sure to tell your friends that I have vintage wedding couture. We're trying to get the word out!"

Rachel waved happily and left, promising to be back soon.

Archer had expected the hard sell from Zoey, and he was pleasantly surprised to see her seem so relaxed about it. Maybe she wouldn't be too pissed that he'd nearly ruined the sale with his dumb comment.

Later, after they'd finished their burgers, Zoey turned to him.

"So, explain the comment about having a brother in the wedding."

"The train," he explained. "It's…long."

"Yes, and?"

"Brothers can be clumsy, especially after they've had a few drinks. Plus, it's hard to dance in it."

"Hmm. Well, the train comes off that dress, but…wise words."

"I had no idea they made dresses with moving parts."

Zoey snorted. "Well, not exactly *moving*, but, yes."

"The thing is I have sisters, as you know. They're all married now, so I've been through the wedding thing a few times."

"Always the groomsman, never the groom?"

Archer shrugged. "Yes, I suppose."

"I wish I'd had a sister," Zoey said dreamily.

While he hated doing this, he would have to pop that bubble. Hard.

"No, you don't."

"Excuse me?" She honestly looked confused.

"Sisters," Archer explained, "are like cats. They like you one day, hate you the next. And God forbid you get drunk at their wedding."

"Ha ha," Zoey said, chuckling. "But I always wanted a sister, because that way we'd both have memories of our mother that we could share. Maybe she'd do something that reminded me of our mother, or I would, and then we'd say, 'Remember when she used to…' That kind of thing."

Shit. The words hit him with a punch. Poor Zoey. She was still grieving her mother. Maybe she always would.

"Tell me again, how long has it been since you lost her?"

"I don't think I told you," she said. "It's been four years."

"Not long at all."

"No," she said, biting her lower lip. "And sometimes it feels like yesterday."

Archer logged in to his call with the agency early Monday morning and listened to the varied and interesting reports from all over the world. When it came time for him to report on his assignment, his boss's tone grew serious.

"Any luck getting that party canceled?"

"Not yet, sir," Archer said. "It would help if I could tell

her the truth. She's not falling for the obsessive boyfriend angle. He's backed off."

"Then we're going to have to think of some other reason to cancel it, because the threat level has increased."

"Here? I have not seen any sign of danger."

"Not in Charming, but her father's security team reported receiving a package with contents that were disturbing. We don't have all the details, only that they might now finally have enough to get this person arrested."

"Does that mean my assignment is over?"

"Not yet—or not until this man is officially in custody. If anything, her father wants her security level increased. Let's just say this package has him worried the guy has escalated his game."

"Got it," Archer said. "I will make sure this party gets canceled, one way or another. You can count on me."

He disconnected the call, and almost the next moment, heard a splash from the pool. She was swimming again, which was a form of torture for him.

He'd had a difficult time winding down after Zoey had asked him to go swimming yesterday morning. He'd been forced to face the facts: he would have gone, if not for his foot. It was humiliating for a man who'd always believed he didn't need anyone. But there was just something about Zoey. She was so beautiful and funny and sweet. Then there was the fact that, at times, he almost felt like she *knew*—about his leg, that is—although he realized she couldn't. She hadn't said anything to him directly, but then she was always so kind. Not just to him, but to everyone.

She hadn't been direct enough with her ex, and the guy obviously clung to the hope that she'd change her mind. Archer couldn't blame him on some level. If it were him, he'd want to keep trying, too. Zoey was truly a prize. But

Scott wasn't the problem anyway, and with every passing day he had the feeling Zoey knew something else was going on. He couldn't keep this ruse going without making stuff up, and he didn't want to lie to Zoey. But now he had to.

He waited for her to finish her swim, shower and dry off. When she strode back into the room, wearing a bright yellow dress with orange polka dots that were actually tiny pumpkins, he couldn't stop staring.

"It's Monday," she reminded him, and he was nearly struck dumb.

Monday: the day she went to the cancer ward to cheer up the patients and encourage the staff. He didn't know how he could have forgotten. It seemed like much longer than a week, since they'd been spending every day together. In some ways, he felt like he'd known Zoey for years.

"I have a check for them," she said, digging it out of her purse and showing it to him. "It's the end of the year and my daddy is making his charitable donation."

He'd never seen that many zeroes on a check in his life. Zoey's father was incredibly generous.

"Then we'd better get that right over to them," he said.

Chapter Sixteen

Walking into the cancer ward a week later felt like a year had gone by. She understood so much more about the man who'd been guarding her. He definitely challenged her and wasn't going to agree with everything she said but also had so much to say. His words to Rachel about the day of the wedding were so deeply personal. It was the way she felt about marriage; it was what her mother had taught her.

"It's not about the dress or the day," she'd said. "It's about the rest of your life together. And it won't always be easy, Zoey, but it will be worth it with the right man."

Archer walked next to her, opening doors. He might be confused for an attentive boyfriend, or…a bodyguard. She was going to assume people believed the first one and let everyone draw their own conclusions.

"Zoey!" Susan, the head nurse said. "You're back so soon."

"Well, it's almost Sweetheart Day." Zoey gestured to Archer. "This is my friend, Archer. He wanted to come along with me today. Is that okay?"

Archer held out his hand to Susan. "Pleased to meet you. I'm Archer Rossi."

"Hey!" a little voice shouted. "Mr. Archer! It's me, Joey. Remember me?"

Zoey turned to see Joey with his mother, Darcy. He was practicing walking with what must be his new prosthesis, while using a small cane for assistance. She remembered the family well, as Joey was one of the few children treated here for bone cancer. Last year, he'd unfortunately suffered an amputation below the knee, but more importantly, shortly after that he was declared cancer free. To Zoey, there was little worse than a child battling cancer, and Joey's parents had gone through all their savings and maxed out their health insurance. They'd been receiving funding from the Patch Lambert Grant since.

She was curious as to how Joey knew Archer. But Archer, for his part, wasn't meeting Zoey's eyes. Instead, he was fixated on Joey. Archer moved closer, ruffled the child's hair, then bent low to fist-bump him.

"Hey, buddy. It's good to see you again."

"Hi, Joey!" Zoey waved. "How do you know my friend Archer?"

"Oh, because Mr. Archer has a bionic leg, just like mine!" Joey said.

After that, Zoey didn't hear anything but a ringing in her ears. It seemed like the entire room had gone out of focus and her legs were made out of rubber. She couldn't move. She couldn't speak. Her heart thudded in her chest like a jackhammer.

It wasn't the way Archer would have chosen to tell Zoey, but in some ways, it was perfect. A full circle moment. There was no one quite like a child to let the cat out of the bag.

"That's right, we're both below the knee amputees and we both have a bionic foot," Archer said.

Joey's mother was smiling, the nurse was smiling, and

Joey was beaming. Zoey, on the other hand, looked like a strong wind might blow her over. Her eyes were wide and fixed. He didn't blame her—it was a shocking way to find out, sudden and unexpected. But this was heavenly timing in Archer's opinion. From the mouth of an innocent child. The truth.

"That's great," Zoey said. "If you'll excuse me, I have to see someone about a check."

Archer gave her a moment, realizing she needed it. He spoke with Joey and his mother for a few minutes, then excused himself. Wandering down the hall, he picked up Zoey's trail, following the flowery scent he'd come to memorize. And then he found her, standing in the break room alone, holding a cup of coffee. Her hands were shaking, and with one of them, she brushed at her eyes.

Jesus, she was *crying*.

"Zoey. *This* is why I didn't tell you," Archer said, walking into the room. "You should not be sad about this. I am *lucky*. Don't cry over me."

She glanced up, confusion clouding her eyes, as if surprised he'd found her. Then anger flashed.

"You think I'm crying because you have a prosthetic leg? Damn it, Archer, I'm crying because you didn't tell me!"

"Because I—"

"Because you had no faith in me. Look, I know it's none of my business, and it's private, but I thought you'd hurt your foot. We ran into each other at the hospital and you wouldn't tell me why you were here. That would have been a good time to tell me, if you wanted to. If you thought I was a big enough person to accept you for *who you are*."

"No, that is not…" Archer swiped a hand across his face. "It was not because of you, it was me."

"I've dated a lot of men, all physically 'whole.'" She

made air quotes. "And all *lacking* in every other way. Did it ever occur to you that I am a lot more than a physically beautiful woman? And that I might want more than looks in a partner?"

He smirked. "I did not think it was my brain you were attracted to."

"No, it was your heart." She locked eyes with him then, raw pain etched across her features. "Maybe you don't know how much love means to me. It's…everything. And love is a lot more than looks or physical attraction. Love is a choice we make every day."

Damn, she was right. He was out of words.

"I saw my parents make a choice to love each other every day, through my father's many injuries and surgeries and rehab and physical therapy."

"What happened to him?"

"He was a football player, remember? *American* football."

"Ah, okay. I understand. But Zoey, that's different. I am starting out with a defect."

"Don't you dare call it a defect!" She gestured toward the last place they'd seen Joey. "Joey has the right idea. Both of you are superheroes."

"No. He is, but I'm no superhero."

"You don't want to be, but you are. You're continuing to live your life, still helping others like Joey."

"You're making me sound like a saint, and I'm not. I've just had time to get adjusted since it happened. But I'm still not proud of this the way Joey is. And there's a difference. What happened to him wasn't his fault, it was cancer."

"And what happened to you wasn't your fault, either!"

Archer cocked his head. She was dead wrong. Maybe

not about the accident, but why he'd been there in the first place.

"Isn't it? I signed up to fight a war in another country. My parents begged me not to go, told me it wasn't my war to fight. But I was a proud first-generation American and I wanted to show everyone that red, white and blue coursed through my veins. I signed up when I was eighteen. And I showed them all right, while I left behind an entire part of myself. I didn't know how much I'd miss it, either."

"Yes, 9/11 got a lot of you young men. I remember guys in my class right after it happened. They were all so… angry."

"And we had to put that anger somewhere."

"Do you ever feel…cheated?"

"Cheated? Because of my *foot*? No, I was lucky. Some of my friends, not so much. But you have to remember, when my family came to this country, I was a kid. By the time the Twin Towers fell, I was in sixth grade. My friends and I thought we'd go over there when we were old enough and win a war. Kick some ass. It meant a lot to me to give back to the country that gave so much to me, so as soon as I could I signed up."

"I admire your courage. I've never done anything truly courageous in my life."

"Except for take care of your sick mother?" He met her gaze. "Courage comes in all shapes and sizes."

"Like the medical professionals who see it every day. I don't have that kind of courage. When they told me about Joey a few months ago, I had to excuse myself. I went home and cried for hours."

"You're a soft touch, Zoey." He reached to take her hand and squeeze it.

She squeezed back. "We were both so young when 9/11

happened. I also had friends who signed up. Your heart was in the right place and you went where your country asked you to go. That's honorable."

"That's all a soldier can do." Archer shrugged. "There's a clear chain of command, and no room to argue with your superior."

Zoey took a step closer to him and grazed his cheek with the back of her hand. "It wasn't your fault."

It was nothing less than he'd expected from Zoey. She felt sorry for him because her heart was too big not to care. Either way, he couldn't regret her knowing the whole truth.

Once they were back at her house, Archer listened as Zoey quizzed him on how the injury happened, when it happened, what kind of care he'd received, and for how long. She was acting like a modern Florence Nightingale, trying to ease his suffering. The tables had turned. She wanted to take care of him, and this time it went beyond the desire to make him feel at home by cooking for him. It was pity, pure and simple.

That wasn't going to work. He had a job to do here, which involved protecting *her*, and he would do it. His feelings and his disability had nothing to do with this. If nothing else, Archer was skilled at compartmentalizing.

"What kind of treatment did you have?" Zoey asked.

"The best there is."

They were in the kitchen and he was seated on one of the stools, trying to get comfortable with all the rapid-fire questions. Part of him wanted to shut her down, to tell her it wasn't any of her business, but he didn't have the heart to do that to Zoey.

"I know quite a lot about extreme injuries and physical

therapy. My mom and I went through this with my father for years."

But he'd bet her father never lost a limb. Kind of difficult to play any kind of football after that. Archer was once more reminded that he would probably never kick a "soccer" ball again, not even with his own children. It was one more of those pictures of his future he'd had to reframe. The physical therapist told him that of course he would be able to. Archer didn't quite buy it. He'd been an All-Star in high school; it was a high bar to meet. In some ways, he didn't want to do something if he couldn't do it as well as he used to.

They had to change the subject to something else.

"We need to discuss the party."

She wouldn't like this but it had to be done. He needed to ax this party—it was far too much of a risk. Ian had made the executive decision.

"What's there left to talk about?"

"Zoey," he said, lowering his head to study his hands. "It's not happening."

She'd been on the other side of the kitchen counter, cutting into some kind of pie, and she stopped and stared up at him.

"Yes, it *is*."

"It *can't* happen. You're going to have to cancel it."

She turned her body toward him, dark eyes flaring, hands on hips. "I won't do it! There's no reason to cancel, because Scott is a nonissue and you and I both know it."

"You're absolutely right."

"I am? About what? The party?"

"No, about Scott. *He's* not the issue."

Chapter Seventeen

Archer understood the need to protect Zoey and keep her in the dark about the reason he'd been hired. But he respected her enough to tell her the truth. She could handle it. Unfortunately, it wasn't his place to tell her about her father's business.

He came around the counter and stepped close, reaching for her elbows.

"Can you trust me and just know my employers know more than you do about this?"

"Are you serious? You're not going to *tell me*?"

"It's not my place, or I would."

"I see," she said. "So, this is my father again, interfering in my life. He can't let me live it the way I see fit. I'm sure he'd rather I still lived with him. Maybe that's the solution."

"That's not what this is," Archer said. "Your father's fears are valid."

"But you can't tell me why?"

Archer scrubbed a hand down his face. They'd certainly not made his position here any easier. The job didn't include a lot of action, but it had become emotionally exhausting. Guilt pulsed through him, because he didn't like hiding the truth from Zoey. His feelings of physical attraction had developed into something far deeper.

"Maybe you can tell me why first," he said. "What is it about this party that's so special to you? Why can't it be canceled? It's just a party, right?"

Zoey strode out of the kitchen into the living room and he followed her.

"It's too late. The invitations went out."

"And all it takes is a few calls," Archer said. "I will help."

"I don't want your help!" Then, as if she realized she'd shouted and been rude to him, she covered her mouth. "Sorry."

"Don't be sorry. Yell at me all you want. Let me be the bad guy. All I care about is your safety."

"Yes, that's kind of your job." She lowered her head.

"No. It's more than my job. I care about you."

"So much that you couldn't be honest with me. I had to find out through a sweet little kid."

"I would have told you, eventually." He cleared his throat and came to sit beside her. "But now you know something about me that not many people do. So maybe you could tell me why this party means so much to you."

"Because in four years I've never missed one."

Four years. There was a connection there, something she'd told him recently. His mind searched for a moment and reached for the association.

Four years ago, her mother had died.

Her lower lip quivered. "I feel her with me every time I celebrate the day with friends. She wanted that for me because she knew how much I value people. She never wanted me to be alone. She wanted me surrounded with love and friendship and family. When she was alive, it was our day, and we invited people to be with us and celebrate connections. I miss her so much, and I don't want to have to give this up, too."

"Aw, Zoey." He drew her into his arms, and that was all it took. "You're breaking my heart."

She collapsed into trembling sobs and held on to him tightly, burying her face in his neck.

Not surprisingly, this all went far deeper than a simple party. The ritual happened to be the way she still connected with her mother, the way she honored her to this day. No wonder she resisted the idea of canceling. He only wished he'd asked sooner and not simply assumed she wanted to get her way. For Zoey, this was not just a party. It was a tradition and a memory.

"I'm sorry," she said through her hiccuping breaths. "I don't usually fall apart like this."

"Don't be sorry. I didn't know how much this meant to you."

She sniffed. "You should have told me about your foot, and I should have told you about my mother."

"Are we even?" He felt a smile tugging at his lips as he ran his fingers through her curls. "Please say yes."

"Yes," she said, and he tugged her against him, not wanting to let go.

There were a couple of things Zoey wanted to do before canceling the party.

First, she had to dry her tears and then phone her father. Archer couldn't tell her the truth, but that didn't mean she couldn't get it out of her father. He *owed* her. If there was danger, she had a right to know about it.

The problem was, she didn't really want to leave Archer's embrace, and he didn't seem to be in a hurry, either. If she had to break down in such a humiliating way, at least she had someone who didn't shy away from tears and honest emotion.

"You're good at this," she said when her sobs ebbed enough to talk, her head leaning against his chest. "A lot of men run the other way when women cry."

"Well, I have sisters. I can't tell you how many times one of them cried on my shoulder."

"And you let them, bless your heart."

"They had me trained well," Archer said with a chuckle. "Worse, I had to listen to them insult every human of the male species. They sometimes forgot to exclude me as the exception."

"But you reminded them?"

"Of course."

"Archer, you know I'm going to ask my father why he really hired you, right after I tell him I canceled the party."

He sighed. "I had a feeling."

"He can't keep me in the dark. It's not fair to you, or me."

"I admit it's been tough pretending this is all about the ex. Not that he hasn't been inappropriate, but you were always right. No reason for a bodyguard. Should we start calling your guests soon?" Archer asked.

"I'll need to tell Twyla first." Zoey stood and walked to get her cell from the countertop. "She's going to be *so* disappointed."

Zoey thought of the beautifully engraved invitations and all the planning which had gone into the guest list. All those unnecessary background checks. She could have done without knowing that Vince Hunman at the post office had been divorced twice and was behind on child support.

In the end, Twyla took the news better than Zoey expected. She was, of course, worried about Zoey, which made sense. But Sweetheart Day wasn't a holiday Twyla had ever celebrated with her mother, so she would have no trouble letting it go. For Zoey, this would hurt for a while. It might sound like an exaggeration, but to her, this signified the end of an era. No one else understood the way Mami would have. It had been their tradition. Had she been there, she wouldn't have let Daddy stop the party. She'd have just made it smaller, including only a few special people. But the day would stand and they would still celebrate love.

While Archer excused himself to the patio, presumably to give her privacy, Zoey made the call to her father.

"Hey, baby girl! What's—"

"I'm canceling the party. Does that make you happy?"

"What party?"

Zoey groaned and dragged a hand down her face. "Are you kidding me? The one I have to cancel for a reason I don't understand. Scott is no longer bothering me, and I doubt now he was ever the issue. He's not the reason you hired a bodyguard for me, is it?"

He was silent for too long and she had her answer.

"I didn't want to worry you."

It didn't take long for it to dawn on Zoey then that the issue might have nothing to do with her at all. There was one main reason her father had bodyguards: overzealous fans. A woman who swore that Patch Lambert was her soulmate had once sneaked into his hotel room. Another had broken into their house and was arrested, but not before she'd declared her love on every mirror of the house. In lipstick.

"Do you have another obsessive fan?"

"Worse than that, but I don't want to talk about it. All you need to know is that it's being handled by my security team. And you…well, you'll be safe, too. That's all I care about."

Zoey closed her eyes and remembered the year her father had received death threats. Surprisingly, the memories weren't horrible for her, possibly because she was too young to understand the gravity of the situation. Her parents had done a good job shielding her from the haters, and her father was still doing it, even though he'd been retired for years.

"I see. It must be pretty bad if you won't talk about it. What did you do? Support the wrong team again?"

He groaned. "I was a guest commentator and criticized the Chiefs' defensive line."

"Oh, no. Not the Chiefs!"

"Most people forgot about it a week later, but someone who is a die-hard Chiefs fan started sending threats. And after a while they got ugly. A few days ago, he crossed a line by mailing a package to the headquarters of my foundation in Dallas. And the FBI is now involved."

"Daddy, are you going to be okay?"

"Oh, I'm fine. I have so much security detail I can't even eat a steak without someone examining it first."

"You shouldn't have to live like that."

"It's something I'm used to, but the fact I'm still in the public eye should not affect you. You have your own life to live, and God knows you never wanted anything to do with football."

"I'm sorry about that."

"Don't be. I've always loved that you are your own person and know exactly what you want, and also what you don't want." He sighed. "And I'm done trying to match you up with someone I like."

"Thank you."

"I realize that who you love is a highly personal choice and everyone is entitled to make it for themselves."

"Awfully mature of you, Daddy."

Zoey had believed that her father wanted to control her life from a distance, but the facts appeared to be different.

He wanted to create a line between his life and hers, so he could protect her from the complications of a public life.

"And I'm sorry about your party."

"You don't really remember, do you? About the party Mami and I had every September 14 for Sweetheart Day?"

"I can't say I do. But September's the start of football season, honey. You probably don't remember all the days I missed being with y'all. Sometimes you came with me, but once you started school that was tougher. It was just you and your mami then, and I know she tried to keep you entertained so you wouldn't notice that I was gone all the time."

The start of football season. No wonder it wasn't a clear memory for him.

"I can't believe this is just now dawning on me. Of course you weren't around for the party."

"I think I might've made one or two over the years. But I always thought it was kind of your mom's thing. Something she did to connect with you."

"Did you know I've been having one every year since she's been gone? Except this year."

There was a long beat of silence before he sighed.

"Maybe you can find another way to honor her memory."

Zoey already had, with the boutique and her mission to make low-cost designer wear available to the average consumer. She had so many ways to remember her mother, in all the memories they'd made over the years. Not just Sweetheart Day but all the trips they took together over the years, laughing at the over-the-top fashions shown on the runways. Mami would want her to be happy and stop putting an emphasis on only one thing, when life was comprised of so many other celebrations.

The party was one small thing, one memory out of hundreds, and Zoey had made too much out of it for far too long.

Chapter Eighteen

Archer surveyed the calm blue water in Zoey's pool. With the mild autumn temperatures, he'd be lying to say it didn't look inviting. He hadn't been swimming with the new foot, but he should be able to, according to the doctors. There were many things he hadn't tried yet, and swimming was only one of them.

He felt lighter now that Zoey would soon know the truth straight from her father's mouth. While he commiserated with the man, he'd never believed that withholding the truth would deliver a desired outcome. But he didn't have a daughter. His poor father had four, and Archer swore the man started graying when Archer's oldest sister turned fourteen. The sense of protection ran deep in Rossi men.

"Whatever you do, do not have daughters, *figlio*," he'd said, shaking his head, clasping his hands together in prayer. "You will live longer."

As if Archer had any control over that. From watching his own family dynamics, he understood that the relationship between fathers and daughters could be a difficult balance. He wondered how Patch Lambert handled his fiery and fiercely independent daughter, because he wouldn't get away with telling her anything but the truth.

When he walked back inside, Zoey was bent by the fireplace moving the pile of decorative pumpkins and gourds over to the side.

"I decided that I want to roast marshmallows," she said, turning to him.

"It's seventy degrees outside." Still, he joined in helping her move her display.

"That's why I turned up the air conditioner," she said, and Archer thought maybe he'd heard wrong.

"You're supposed to wait until it's cold enough to make a fire."

"That's not how Texas works. I need a little pick-me-up, and I want something to make me feel like it's truly autumn, and I'm tired of waiting for the rain."

"All these pumpkins, orange lights and leaves aren't doing it? What about the pumpkin spice you put in everything?"

She made a face. "That's a good start, but fires are cozy. I'm indulging in a little self-care today, if you don't mind."

"Okay," he said, putting up his palms in an "I give up" gesture. "You had to forgo the party, I get it. You deserve to get what you want. I'll take care of this."

"I've got the fire logs," she said, going to the closet nearby and pulling one out with a smile.

"Don't you want a *real* fire? A roaring fire?"

"Yes, but beggars can't be choosers."

"I can use the wood you have piled outside," he offered.

"The decorations, you mean?"

"Don't tell me they're not real."

"Oh, no, they are. They give the house a woodsy feel, but I never thought of actually burning them."

"Well, I could hack down your furniture, but I don't think we need to go that far." He hooked a thumb to the decorated porch in front. "I'll go get the wood."

Zoey helped, and together they carried several logs inside. If she was worried about her father, he assumed she might not share that with him. The fewer questions she asked him, the better. At least the real danger was faraway and would never come close to touching Zoey.

The fire—nutty though the idea was—could be a good distraction, and he'd indulge her.

"Fortunately for you, I grew up in Connecticut," Archer said. "I'm going to need some kindling and some paper. And a match."

"Absolutely!" She turned to him with a big smile. "Now, what is *kindling*?"

Archer laughed. "I'll see what I can find."

He went into the back garden and gathered a few twigs by the oak tree that would work. Zoey's face brightened when he walked inside. She held a box of matches and some paper.

"I bet fall is lovely in Connecticut."

"Sure is, but I prefer Texas weather myself."

"You say that because you didn't grow up here. Texas is great, don't get me wrong, but I don't have many chances to wear my sweaters and boots except when I visit Amarillo in February."

This gave new meaning to fashion: going somewhere where the weather suited your clothes. No doubt about it, Zoey made him smile. He'd never seen anyone so enthusiastic about a season.

"If sweater and boot weather is what you'd like, I'll have to take you with me to Connecticut. Preferably in winter. But you're also going to need a parka."

Damn, that had just slipped out. He hadn't mean to make such assumptions. When this job was over, he'd likely never see Zoey again.

"I'd like that."

As usual, Zoey was being kind, especially since he was about to make her dreams come true.

"You say that now, but wait until you're housebound for days because it's below zero and we're expecting a nor'easter."

"I imagine people can find fun things to do while indoors, too." She nudged him playfully.

"You would be right about that. Nine months later, there are plenty of bambinos born."

Archer angled logs of wood strategically and placed crunched up pieces of paper between them, then struck the match. The flame immediately caught but didn't spread, so he blew air on it to get it going. Within a couple of minutes, they had their roaring fire. Of course, this meant that they were both feeling a little too warm, even with the air conditioner on. He took a step back from the wall of heat. Zoey did, too, but their timing was off so they bumped into each other, both chuckling.

"Too hot for you?" he said, hand on her waist to steady her.

"No comment," she said with a smile. "But I love the aesthetic."

"Wait a little while and you'll have embers for your roasted marshmallows." Somehow, he now had his arm low on her back with no desire to move it.

Then she turned to him and reached up to ruffle his hair. "You're a regular Boy Scout. Thank you for the fire."

"Though I question your methods, you have a point. It probably never gets cold enough in this part of Texas. I suppose sometimes you have to take matters into your own hands."

He lowered his arm from her waist, then reached to loosen his tie. As a rule, for work, he always wore slacks, a button-down and tie. But more often than not, he rolled up his sleeves to the elbows. At the moment, rolled-up sleeves weren't enough for this heat and he wanted to rip his shirt off. But he wouldn't breach decorum with Zoey nearby.

He squatted on his haunches near the fire. "You talk to your father?"

"Yes," she said, sitting cross-legged beside him. "He finally told me the truth, and suddenly everything makes sense. Another unhinged football fan. It's something we've been through before as a family. I remember those days clearly, being chauffeured to and from school, a bodyguard always on standby."

"That must be especially tough for a child."

"It's no way to live but I got used to it. Like I said, after a while they were like family."

"And your father. You're not worried about him?"

"Of course I am, but I know he's well protected. It's something he needs to learn, apparently. How *not* to worry about me."

"Yeah, not sure a parent ever does that. Least of all the father of a daughter. My father had four, so I've seen it firsthand."

Zoey studied him through narrowed eyes. "*Riiight.* You're the one who got away with everything while they were probably interrogated about every move they made."

"Maybe not every move, but close." Archer winced. "I admit there's a double standard with my father's generation."

"I understand not wanting to know what I do in my personal life," Zoey said. "Like me. I definitely don't want to know about any of the women he dates. There's no shortage of women interested in my father, both young *and* old."

"I can imagine."

"A few months ago, there was a woman."

"Yeah?"

"I didn't like her much but I decided I might be being unfair. It's not like me to dislike someone. It was the last time I went up to see him. We don't talk about her. I don't want to know what they do together in my mother's house."

Archer heard the sharpness in that sentence, which didn't sound like the Zoey he'd come to know. Apparently, there was at least one person who wasn't the recipient of her kindness, but he could understand why not.

"It's got to be hard, seeing him move on."

"Oh, he never will. The women come and go. My mother will always be his true love, his number one. Forever and ever."

Archer chose his words carefully. "And...you think that's fair to him?"

"Maybe not, but you can't change the truth. No woman will ever match up to my mother, mark my words."

"I don't doubt it, but maybe he could find someone who would make him really happy."

Zoey gave him an "Are you for real?" look, swiveling her neck and chuckling.

"It's a thought." He shrugged. "Don't you want your father to be happy and find love again...someday?"

"Looks like the fire's died down. Time for marshmallows!" Zoey exclaimed, jumping to her feet.

Great way to avoid answering the question, he'd give her that. She ran into the kitchen and came back with a bag of marshmallows and what looked like shish kebab skewers. He took a couple and started spearing marshmallows. There was a trick to this and he had it down to a science.

Zoey, on the other hand, like a true-blue Texan, put the marshmallow so close to the fire it burst into flames.

"What did I do wrong?"

"Haven't you done this before?"

"Well…a long time ago. It shouldn't come as a shock to you that we didn't do much real camping as a family."

"Don't tell me the bodyguards did it for you."

"Ha, ha. But you and I are actually christening this fireplace. It's my first time in the new house."

"I'm honored. Let me show you how this is done."

He demonstrated with his own skewer, not getting too close to the embers, turning it when one side got brown, then the other.

"Here," he said, handing one to her. "It's all about timing, and patience."

"Oh, my gosh, you're so *good* at this!" She bit into the toasty and melting marshmallow, licking her fingers. "I'm going to keep you, or at least send for you every autumn."

Then, as if she realized what she'd said, she smiled but lowered her head. She didn't take it back, but he hadn't taken back his statement of bringing her home to Connecticut, either.

"Sounds good to me." He bit into his own treat, and the sugary sweetness reminded him of easier times.

He'd loved camping trips with his large family in the woods of Connecticut and upstate New York. The Finger Lakes region was a favorite area of the family. He should get home soon, Archer decided, and let his family see with their own eyes that he wasn't an invalid. They claimed to understand, but on every phone call home he heard the sadness in his mother's voice, as if what he'd lost, he would never get back. She meant well, but she worried about him so much that all he'd wanted to do as a young man was leave. But he supposed mothers and sons had their own issues.

Zoey reached for Archer's chin with a sweet smile. "You have something…right there."

A jolt of pure heat slashed through Archer that had nothing to do with the fire.

Chapter Nineteen

Zoey desperately wanted to kiss Archer and this moment felt ripe for it, but at the last second, she chickened out. After she'd spent several seconds staring at his mouth, he didn't make the first move. She liked to think of herself as bold and ready to take charge in every area of her life, but when it came to Archer, she froze every time. Instead of kissing him, she scooted closer as they both stared into the flickering yellow-and-red flames.

"We should really be doing this outside." Archer stoked the fire the way she'd seen done in countless Hallmark movies, then returned to sit beside her. "Have you ever slept under the stars?"

She had a difficult time admitting the truth: She'd led a privileged life. Her mother's idea of camping was a four-star hotel, and her father claimed he hadn't worked so hard all his life to pretend he was literally unhoused for a week.

"No, I'm afraid not." She sighed. "My parents weren't into camping."

"I should take you camping and show you what real roughing it is like. Do you think you could handle that?" He chuckled.

"Yes."

Her heart raced every time he talked about a future that

included her in it. She'd mentioned keeping him on or sending for him every autumn and then worried she'd overstepped. But whether joking or not, the words rang true. She didn't want this time with him to end but didn't see how they could continue. Sooner or later, this assignment would be complete.

They were quiet for several more seconds and were close enough for Zoey to lay her head on his shoulder. And she did, because it felt easy. Natural.

"After a while, I resented my father for wanting to keep me home after my mother died. He didn't recognize that we were each handling our grief in different ways. His idea of grieving was to make our world smaller and to retreat, to hide. He grew paranoid, worrying he had enemies everywhere. He fired a bunch of people that first week. It was awful."

"When you're in the public eye, with people talking about every aspect of your life and taking it all apart to be examined…that's got to be difficult."

"Until then I hadn't realized how much he'd counted on my mother, but I guess we all did. She was our balance, our center. With her gone, he fell into an abyss. Instead of dealing with my own grief, I had to rescue *him*. I didn't mind, because he needed me. He deserved my compassion. But when I wanted to leave, when I wanted to find something for myself, the guilt trip came and it came hard."

Somehow, Zoey had wound up in Archer's arms, him sitting right behind her, pulling her into the circle of his arms. She leaned back, feeling safe and protected. Everything felt so easy with him, the affection and emotional intimacy. It was as if she'd known him for years.

"Funny," Archer said. "One of the reasons I haven't gone

home since my injury is my concern that my family won't let me go once I get there."

"You haven't been back?"

"No. They came to see me in the hospital, but I made them go back home. If I hadn't, I would have never been able to pull out of it on my own. I have a hard time relying on others."

"No kidding."

"The truth is I own my decisions, even if there are times I've regretted some of my choices. But when I look at where I am, how far I've come, it has all been worth it."

"I like the sound of that. No regrets."

"It's the only way to live."

They were quiet then, watching the fire until it faded away.

Still thinking of Archer's words to her last night, Zoey pulled a shipment of sweaters out of a box. She'd probably only sell these to customers who were leaving town to visit family and friends during the holidays. The weather was still in the seventies today, bright and sunny, although there was some rain in the forecast. She'd love an excuse for another fire like the one last night. She wondered what the weather was doing in the Panhandle.

Until Archer mentioned it, Zoey hadn't really considered whether she was being fair to her father. He was the kind of man who had everything: wealth, a legacy, family, fame, love. But without her mother, and now without her, he might be lonely. He hadn't taken her leaving Amarillo well, and yet she had, eager to get away from his control. She'd also gotten away from Peter, which at the time seemed most important because he'd ingratiated himself once again with her father. In retrospect, she'd simply walked away from *two* men who thought they knew the kind of future she should have: A safe and predictable future as little more than a trophy wife, throwing parties for her father and her husband. Traveling to places predetermined by her husband.

She'd wanted and chosen *this* life, starting over in a small coastal town, with her found family, creating her own legacy of love. Now that the party was no longer in her immediate future, she had to wonder whether she'd been celebrating the day to honor love or her mother. When asked, she had to face it: the party was *all* about her mother. And there were many other ways to honor her.

Last night, after the fire had died out, she and Archer made phone calls. She took most of the list. He'd offered to take half, but Zoey thought it best her friends hear it from her.

"Aw, no party? But we do this every year. Why not? Are you sick?" Debbie had asked.

"No, it's just… I'm…" *Having a change of heart, moving on, making different choices?* "Having some remodeling done, and it's just gone over time and budget. I'm so upset."

She didn't have the heart to tell them she had to cancel a party because of a lone obsessive football fanatic. Zoey was beginning to hate the sport. Thankfully, the shop kept her busy as customers came in droves. Some were shopping for Governor Tippy's annual gala, others were already Christmas shopping, and she suspected there were women who were still coming to check out Zoey's new "employee." Rumors were rampant around town that he was a former model interested in opening up a men's boutique in town, or that he was designing his own cologne and looking for investors. She thought it was hilarious.

"It is my understanding that women love leather," Archer was saying a few feet away from Zoey. "So, I recommend this jacket."

"But do you think it would look good on me?" This came from Tee, a young man who worked for Noah in his charter boat business.

Recently, there'd been more men coming into the shop than the norm. But it made sense, since they'd heard Archer was making suggestions and doling out fashion advice. They assumed that he had plenty of game and wanted to emulate his ways. She'd had to order button-down shirts like the ones Archer wore every day, when both men and women started asking about them. Zoey's shop might wind up having the best last quarter of the year on record if this kept up. In just a few days, she'd sold several designer men's dress shirts. She might run out of stock before the holidays.

"Do we have this in another size?" Archer asked Zoey, holding up the leather jacket she'd made him model for her a few days ago.

It would definitely be too large for Tee. "I think so. Let me look in the back."

She went to the dark stockroom where she kept most of her poorer-selling items. A marked box on the top shelf was labeled "Men's Jackets." She'd just reached for it when she felt Archer come up behind her. His hand low on her back felt like a brand, heat searing through her clothes.

"Here, let me." He reached for the box easily and put it down beside her.

But he didn't look at the box or inside of it, simply locked those amber eyes on hers and cupped her face. His gaze lowered to her lips, and in the space of a moment, he kissed her, long and hard and deep. She responded eagerly to let him see this was what she wanted. The two of them together, locking lips, holding each other tightly in the low light.

Then it was all over as quickly as it had started when Archer pulled away. “Sorry. I am sorry.”

“No, don’t—” But he was already out the door with the box.

Damn, what a screwup.

Archer needed to get a hold of himself or he would soon earn a reputation in this business. First, for being a hothead, overzealous for the job; second, for being a Romeo and kissing his beautiful clients. The truth was, his previous assignment, the reality TV celebrity, was another beautiful woman. But not only had he never kissed her, he’d also never been *tempted*. It was different with Zoey because it wasn’t just her looks that drew him to her. There seemed to be an electric current firing between them that he could almost touch.

He told himself that was why he’d kissed her in a quiet moment filled with lust and weakness. She’d returned the kiss with enthusiasm, and this worried him even more. He couldn’t afford for her to get the wrong idea. He wasn’t ready to sign up for an intimate physical relationship, and Zoey wouldn’t accept anything less.

Archer cleared his throat after digging through the box and finding another jacket for Tee. “Maybe this will fit better.”

Tee slipped it on and shrugged into it. He straightened and strode around the store a bit, modeling it.

“Yeah, this is sweet. I *like* it!”

“Looks good on you,” Archer said, though he had absolutely no idea. The point was it seemed to be the right size.

At the moment, he could only think of how good Zoey

had felt in his arms a few minutes ago and how much he hated the fact that he'd met her under these circumstances. He could do nothing about the way he felt, nor should he.

"How much?" Tee said, looking for a tag.

There was none. "No idea, but I bet Zoey would give you a good deal."

"I hope so." Tee glanced in her direction, where she was now back to folding sweaters in a stack as if nothing had happened in her storeroom. "Hey, do you think I'd have any luck asking her out? Is she seeing anyone?"

"Don't ask her out," Archer said, shaking his head. "It's not a good time for her."

"Really? Why not? I heard she and Scott broke up."

Archer's illogical mind shouted: *If you touch her, I will kill you with my bare hands.*

Instead, he said, "That's why it's not a good time. She's taking a break."

"I guess you have the inside scoop, working with her daily and everything." Tee looked longingly in Zoey's direction.

Get in line, buddy.

"That's right. We work well together."

And they'd be good together at many other things, too, if they ever stood half a chance.

"Would you let me know when she's ready to start seeing someone again?" Tee said. "I mean, before anyone else has a chance?"

It was an awful lot of trust from the kid.

"Yeah, sure. Just drop by the shop, buy something, and I'll give you the 4-1-1."

"Thanks, bro." Tee clapped Archer on the back and

headed to Zoey. "I'll take it," he said, bringing the jacket up to the counter.

Her face lit up with a smile. "Good choice!"

She exchanged a wink with Archer and rang Tee up.

Chapter Twenty

After they'd closed the shop, Archer suggested dinner before heading home. He would now do everything in his power to cheer up and distract Zoey from the canceled party. She wasn't fooling him. Last night, he'd heard her crying in her bedroom. He'd been about to knock on her door to check on her when he heard the quiet sobs. Suddenly, he hated himself, American football, social media, sports fans and everything in this messed-up world. If a woman wanted to celebrate a day for sweethearts, she should be able to do it.

"My treat," he said, after suggesting they go out to eat.

"What did you have in mind?" Zoey settled into the passenger side and put on her seat belt. "We have our pick of food—Japanese, Tex-Mex, Italian, Chinese."

"I refuse to eat Italian. They never cook the food right. What's your favorite place around here? Let's go there."

"Well, I like the Salty Dog Bar and Grill. They have the juiciest burgers."

"As it turns out, I like that place, too." He pulled out onto the road and headed to the other side of town.

The boardwalk along the seawall had one side with carnival rides and games and the other was lined with restaurants.

"Are we seriously not going to talk about the kiss?" Zoey said after a few minutes on the road.

He winced, grateful she'd chosen this moment to ask. At least he was forced to keep his eyes on the road. "Please, forgive me. It was a terrible breach of decorum. I regret it."

She huffed. "*I* don't. Maybe you noticed I kissed you back?"

"I did…notice that." He cleared his throat. "But it was unprofessional of me. I'm sure you agree. Just because you're a grown woman with the ability to consent doesn't mean it's ethical for me to cross the line."

"We crossed it *together*, Archer."

He sighed. "Believe me, I wish it were different."

She was quiet for a long moment, staring out the window, so Archer decided to tell her something about himself that he'd only now realized.

"And the truth is, I've never just been friends with a woman before you."

The statement felt like a bomb, given the utter silence that followed his truth explosion.

Then Zoey snorted. "You're kidding."

He didn't change his expression.

"Oh, you're *not* kidding! Are you serious? No women who were just your friends?"

"It sounds ridiculous, but there was rarely an opportunity to stay friends."

"Oh, I see," Zoey said, giving him the side-eye. "*Now* it makes sense."

"What do you mean?"

"I mean you didn't *want* to stay friends, and you get what you want, don't you?"

"Well, that is probably true." He cleared his throat. "All

in the past. The thing is, and I know it's hard for you to believe, but before my accident…let's just say I dated a lot."

"Color me *not* surprised!" She chuckled, then turned her entire body toward him.

"The thing is, I've recently understood how truly stupid that is."

"Dating a lot is stupid?"

He shook his head. "No, not knowing how to stay friends. You've been good for me, Zoey. I'm learning a lot."

"Wow, bad timing for me."

"*Good* timing for you. I'm not willing to risk going all in with the physical stuff, even though I'm attracted to you. I know now how important it is for a couple to be friends first. I mean, that's how it should work."

"Sometimes. That's how Twyla and Noah got together. They were friends for years before anything happened."

"Years?" Archer tried not to choke on his own spit.

This had not been what he had in mind, but he admired Noah for his restraint.

"Yes. Well, they were young when they met. And over the years, they dated other people. Still stayed the best of friends."

"That had to be tough for Noah."

"More so for Twyla, actually."

Archer doubted this but didn't want to argue the point.

Now Zoey cleared her throat. "Just, um, out of curiosity, where will you go after this job with me is over?"

The truth? He didn't know. He'd have to go where the agency needed him to be. It might be California, or it might be the Middle East. The job involved travel, even if some jobs would undoubtedly be local, like this one. But that wasn't the norm.

"It could be anywhere."

"Anywhere?"

"Yes. Literally anywhere."

"So…you might be sent thousands of miles from Texas. Is that what you're saying?"

"That's what I'm saying."

She was quiet, presumably absorbing that information, allowing him to focus more on driving, a mindless activity that gave him some degree of comfort. He found a parking space on the restaurant side of the boardwalk, the cries of children echoing from the carnival side. It reminded him of his childhood, trips to the Jersey Shore and Coney Island, and a wave of melancholy swept over him.

The Salty Dog Bar and Grill had a bar section on one side, separated from the restaurant section by a short hallway. The walls on the grill side were red brick, and there were handwritten chalkboards announcing the daily specials. The hostess greeted them at the door and led them to their table. As Zoey walked ahead of him, heads turned. He was not surprised, though some caveman instinct in him wanted to throw a blanket over her so no one else would appreciate her the way he did. Their server came, and they placed their orders.

"Question from a newcomer to your town," Archer said when their server had left. "What in the world is up with the wood placard in the front window that says, Mr. Charming, and lists a bunch of years?"

Zoey laughed. "That's an annual contest we have here during the summer. Both men and women compete for the title of Mr. Charming. It's Ava Del Toro's brainchild. She used to run the Chamber of Commerce before she got married and opened her coffeehouse."

"So, one of the workers here won it?"

"Yes. Cole Kinsella, one of the owners, was the most recent Mr. Charming. He's actually won a few times."

Archer had met Cole before. He was definitely gregarious and friendly, so it made sense. He'd heard him more than once refer to an elderly woman as "darlin'." There were probably not many people who didn't love that guy. Were Archer to enter a Mr. Charming contest, he'd lose handily. He identified far more with Max than he did Cole.

"I've met the owners," Archer said. "I'm especially fond of Max."

"Yes, I can see why you would be. He's a good guy."

"You know, Zoey, there's no reason you can't have Twyla and Noah over on the fourteenth, in place of the party."

"And you'd be my plus-one?" She smiled.

"Of course, if you don't mind."

"Obviously, I don't mind, but actually, I was thinking about taking the day to do some quiet reflection instead."

"Also a good idea."

"Maybe it's time for me to rethink the importance of having a silly grown-up version of a party like the one I used to have with my mother as a child."

"I don't think it's silly," Archer protested. "No one does."

"Really? *Sweetheart* Day?" She gave him a wry look. "I don't know what I was thinking. I'm not ten anymore."

"It's not silly to celebrate love." He reached for her hand and squeezed it.

"We have February for that."

He was about to tell her she could celebrate it all year long if that's what she wanted, and he'd fight anyone who said otherwise, when a couple joined them.

"Hi," said a pretty brunette. "I was sorry to hear about the party."

"We were looking forward to it and already had a sitter," said the dark-haired man with her. He turned to Archer. "Hi, I'm Adam Cruz and this is my wife, Stacy. Heard a lot about you."

Adam was the sole restaurant owner Archer had not met yet, but apparently Max had been talking about Archer. Adam had previously worked as the chef and now supervised the kitchen, so it made sense for him not to be as visible as Max and Cole. He also ran the support group Archer had been avoiding. Even if he had wanted to attend—and he didn't—he didn't have time. After all, he couldn't very well leave Zoey to go to a meeting.

He was still on the job even if these days it felt too pleasant to be called work.

"Join us," Zoey said. "At least we can hang out a little bit tonight."

Archer stood to give the couple the opportunity to sit together on the opposite side of the bench. He took the seat next to Zoey.

"So, I hear you're working for Zoey now," Stacy said. "And business is booming."

"Well, I do what I can," Archer said, biting back a smile.

"I thought you were former military," Adam said, which meant he knew exactly what he did for a living. "This must be a change for you."

"Yes, it's definitely a change." He winced.

"Actually, can you two keep a secret?" Zoey leaned in. "That's just a cover. Archer is my temporary bodyguard."

Next to her, she literally felt Archer's body relax. Zoey felt better about the truth now. There was no shame in needing protection.

"He's been a good sport about pretending to be my employee." She reached to squeeze his forearm. "And the truth is, the party was canceled because we thought it best, since my father has one of those obsessive football fans after him again."

"Good ol' Patch." Adam chuckled. "He tells it like it is and doesn't pull any punches. The Chiefs defensive line has issues this year and somebody had the nerve to say it."

"My father has never been shy when it comes to football," Zoey said. "And when he talks and he gets haters, I'm punished for it, too."

"You're his only child," Stacy said, and then gave Adam the side-eye. "We have two daughters, and though they're little, I already see Adam is the same way."

Adam made a face but nodded. "It may be a little retro, but fathers still want to protect their daughters whether they need it or not. I'm glad your father hired Archer."

Actually, Zoey was, too, if for no other reason than she would have never met Archer otherwise. Not that it mattered. When he finished this assignment, he might actually leave the country. There was no room for any kind of relationship with him.

Falling for him would be the single most impractical thing Zoey could ever do.

Driving home, they talked about what a nice couple Adam and Stacy were.

"He runs a support group for veterans," Archer said. "Max told me about it and gave me Adam's number to give him a call about it sometime."

"I didn't know that, but it makes sense. Adam was a widower before he met Stacy, and he also had a lot of survivor's guilt from his time as a soldier, apparently."

"Yeah. I'm fine, though."

"You seem fine. But, of course, sometimes it's difficult to tell what's going on inside."

"I've already had therapy. Lots of it."

He sounded a little defensive but Zoey let it go.

"Then maybe you could help the other guys in the group, offer your insight."

"Yeah, I guess. I'm an encyclopedia of information when it comes to prosthetics, analgesics and physical therapy."

"I bet you have a lot more than that to offer."

He seemed resistant to talking about all the other losses he must have had. The friends he lost. Grief, she knew well, was not something that disappeared with time. It became a part of you.

"You seem thankful despite what you lost. I admire that." She took a breath. "How many friends did you leave behind?"

"None," Archer said, patting her chest. "Never leave a man behind. They're still with me."

It was something she understood far better than he realized.

Chapter Twenty-One

On the morning of the party, Zoey woke up early and managed five laps in the pool. It was official. She would be doing this every morning, not just on her day off. Why not make every day a "me" day? Swimming was a great way to recharge and she vowed to make the time to squeeze it in in the mornings. Last night, after dinner, Archer had retired to his bedroom and she'd downloaded several meditation apps. She looked forward to meditation and possibly yoga, if she could locate her pants.

She'd had a good cry over the loss of this year's party, but hanging out with Archer was a good consolation prize. Archer gave her space when she needed it. The kiss in the storeroom had been amazing, but he was right, and nothing could come of this flirtation between them. They had chemistry for days, enough to start an electrical fire, but it didn't matter. She had to put it out of her head and focus on self-improvement. Maybe love *was* everything, but she'd focused too much on romantic love. Showing Archer how a man and woman could simply be friends could only help both of them in the long run.

When she climbed out of the pool and toweled off, she witnessed an incredible sight and thought this day might be salvaged. The sky had darkened to a beautiful indigo, clouds laced with gray. Her heart soared: It might actually *rain* today. Last night, Archer had checked the forecast on his phone when they were sitting in front of the TV watching *Frasier* reruns, and he had seemed irritated about the possibility.

"But if it rains, we can do another fire," she'd said, and he'd scowled.

Now she strolled inside and saw Archer was already up and settling a few packages inside. He'd been receiving packages for two days now and remained cryptic about them. Zoey had most of her packages, personal or otherwise, delivered to the boutique, but today of all days she'd hoped to get something to cheer her up. Maybe something she'd ordered a while back and forgotten about.

"For *me*?"

"Just a few things I had delivered," Archer said, and then carried them into this bedroom like they were a state secret.

Fine. If it was a secret, she didn't need to know. Maybe it was some kind of bodyguard paraphernalia, though she couldn't imagine what. A new suit, so he'd look even more like James Bond? She could do without anything that made him more attractive. It hadn't helped at all when he'd kissed her in the storeroom with such passion she'd lost her footing. They would be so good together, if they ever had a chance. But she didn't see how it could happen with him taking off so soon. When it came to romance lately, she was in one of those "shutouts" Daddy used to talk about, where one team got all the points and the other, zip. She was in the zero column. It was time to give up.

After showering and styling her hair, Zoey sat cross-legged in front of her flat screen and pulled up an app. She'd closed her eyes and had started the guided meditation when the ring camera went off again. *Another* delivery for Archer? What in the world? She went and retrieved the package, then knocked on his door. “Hang on. Be right with you,” he said.

When he cracked open the door, she tried to look over his shoulder. “Another package for you.”

She hadn’t opened it, but the box was from a major retailer, so it could literally be anything.

“Thanks,” he said, took it and shut the door.

How mysterious. If he wanted her to lose interest in him, this was not the way to do it; the deliveries only had her more intrigued. Meanwhile, outside the sky continued to darken, the wind kicked up, tossing leaves around, and Zoey’s hopes soared. She went back to her meditation practice.

“In through the nose, and out through the mouth. Picture your happy place…”

Zoey focused on New England in autumn, falling leaves and cozy fires—but the image of the dark storeroom kept interfering. Archer pulling her close against him, his hands low on her behind, his lips pressed against hers, kissing her deeply.

Zoey had no idea how much time had passed; it could have been thirty minutes or thirty hours when she heard Archer’s voice.

“Zoey,” he said, sticking his head in the door. “Sorry to interrupt.”

“No worries,” she said, turning around to face him. “That was *relaxing*. How long was I meditating for?”

He glanced at his watch. “About two minutes, give or take?”

“Excuse me?” Zoey stood. “That has to be wrong. I feel like I’ve been sitting here forever!”

“Sorry,” he said, and once again seemed to be fighting

the urge to smile. Or laugh. "But maybe that's the point with meditation. You lose track of time."

Ugh, whatever. "I was hoping it would be longer than *two minutes*. Did you need something?"

He walked to the window facing the patio. Sunlight poured in and once more South Texas weather had failed her. It was barely cracking the low seventies today.

He pointed. "Look. It's not going to rain after all."

"I can see that," she huffed.

"That's actually for the best," he said. "Did you really want it to ruin your party day?"

"Don't you mean *former* party day?"

"No, I mean party day. There's a whole 2.0 happening."

"Since when?"

"Don't worry about it," Archer said. "Just be ready tonight, about six o'clock?"

"Are you kidding? We're seriously having a party? Um, thank you, but I'm not ready! I need to find an outfit."

"About that...dress is casual."

"How casual?"

"Jeans," he said.

"Do *you* have jeans? Because I've never seen you wear them. You're always in a suit and tie."

"I've got something, don't worry."

Excitement poured through Zoey. Maybe Twyla had figured out a way to surprise her. She clasped her hands together.

"Who's coming?"

Archer held up two fingers.

"Two people? Is it Twyla and Noah?"

Then he pointed from himself to her and once more held up two fingers.

"Just you and me?" Zoey swallowed hard and he nodded. A party of two.

He was *torturing* her with what she couldn't have.

Finally, Archer had everything ready.

He'd been working on this plan since the decision was made to cancel the party. A bright idea came to him while lying in bed, staring at the cracks in the ceiling and trying to sleep.

What if he threw the party for her?

He wasn't much of a party planner. He could have asked Twyla for help, but he wanted this to be his baby, his plan. It had taken a little time and imagination, but he was pretty proud of himself, considering he'd never done anything like this before. He'd pulled out all the stops.

"Why don't you go and change, and I'll meet you outside at six?"

"Outside?" She blinked, eyes wide.

"Yes. Stop asking questions. This is a surprise, okay?"

"O-kay, Mr. Bossy." She brushed past him on the way to her bedroom.

"And don't forget, *casual* is the word of the day."

"Right."

He hadn't seen Zoey in anything but a dress—or a swimsuit—during the day. She was always polished and put together. And her hair might be called a work of art, as he knew she spent hours in her bedroom getting it just right. All these things he knew simply from the gift of living with her for the past two weeks. There was so much more to know, and he wanted to, even if he didn't see the point. As he'd told Zoey, he might well leave the state when this job was over. Ian was the only member of the team centrally located in Houston because he'd started the satellite office, and though Ronan Sheridan was based in Charming, he still traveled a great deal. He'd made Charming home because of his family, and now his wife.

Archer would love a reason to make Charming his home base, but at the moment he didn't really have one. He was ready to travel again, ready again to see other parts of the world in a different way than a soldier, this time, under less duress. Yeah, it would be nice to have a family someday, but he couldn't think that way. It wasn't time. First, he had to work on a career postmilitary that would support him and a partner.

He didn't have forever to offer Zoey, but he certainly had right now. This day. This moment.

Setting up the two-person pup tent in a corner of Zoey's massive backyard didn't take long. It had been the first box to arrive followed by several boxes of camping supplies. One night, he'd searched the garage, finding it so clean and pristine it could be an extra bedroom. Clearly, a man did not live in this house. Even the gardener didn't keep his supplies in here. Archer had to order everything. He now had a lantern, flashlights, a portable firepit, sleeping bags, even a small gas stove and "cowboy" coffeemaker.

Thanks to him, Zoey would spend a night under the stars.

He had everything set up by six o'clock, and when Zoey strode through the patio doors and past the swimming pool—wearing a plaid shirt and jeans, but still looking every bit a supermodel—he called out to her from the side.

"Over here," he said, emerging from the tent. "What do you think? We're going camping!"

His chest pinched when Zoey's jaw went slack. She walked toward him slowly, each step measured as if stepping into a different timeline. When she smiled wide and held up her hands to cover her mouth, Christmas came early for him.

She lowered her hands. "Oh, my gosh! What a surprise! Are we seriously doing this?"

"You're sleeping under the stars tonight! Now you see why I didn't want it to rain and ruin my plans. You're getting a fire, campground style." He pointed to the firepit he'd loaded with wood he'd also had delivered. "Do you realize you can practically order anything online now?"

"I'm a business owner, what do you think?" she replied, but she was grinning, as she simultaneously took in the entire setup. "My little baby boutique has to compete with the giants, which is how I got the idea to sell one-of-a-kind items. Even so, I can't offer free shipping or I'd always be in the hole."

"Yeah. And there's all the damn packaging." Archer shrugged. "Well, I'll plant a tree."

"This explains all the packages the past few days." Zoey bent down, peeking into the tent, then straightened and caught his eye. "There are two sleeping bags."

"Did you think I'd let you do this alone?"

"We're going to sleep together, in the same tent?" She quirked a brow. "Buddy?"

"There are two sleeping bags," he protested. *"Buddy."*

"Gotcha." She elbowed him. "Well, you had better not snore."

"If I do, I'll just move outside and literally sleep under the stars." He moved toward the gas camping stove. "And *I'm* cooking tonight."

"On this?" Zoey looked incredulous. "But I have a state-of-the-art kitchen only a few feet away from us."

"Cheating," Archer said. "This experience has to be honest or you won't get the full Monty."

"The full Monty?" Zoey quirked a brow, and Archer remembered the premise of that movie.

"I mean the full experience." He bit back a smile.

She winked. "Um, yeah. The full experience. That would be nice."

Ignoring her flirting, Archer opened up the ice chest in which he'd placed a couple of steaks he'd already presalted. He handed Zoey a cold beer from the chest.

She accepted it and twisted off the cap, then seemed to be thinking something over, her gaze looking up and to the right.

"I'm going to need a few things if I'm spending the night here." She took a pull of the beer. "With you."

Yes, they would be spending the night together, but only in a similar way as they'd already been doing this week. With the exception of sharing a very small space.

"Go pack a bag."

Chapter Twenty-Two

Zoey had never been as thrilled as in the moment she realized she'd be camping for the first time in her life. Sleeping under the stars, too, because she planned on lying outside of the tent in a sleeping bag. Daddy would think she'd gone bananas if he could see her now.

"You have a beautiful home, why would you sleep on the lawn?"

She understood, on some level, because her father had not grown up with the kind of luxury Zoey had. His mother, a single mom, had worked hard for everything they had. If Zoey had to sleep in a tent year-round *of course* it wouldn't be fun. But she wanted this experience and couldn't believe a boyfriend or friend had never suggested "roughing it." They might have assumed she wouldn't be interested but they'd be wrong.

Zoey hadn't asked if electronics would be allowed on this excursion, but just in case, she FaceTimed Twyla before beginning the adventure.

"I'm going camping!"

Twyla's happy face lit up with a smile. "Really? Where?"

"My backyard."

"Oh." Twyla seemed stunned for several seconds, just staring into the phone. "Okay."

"It was Archer's idea and he surprised me. You should see it. There's a tent and sleeping bags and a firepit…it really feels like autumn arrived in my backyard."

"Aw, I hope you have fun," Twyla said. "Eat a s'more for me!"

After she disconnected, Zoey packed an overnight bag with a few essentials, like her toothbrush, hair bonnet, slippers and pajamas. If she forgot anything, she could simply walk a few feet and get it, although that might be considered cheating. If she were miles away from home in the woods, she would have to make do. Either way, she took off her makeup and washed her face ahead of time. She didn't want to have to do so with the garden hose.

When she rejoined him, Archer was grilling two steaks on a grate over the firepit.

"Smells delicious," Zoey said, throwing her bag in the tent.

"Wait until you taste this," Archer said. "I'm not kidding, somehow everything tastes better when it's cooked outside."

"Should I get plates and cutlery?"

"Nope, already did."

"You have definitely prepared for this, and I am truly surprised." She took a seat on one of the folded lawn chairs he'd placed in front of the tent. "Thank you."

"I felt bad about canceling your event," Archer said, turning a steak. "It isn't fair that your father's problem became your own."

"If only y'all had told me the truth instead of blaming it on poor Scott—"

"You would have gotten on board?" Archer gave her a quirk of the eyebrow suggesting he didn't buy it.

"Well, maybe not, but it would have made more sense to me."

"What about Scott? Is he texting or bothering you anymore?"

"Not since your very direct message on my behalf."

"I had a feeling that might work."

"And I suppose I should thank you for that," Zoey said, leaning toward the fire. "I never would have been so blunt, but I see now where sometimes it's necessary to get the message across. I've never been good at that."

"I'll tell you what—you continue to be kind and leave me to be the ass on your behalf. I can pull it off far more easily than you ever could."

"Yes, but…you won't always be around, will you?"

"That's true, but let's not think about that tonight."

When the steaks were ready, they ate them from their plates right on the ground, on which he'd laid a large plaid blanket. Granted, she had a patio table on the deck they could drag over, but this was roughing it and she wouldn't complain. The steak tasted charbroiled, almost as good as what she'd order in a restaurant. Archer had also boiled some potatoes and vegetables, which would normally taste bland to her. But damn, he was right, everything tasted better outside. Such a mystery!

"So tell me, Archer. You and your family did this all the time? How often did you and your family go camping?"

"Just about every summer. Naturally, my sisters would complain about not having running water and facilities. I loved it, though. As a kid, I probably spent half my life outside, taking every dare I ever got. I broke my leg once." He moved his prosthesis. "I suppose I should say twice. Once, rather more permanently."

They hadn't talked about this. For all practical purposes,

Archer was a man without anything notably missing. He certainly no longer had a hitch in his step, but they both knew the truth. Because of an accident, his life would never be the same. For someone who'd lost so much, Zoey remained impressed with how little it seemed to matter to him. She assumed, however, that was a front for his real thoughts and fears.

"Does it hurt?" Zoey whispered.

"Nah. It took some getting used to, but it's been months now. The only issue was just before I got here, I'd been given a newer model. It took some adjusting. Funny how I can trade in my old foot for a new one. Kind of like a car. More bells and whistles."

"You deserve the best," Zoey said, scooting closer to him. "Like the Cadillac or Rolls-Royce of prosthetics."

He chuckled and their shoulders touched, leaning into each other. "Pretty sure I have it."

When the flickering flames died back to red glowing embers, Archer reached for the bag of marshmallows. He had her dialed. This time Zoey ate far too many and may have had a sugar high because she kept reaching for Archer's lips to clear off something that wasn't actually there. If he questioned it, he said nothing.

"My parents never took me camping. I don't know why. It just seems like the seminal American vacation and I missed out on it. I never had the s'mores and campfires and ghost stories."

"But you got to see other things instead."

"True, and I'm not complaining. I've had a privileged life and I accept that. But I never asked for this. I just happened to wind up in this family with a famous athlete for a dad. He gave us everything he could, even if sometimes he failed to give us more of himself."

"He was gone a lot, I take it?"

"Yeah. It was far from ideal. We were the pretty picture to the public—Patch Lambert, his wife and daughter. With the bigger games, we were always there for the photo ops. Super Bowl wins and parties, those were the high times. No photo ops of the times my father was sidelined with an injury, miserable and angry. My mother handled it well, even if looking back, it was almost like she was a single parent during football season. I don't want to sound ungrateful. We had so much of everything, but sometimes it's the small things that matter the most. Having a father home to tuck you in every night, tell you a bedtime story, just be there. My mother did all that for me. No wonder we were so close."

"In our family, my mother never let my father off the hook. Of course, he didn't travel, though I bet there were times he would have liked to get away from us all for a week or two. When he got home every night it was his job to give the younger kids baths and tuck them into bed after dinner. He wasn't allowed to say he was tired from working all day, commuting home from the city. She'd say, 'And what do you think I have been doing all day? Eating chocolate bonbons?'" He laughed. "I grew up in an equal opportunity household, and that's how it's going to be when I have a wife and children. It's only fair."

The thought of Archer with a wife and children sent a swift kick to her belly. She didn't like the thought, unless she was in the picture. Now *that* would be a nice photo op.

"You're going to have a wife and children?"

"I'm Italian, what do you think? I think it's written in the contract at birth." He snorted.

"Well, I'm half Mexican and half Black so it's probably

in my contract, too." She chuckled. "I have to tell you, this is probably the best Sweetheart Day *ever*."

"Yeah? That's high praise."

"Except for the ones I had with my mother, of course."

"Naturally. I can't compete with that, nor would I want to."

"Had I known *this* would happen, I would have canceled sooner. It's better than a party."

"You say that now," Archer said with a smirk. "But wait until you wake up after a night sleeping on the cold, hard ground."

"I won't mind."

"We'll see about that."

Archer bit his lower lip to keep from breaking into a full-blown smile watching Zoey struggle with zipping up her sleeping bag.

"I'm going to sleep outside the tent, I've decided." She positioned her bag a foot away from the smoldering firepit. "And truly see the stars."

"I might join you. If it gets too cold, just climb in the tent. It's not like we need protection from dangerous animals or anything."

"My gardener sprays regularly for snakes and mosquitoes."

"I meant a coyote."

Her expression was priceless, eyes round, brows scrunched together. "But I don't think—"

He grinned. "No coyotes out here. Or lions or tigers and bears."

"Oh, my." She giggled, having now curled completely into her sleeping bag and zipped up. Only her pretty face showed.

He certainly wasn't afraid of anything out here. He had his gun nearby, locked and loaded, though he hardly needed to bring that up to her. She'd seen him carrying the entire time. But just because they were outside in a perfectly landscaped backyard in a wealthy neighborhood didn't mean he'd let his guard down. Protecting Zoey was still his number one job.

It didn't take much longer for the sky to darken to inky black, and with the cloud cover gone, the stars twinkled brightly against a perfect velvety backdrop. This was the way Archer loved to see the sky, and the range and depth of space itself. It reminded him that this earthly life was temporary and transitory. He'd already lost so many friends who would never experience the pleasures and pains of growing old. Archer could only hope he would be one of the lucky ones who did.

He covered the fire, took off his boot, then his foot, placed both in the zipped-up tent and climbed into his own sleeping bag not far from Zoey's.

Zoey took out her arm to point. "That's the Big Dipper."

"You're not a true novice." He chuckled.

"I'm still a camping virgin," she said, scooting her body closer to him.

He snorted. "Proud to be here with you for your first time."

"Archer, this is the best thing ever." She reached for his hand and squeezed it.

He squeezed hers back, not letting go. He'd been all over the world and slept under the sky countless of times, but without a doubt, this would be the one he'd always remember.

They fell asleep holding hands.

Archer heard the sound before he felt the first sprays

of rain. Wait. No, not rain. He opened one eye to the first rays of sunlight just as water hit him. Sitting up, he saw the problem. The garden sprinklers had gone off. They were probably on a timer, which was smart, and which he should have considered when setting up. Pretty soon, he imagined, everything out here would be wet.

He reached for his foot and boot inside the tent, when he heard Zoey squeal.

"Oh! It's raining!" She sat up, looked up at the sky, then climbed out of her bag.

"Sprinklers," Archer said. "My fault. We should have turned them off."

The sprinklers really packed a punch but surely they'd be going off momentarily.

"In here."

He crouched and helped Zoey climb into the tent. They could just run inside the house, only feet away, but this was the experience. They were only slightly damp and not totally drenched, and more importantly, both laughing hard at the idiocy of the moment. Such careful planning on his part, then forgetting something as silly as turning off the timed sprinkler system.

"You almost got your rain," Archer said, throwing his arm around her in the tight space. "Wish hard enough for something and maybe it will happen."

"If only that were true," she said, curling into his chest. "I'm wishing for something else right now."

"Zoey," he said quietly, but it was too late.

She raised her lips to his, and they were kissing in a way that reminded him of other carnal pleasures in life. He'd been denying himself those, too, for what felt like far too long. One of the greatest pleasures in life: a beautiful woman who knew how to kiss. They kissed for so long that the sprinklers finally stopped their pulsing waves of water. And just like that, Archer woke out of his trance. He pulled away.

"We shouldn't."

"Look," Zoey said. "I don't care if it's unprofessional. You know I won't tell anyone. It'll be our secret. You want me and I want you. What could be simpler?"

"It's not that easy. I wish it were."

He unzipped the tent and climbed out. Together they began to clean everything up. They worked together well, and after an hour, a person wouldn't know they'd been camping last night. Archer stuck all the supplies he'd bought in Zoey's pristine garage.

After showering, he changed into his uniform of white button-down with tie and black slacks. Zoey had also showered, and he found her in the kitchen chopping potatoes. As usual, she was making him breakfast. He'd told her a million times she didn't have to include him, but she always did anyway.

Both the ring camera and doorbell sounded at once, and Archer stood.

"Expecting anyone?"

"Nope," Zoey said, moving to the door. "But I'll get it."

He hoped it wasn't Scott, trying again, or even worse, the other guy Zoey used to date coming around to try again. If that were the case, he'd have to do better at scaring him off for good. Glancing at the ring app on his phone, Archer saw three men. He moved behind Zoey.

She opened the door to a tall, muscular African American man flanked by two smartly dressed equally large men.

"Daddy! What are *you* doing here?"

Chapter Twenty-Three

Zoey stared at her father, surrounded on either side by his regular bodyguards. She recognized them both since she'd grown up with them.

"Hey, baby girl," Daddy said, holding out his arms. "Decided to surprise you."

His eyes narrowed. "Aren't you going to let us in?"

"Sorry, of course. Please, come in. Hello, Harry. Alec."

She waved her father and his small entourage inside. These two had been with her father for years and had known her mother, too.

She nodded at everyone. "We were just going to have breakfast."

Archer came up right behind her and offered his hand. "Pleased to meet you. I am Archer Rossi, at your service."

"So, this is the guy!" Her father stood back after shaking Archer's hand. "You're awful young, aren't you?"

"Aw, c'mon, Patch," Harry said, clapping his back. "We were young once."

"Until you got a hold of us," Alec joked. "Now I look like I'm ninety."

"Don't listen to these jokesters," her father said. "I'm hardly any trouble at all. Never planned on my bodyguards meeting my *daughter's* bodyguard, though. It's good to meet you, young man."

"Would y'all like something to eat?" Zoey said, leading them into the kitchen.

"She's just like her mother," Alec said. "Already feeding us and we just walked in the door."

"That's my girl," her father said. "Just like her mami."

Zoey smiled at the compliment. "I'll chop up some more potatoes."

"Don't bother," Alec said, patting his potbelly. "At least, none for me. I'm cutting back on the carbs."

"I'll have his portion." Harry raised his hand.

Her father was already chatting with Archer, both of them chuckling at something or other.

"Don't worry about cooking for us," Daddy said, waving his hand dismissively. "Can we talk?"

Her father *never* wanted to talk. Her mind started conjuring up all kinds of terrible scenarios. He was here to tell her that he'd been diagnosed with some terrible ailment. Maybe not cancer, but Lou Gehrig's disease, or diabetes, or Alzheimer's. What would she do if she lost both her parents?

She followed her father into the living room, where he took a seat on her L-shaped leather couch.

"What's wrong? Are you *sick*?"

"God, no, baby. I might need another knee replacement and I could always use a brand-new spine, but otherwise I'm healthy as a horse."

"Oh, phew." Zoey touched her chest. "You had me worried for a minute because you *never* want to talk."

"Well, I wouldn't say never." He coughed into his fist.

"Never." She quirked a brow, not letting him off the hook.

Mami used to say to him, "*For God's sake, Pat, if something is bothering you, say it. Don't just let it fester.*"

But he never did talk about it. His way was to keep it close to the vest and deal with it himself, even if that meant taking time alone. Now he wanted to talk. He was probably worried about her. She prayed he didn't have someone new he wanted her to date.

"So…that bodyguard," her father began. "I think it's pretty interesting you didn't mention that he looks like a matinee idol."

Zoey crossed her arms. "First, his name is Archer, and what does *that* have to do with anything?"

"He's the kind of man you've always been attracted to."

"How would you know that?"

He flinched like she'd wounded him. "Your mother told me."

"Oh. Well, he's Italian, if that's what you mean."

"A foreigner. Your type."

"He's Italian-American." She straightened. "And actually a Texan for the past decade or more."

He waved his hand in the air. "Whatever."

"I'm sorry, did you come all this way to check up on me? Do you think I'm taking liberties with my bodyguard because he's attractive?"

Her nerves pulsed at how close he'd come to the truth. Funny how well he knew her for having spent so little time around her growing up. Her mother must have shared more than Zoey had ever imagined.

Daddy's ever-present grin momentarily cracked. "No. I trust you to always do the right thing."

"Good."

"And you trust me, right?"

"Of course, you're my father. I know you want what's best for me."

This wasn't the time to remind him that he didn't always know what she wanted *or* needed. That was beside the point.

"I always have." He cleared his throat. "And I'm sure you also want what's best for me."

"Well, of course. Why? Is something wrong?"

"Nothing's wrong at all." He straightened and tugged on the collar of his shirt. "Something's very good."

"Are you getting elected to the Hall of Fame?"

"*Inducted.* And I'm already in the Hall of Fame."

He scowled, and Zoey feared she'd insulted him. "Oh, right. I forgot."

"Here's the thing. There's no point in skirting around the issue so I'm going to come right out and say it. I'm getting married."

All the oxygen was sucked out of the room, and Zoey couldn't catch her breath as she stared at him. She had to have heard wrong. It had only been four years since her mother died. What was the damn rush? Who was this woman he was going to marry? She hoped not his last girlfriend because she was far too young. But it didn't matter, because no one would ever be as good as Mami. No woman would ever love her father the way Mami had. No one could.

"Are you okay?" her father said, and suddenly he was next to her, holding her hand.

That's when she realized she was gasping, trying to find words.

"You…you…you're getting married? When?"

There were too many other questions, like why? And to whom? But she was afraid to ask to whom, because she feared it was the woman he'd been seeing on and off, the one Zoey didn't like.

"We're not eloping but as soon as we can make it happen." He patted her knee, as if that made it all okay. "I had to tell you, because I've waited too long."

"Waited too *long*?" Zoey stood. "You haven't waited too long! Mami died four years ago. That's no time at all."

"It feels like forever to me," her father said. "I'm alone, Zoey."

"You and your bodyguards, you mean."

Somewhere in the far reaches of her mind, Zoey became aware her voice was gradually increasing in volume.

"My bodyguards are my friends, but they have their own wives and families. I miss having a partner, someone who'll stand beside me and support me."

"So, that's it? You're going to forget all about Mami?"

Unfortunately, she'd not so much said this as screamed it.

Why would he come here on the day after Sweetheart Day to further slash her illusions about forever love? Yes, she got it: Her mother was gone and would never be back. Some things had to change. No more stupid Sweetheart Day, for one. But this was just too much. Her father remarrying put a stamp on it: Her mother was gone forever.

All three bodyguards were suddenly in the living room with them, foreheads creased, jaws tight. With her scream, she'd activated alarm mode in bodyguard language.

"Everything okay, Patch?" Alec said.

Her father nodded. "We're fine."

Archer came to stand behind her, bless his heart, as if he could somehow fix this. He couldn't. No one could.

"One of y'all get my daughter a glass of water, would you?" Patch asked.

Harry beelined it to the kitchen, Alec following behind. Archer wasn't moving. He didn't move when the guys left, and he didn't move when Harry returned, offering her a glass.

"Thank you," Zoey said, taking a long swallow. She glanced behind her at Archer. "I'm okay."

He nodded, then moved closer to the rest of the men.

"Some privacy, please?" her father asked.

"We'll be in the kitchen," Alec said.

Zoey's regular breathing returned, and with it, the knowledge she'd acted like a child. Just like back in the day, when her parents stood together, a united front, and refused to let her drive the cute little coupe she'd purchased with her own money, declaring it "too dangerous." She had raged at them then. Sometimes their love had been a suffocating vice around her neck.

But she wasn't a child any longer. These were grown-up problems. Her father was getting remarried, and she should want that for him. She wanted him to be happy, but it just hurt.

"Is it Veronica?" Zoey asked, knowing the answer, and making the reluctant choice to accept it.

Daddy blinked. "Good Lord, no! She's twenty years younger than I am."

The spike of relief that went through Zoey delighted her, until she realized the situation might be worse. Who else could it be? He didn't have much time to date or meet new people, so it had to be someone he knew. Surely not her mother's best friend!

Zoey took another gulp of water for fortification. "Then *who*?"

Daddy studied his nails. "Well, it's someone you don't know."

At least it wasn't her mother's bestie. "I know a lot of people, so you might as well try me."

Daddy leaned back with a chuckle. "Well, I hadn't talked to this person in a long time because we lost touch."

Hmm. So someone from his past.

"Just tell me. If you're getting married, I'm going to assume you've been dating her for a while."

He wouldn't look at Zoey and seemed suddenly very interested in her carpet. "A few…weeks?"

"A few *weeks*?" Zoey set her glass of water down on the coaster beside her with force. "How well do you know this woman? What would you tell *me* if I was going to marry someone after only knowing him a few weeks? Really, Daddy?"

"There are about thirty years between us, young lady, and I know my mind. I'm old, honey. I know things. It doesn't take long to know when you're my age. I know when it's right."

"Okay, wow." Zoey crossed her arms. "It sounds like you're just coming up with excuses now. Maybe you should take five and think about this. What's the rush? If it's love, she'll still be around in another year or two, right?"

He smiled and shook his head. "We don't want to wait."

Zoey blew out a breath and tapped her foot. "I still don't hear a name."

"Right. Her name is Robin Brown. She was my high school girlfriend."

Chapter Twenty-Four

"Your *high school girlfriend*?"

"We broke up when we went to different colleges. I went to A&M on my football scholarship and she went back East. I met your mami, and the rest is history."

Okay, so this woman couldn't be all that wonderful or her father would have kept in touch. He wouldn't have dropped her. Obviously, Zoey's mother was "the one" and he realized it. No point in looking back. Relief spilled through Zoey. This was simply some kind of rebound relationship. Those second-chance love stories never worked in real life, only in books.

"I thought you never went back to high school reunions. The last time you went, they had to hire extra security."

"I don't."

"Did you reconnect on classmates dot net or something?"

"Believe it or not, it was through a celebrity dating app."

"You joined a dating app?"

"Yeah, I was…talked into it."

"So this Robin is a celebrity?"

He shook his head. "Not at all."

That meant she'd somehow lied to get herself on the celebrity app. It sounded like Robin just wanted to marry someone famous. Zoey didn't understand how her poor father couldn't see through this ruse. She obviously had an agenda.

"She has a good friend who's a movie producer," her father continued. "And when this friend was scrolling, she saw my name and told Robin. Apparently she…used to talk about me."

"Hmm. No doubt. So, this friend simply got you two together, off the app?"

"Exactly. She made the connection, told Robin, then when Robin said she'd be happy to meet, her friend told me through the app. We decided we'd just get together, you know, catch up. We'd definitely lost touch." Daddy cleared his throat. "We had one date, and it felt like we just picked up where we left off. Like no time at all had passed."

"She's your age?"

"Actually, she's a year older." Patch chuckled. "She never forgot me. But she was married, too, just like me. She's a widow. All these years later, we have a lot in common. Even our pasts are similar."

Zoey's stomach hurt. More and more, this sounded like one of the second-chance reunions she loved reading about. It was different in real life, watching it happen to your own father.

"Anyway—" her father sighed "—that's why it happened so fast. We know each other, we fell back in love, and I'm not willing to waste any more time."

Zoey felt like a hypocrite. She didn't want this kind of love for her father, not now. It was too soon, but she didn't know how to stop it. It wasn't in her nature to be cruel and accuse Robin of being a gold digger, even though that's what she thought she was. But she'd have to thoroughly vet this woman who dared to take her mother's place.

Her daddy left not long after dropping his truth bomb.

Zoey walked him to the door, hugging him goodbye. Even if she hated all this, she loved her father. She would try to give this woman a chance, for his sake. Robin would be flying in tonight, and he wanted Zoey to meet her tomorrow. They were to have dinner at Le Ouragan the restaurant at the hotel where they were staying. Just the three of them and their three bodyguards. Perfectly normal. They were simply a normal, average, American family. *Right.*

This was all so unexpected that Zoey's brain had a ton of rearranging to do. She was going to have to remodel and build entire new rooms in her mind for this to fit. She didn't even know her father had *been* on dating apps, or that there was some exclusive dating app for celebrities called *Shhh.* Really?

What a strange experience. Surreal. Her father had loved somebody else before he met Zoey's mother. She'd always thought they were each other's first love, but they'd met in college.

Zoey didn't know how long she'd been sitting on a stool in the kitchen when Archer walked in and said, "Are you okay?"

"I had never heard of this woman before. Why did I never hear about her?"

"Just going out on a limb here, but maybe because she was firmly in his past. He married your mother. Robin wasn't important before."

"But she is now."

"*Zoey,*" Archer said, voice low and filled with compassion. "I know this is hard."

"No, you can't imagine! Hard? This is like a root canal without anesthesia!"

"That bad, huh?"

"I don't want him to marry again so soon. It's not right."

Archer cocked his head. “Is this coming from the lover of love? From the woman who decorated her store with yellow and orange hearts for the season? Who mailed out engraved invitations to a *house* party? Who celebrates Sweetheart Day because Valentine’s Day isn’t enough?”

Zoey flashed him a scowl. Oh, gosh, she hated when people called her out on stuff. That had always been her mother’s job. Sometimes Twyla tried, but she didn’t have the temperament for it. Too sweet and understanding.

Archer didn’t have that problem.

“This is different. It’s my *father.* He should have had me meet her first before he asked her to marry him. Maybe he’s slipping in his old age.”

“I didn’t see any sign of that.”

She crossed her arms. “Well, I worry about him.”

“And he worries about you. Hence, my presence here.”

“You don’t know. I’ve personally witnessed women of all kinds throwing themselves at my father. Right in front of me, as if I wasn’t even there. His only daughter. He has money and they know it. Maybe I should have never moved out of the house. That way, I’d have been there to stop this from happening.”

“At least give her a chance.” Archer tipped back on his heels. “If she’s horrible and an obvious gold digger, I’ll help you get rid of her.”

“You will?” Zoey smiled for the first time in hours.

He nodded and said mysteriously, “And I know how to make a person disappear.”

“You better be kidding,” she said.

The facetious grin on his face assured her that he was—*thank God*—but she appreciated that he had her back.

Archer found it funny that Zoey didn’t think her father should find love again, or that four years was long enough to grieve someone. Part of him understood. He'd like to think he'd be accepting if the situation happened in his family, but his mother was also irreplaceable, so…he understood. Archer also saw that Zoey hadn't entirely worked through her grief, and this latest development might be pushing it. She'd given up the day she'd shared with her mother, and now this. Her father was getting married, just like that. Archer sympathized, even if he'd continue to play devil's advocate.

He agreed that her father's timing could have been better. Zoey had just had to cancel an event that meant a lot to her due to her connection to Patch Lambert. Then again, the man wasn't getting any younger. And he'd fallen for someone his own age when he could probably have any woman he wanted. The truth was, it sounded to Archer like it could be a real relationship, and maybe that was the part that bothered Zoey the most. This wasn't a fling, and it wasn't temporary. There was a lot of good in that, but unfortunately, Zoey only saw this woman as a replacement for her mother, and not as someone who could simply make her father happy for however long he had left.

The next afternoon, Rachel returned to the boutique and chose the dress without the long train. While Zoey was in the back with her, Archer minded the store, giving advice when and where he could. He'd become better at this, understanding that women wanted simply to be seen. And he could do that.

"Which one?" A young woman held up a sparkly pink dress next to a black one with a scandalous slit up the side. Archer's inner big brother reared his head.

"This one." He pointed to the pink dress. "Black is boring."

It would also make this girl look far too sexy for her age. Better for her to look like someone's prom date.

"*That* was interesting," Zoey said from behind him. "I thought you liked black."

"It looks good on most women, but that one was too risqué for her," he said. "She's too young."

"Hmm, yes. I agree."

Later, after closing up the shop, Archer and Zoey headed to the restaurant to meet Patch, his bodyguards and his new fiancée. Zoey's nerves were on full display as she drummed her fingers anxiously against the console of his car.

"The truth is, I'm trying to keep an open mind," she said, fingers tapping. "I want to be fair."

"Good."

"*She* might be nervous, too."

"Naturally." Archer reached for her hand as much for comfort as to still it. "You're the most important person in his life. If she doesn't win you over, this isn't going to work."

"Right," Zoey said, squeezing his hand. "But the thing is, I have to look out for my daddy. He's been lonely, so he might fall into the clutches of a woman who wants his money or his fame. And to be honest, he grew up in Section 8 housing. He got out of that neighborhood with his talent, but I'm not sure the same could be said of most people at his high school. Like Robin."

They arrived minutes before Patch pulled up with his entourage, and Archer received another crash course in the world of celebrity. He'd already had a taste of it with his first job. People in general could be funny when it came to seeing a celebrity walking around like a regular person. Eyes bugged and jaws dropped. Archer had never been privy to this before becoming a bodyguard. His closest experience had been when a four-star general visited his platoon.

But this was different.

He hadn't anticipated just how popular an NFL Hall of Famer could be.

"Oh, my God, Patch!" someone said as he walked toward the entrance, flanked by his bodyguards.

"I can't believe it's you!"

"You're the best running back that ever lived!"

"Thank you. Thank you, folks." Patch made his way through with grace, nodding, waving. Then he stopped and turned. "Just here to have dinner at this fine establishment."

"No pictures," Harry ordered, holding up his palm.

It was always the bodyguard's job to be the bad guy, and no need to let Patch's stalker know he was in Charming. Last night, Archer had checked in with Ian to advise him of this latest development. Ian hadn't known about it, and he was definitely not happy. Archer saw his point.

"He came to see his daughter? When he's got this stalker possibly following him?"

But Archer had discovered, through Harry and Alec, that the police would be making an arrest today. Both law enforcement and Patch thought it best he leave the area when that happened. The arrest would make public what had been happening and might elicit sympathy for the man from Patch's other haters.

Now here he was, staying close to Zoey, while they waited for Patch to get through his sea of admirers. Inside, he shook hands with the lined-up staff, even the cook, broke rank and graciously took some selfies.

"Is it always like this?" Archer whispered to Zoey. He hadn't been with his first celebrity assignment long enough to know.

"You have no idea," Zoey said. "I'm sure we have a table in the back for some privacy, but believe me, it won't stop them. It's like my father belongs to everyone. And honestly, he likes it. Loves the attention, all the fawning and interruptions. It's tougher for those of us in his life who would like his exclusive attention."

When they were shown to a table in the back, a group of patrons sitting nearby clapped for him and called out his praises.

"This is going to be tough for Robin to get used to, believe me," Zoey said, and he detected a hint of pleasure in her voice. "She'll have to share him. They don't want to see her, or anyone else. They only want him. That's how it is."

Archer was about to say that she might not mind but thought better of it. He sincerely hoped the woman was kind—like Mother Teresa kind—or she didn't stand a chance.

Archer pulled out a chair for Zoey to sit, then made his way to stand a few feet behind her. Enough to give them privacy, but not too far, in case he was needed. Harry and Alec did the same for Patch.

"We'll take turns eating," Harry said, motioning for Archer to take a seat. "Go ahead."

Zoey looked up and patted the seat beside her. No sign of Robin, but Archer figured she was coming on her own to avoid the attention. No sooner had they sat down than they were served with an appetizer...and they kept coming, one after another. Platters of stuffed mushrooms, calamari, barbecue. Zoey didn't touch a thing.

After about fifteen minutes, a tall, svelte, beautiful Black woman dressed in a conservative green dress joined them. Patch stood and so did Archer.

"Hello, sweetheart," Patch said, embracing her. "Robin, meet my daughter, Zoey."

Zoey didn't get up, but Robin went straight to her, offering her hand and a beaming smile. "I've heard so much about you. You look *a lot* like your mother."

"She does," Patch said, beaming with pride. "I'm so glad my two girls finally get to meet."

"Just in time for the wedding," Zoey said with a bite. "A little later and we might have had to meet at the altar."

"Patch, you told her we're getting married?" Robin said. "You could have eased her into this."

Zoey straightened the cloth napkin on her lap. "I didn't even know you were *dating*. Had no idea my daddy signed up for the dating apps."

"That's not actually how we met," Robin said, turning to Patch. "Did you tell her?"

"She knows you were my high school sweetheart," Patch said, softly touching her shoulder and helping her into her seat next to his.

Archer elbowed Zoey, hoping she'd get the message.

Be nice.

"That sure was a long time ago," Zoey said. "You two are probably not the same people you were back then."

"I think she just called us old, Patchy." Robin chuckled. "And she's right. We are *not* the same people."

"Indeed, we are not." Patch shook a finger at Zoey. "But close enough. And we are not *old*, young lady. I still have plenty of good years left in me."

"As long as you take it easy and pace yourself," Zoey said, and Archer wished he could get her to stop talking. "You don't want to act like too much of a young man and wind up with a heart attack."

Archer internally face-palmed and gently elbowed Zoey again, this time while clearing his throat.

Robin's eyes were wide saucers when she turned to Patch. "You have heart problems?"

"Of course not. Just a little hypertension but I take my pills. The only problems I have are orthopedic ones. But you know all about that." Then he turned and focused his attention on Zoey. "Robin is a doctor. An *orthopedist*."

Chapter Twenty-Five

Patchy?

Robin had just called her father, a six-foot-five giant of a man, Patchy? *No one* called him Patchy. Her mother never had, nor had any of their family and friends. The name was ridiculous, a joke. For crying out loud, "Patch" was a dorky enough nickname.

And now, this woman, who was the antithesis of Zoey's mother, was a *doctor*?

When Archer elbowed her again, she was tempted to elbow him back…in the gut. Zoey was being nice, sweet as potato pie, but this woman was arrogant. Confident, full of herself, beautiful. She hadn't walked in, she had *stridden* in, à la Olivia Pope in *Scandal*. As a doctor, she must have money. Why did she want her father? What was her endgame? Maybe she was simply trying to recapture her youth. Yes, that had to be it. Maybe they were *both* trying to do that. It made sense. Zoey was here to remind them both that Patch Lambert was the daughter of a thirty-year-old woman. He couldn't lie about his age.

"I always wanted to be a doctor," Robin was saying. "But I didn't know where I'd specialize. Patch went off to college to play football and I did premed on the East Coast. Then in medical school, I decided to specialize in orthopedics, which must have had something to do with the affinity and connection I always felt to Patch. Naturally, I kept up with his career and saw all the injuries he endured as he played his heart out on that field. Patch inspired me to want to fix all those injuries, I guess."

Her father gave her a goofy smile.

"Where did you attend school?" Archer asked, like a normal human being engaging in conversation.

"Howard for premed, then Johns Hopkins," she said proudly. "I did my residency there, too."

It was odd the way her father was staring at Robin with stars in his eyes. It was the same way he'd looked at her mother. With simple adoration. He must be under some kind of spell. There could be no other explanation for this.

"Did you just call him 'Patchy'?" Zoey said.

Robin laughed behind her hand. "That was his nickname in high school. Sorry."

"Only you were allowed to call me that," her father joked. "And I called her 'Birdy' for a long time."

Birdy and Patchy? Zoey threw up a little in her mouth.

"So, when is the wedding?" Archer asked, again making conversation as if this was normal.

"We haven't set a date yet," Robin said. "At this point, for us, it's just a formality. We've both been there, done that. I'm respectful of Patch's need for privacy. And of course I've already done this once. Did I tell you I was married for twenty years? Just out of medical school. We were too busy to have any children, which I regret."

"Robin lost her husband not much before I lost your mother," her father said. "We connected, both being widowers."

But Zoey's mother wasn't *lost*, and she hated the euphemism. She knew exactly where to find her at the cemetery. She'd died and gone to heaven but wasn't "lost" to anyone.

"That makes sense," Archer said, probably because Zoey wasn't talking anymore. "You both have something traumatic in common."

"In addition to going to the same high school," Robin said. "I've always followed Patch's career, naturally, but it was my late husband who was the real football fan. I used to tell him, 'I know that guy.' Of course, he knew all about me and Patch. It was a badge of honor for him."

"Did you know that Zoey has wedding dresses at her boutique?" Archer said. "In case you're looking for one."

This time Zoey nudged his thigh under the table and gave him a glare. Both her father and Robin turned to her with wide, eager eyes. Zoey squirmed.

"Do you?" Robin said.

"One of a kind," Archer said, biting back a smile. "That's what she tells me, anyway."

"You won't believe this, Birdy," Daddy said, chuckling and pointing to Archer. "He's the bodyguard I hired for Zoey when all this mess started. But Zoey lets people think he works for her at the boutique."

"Ingenious," Robin said. "I would expect a smart girl like Zoey to think of everything. And what kind of dresses do you carry, if I might ask? Anything vintage? That's what I'd love. Obviously, I'm no blushing bride. I'm sixty-one years old and getting married for the second time. I want a dress that's old, too."

Archer and her father laughed at this, but Zoey didn't think it was funny.

"I have vintage dresses," Zoey finally said, and Archer gave her an encouraging smile. "But I don't think there's anything you would like."

"I'd love to see what you have," Robin said, leaning forward. "I'm going to be in Charming for a few more days so maybe I could drop by."

When Zoey didn't respond for a second or two, Archer piped in. "Drop by anytime, except she's closed on Mondays."

Finally, the food was served, and Zoey picked at her pasta carbonara. She'd lost her appetite. After Archer finished his steak, he switched with Alec, who ate a quick meal. Harry took his meal to go. The conversation was pure agony, having to listen to Robin and her father discuss their past and how much they had in common. Their families went to the same church, their mothers were friends, their siblings were friends. It all sounded ideal.

On the drive back, Archer had decided to be quiet for a change. Maybe he was giving Zoey space to gather her thoughts. She didn't say anything for a while, simply stared out at the landscape as they passed the sea wall, the lighthouse and the piers.

It was only when she could form her thoughts in a coherent fashion that she finally spoke aloud what was in her heart:

"I really, *really* don't like her."

Archer had tried his best, but when forced to take sides, he was decidedly and firmly Team Zoey. There was no other choice. He was on her side, no matter what, in everything. It didn't make sense, but somehow it didn't have to.

When Zoey had asked him if she thought Birdy and Patchy were reasonable nicknames for "people of their age" he had to admit no, he didn't think so, either. When she said Robin was so beautiful she had to be stuck-up, he had nodded and agreed that might be true. Personally, Archer thought she'd been very nice, but she did carry herself with confidence, which he supposed could be interpreted as arrogance.

"Why did you offer her my wedding dress services?"

They were back in the boutique the next morning. Zoey was hanging up dresses according to a color scheme and he was standing guard, because there was no one else in the store.

"Aren't you trying to get the word out about your wedding dresses?"

"Yes, but these vintage designer dresses are deals I scour, and they're for women like Rachel, who couldn't otherwise afford them. I do this to honor my mother because, before she married my dad, she used to shop secondhand everything. Robin can afford a designer dress. She's a doctor, after all!" Zoey huffed.

"Well, the good news is that she's not after your father's money," Archer offered, and when Zoey scowled, he added, "I don't like her, of course. But still."

"My father still has a lot more money than she does, I'm sure." She stopped and looked up at the ceiling as if something had just occurred to her. "He *better* sign a prenup."

"I'm sure he will." Archer didn't think any good business manager would allow the marriage otherwise.

She shook a finger at him. "Don't be so sure! She's got her hooks in my father, I can tell. He's got this dreamy, 'I've lost leave of my senses' look in his eyes."

"And what does that look like?"

Zoey actually tried to show him, shimmying her shoulders, fluttering her eyelashes, making such a silly face that Archer had to laugh out loud.

"Like that!"

She turned back to her dresses.

He shook his head, chuckled and wondered if that was what he looked like every time he stole a look at Zoey. He did so often, when she was busy with a customer, swimming laps in her pool, cooking or sitting on the couch with a bowl of popcorn binging old Frasier episodes. This assignment would be over soon, any day now, and he'd have to leave her behind. He'd have to abandon the sense of home she'd created for him in the course of just over two weeks. To say he'd miss her would be an understatement.

Last night he'd spoken with Ian, who'd said he would let him know of his next assignment today. He was impressed with his handling of this one. There was a chance he could be sent to China to be part of a liaison team for the Chinese ambassador. Not a small job.

A part of Archer wanted to move on, so he wouldn't have to live in this space between desire and helplessness anymore. His inclination, when it came to Zoey, was to protect her at all costs, and that didn't only come from his job assignment. He'd probably never stop worrying or thinking about Zoey. She'd had a life-changing effect on him, because he now saw clearly how someone could need him, and he could also need them. He needed the way Zoey made him believe in that part of himself that carried and held deep emotions. He had never let himself be as vulnerable as he had been with her.

"Welcome," Archer said when a new customer came in. "Let me know if I can help you find something."

Most of the time, this was all it took. Shoppers had something specific in mind when they entered the shop and only wanted to find the right size.

"I heard you can help me," said the well-dressed elderly gentleman. "Name's Roy. Roy Finch."

He offered his hand and Archer shook it and introduced himself as Zoey's co-worker.

"Anything in particular you're looking for?"

"Something for my wife," the man said, and pulled his gray English cap lower on his head. "I always shop ahead of time."

"So, a Christmas gift?" Archer moved toward the counter with all the costume jewelry.

His eyes flashed on the necklace Zoey had held up for him when she mistook him for a customer. He'd been tongue-tied by her beauty and grace. Now he could talk to her but not much else had changed. She still took his breath away half the time.

"She has too much jewelry." Roy Finch waved a hand. "I always get her a book, which she says isn't all that romantic. This year I'm truly stumped."

Normally, Archer would try to catch Zoey's attention. But she was with another customer at the moment, holding up a sweater.

"It's finally sweater weather!" he heard her squeal.

"Um, how about a sweater?" Archer pointed in that direction, hoping he could at least get him closer to Zoey.

"My wife runs hot." He shook his head. "It never gets cold enough around here."

Archer took him through the list of items in the store: dresses, pants, shoes, skirts. No dice.

"What about that?" Roy Finch pointed.

It was the small display Zoey had of lotions and perfumes. Archer avoided this part of the store since it was far in the back and no one had asked for his help in "smelling" them yet, thank God.

"Yeah, you can't really go wrong with something that

smells good," Archer said, leading the way. "These seem to be popular."

Before long, he discovered why this corner was so popular.

Everything smelled like Zoey.

As Mr. Finch picked up the samples and smelled each one, Archer figured out which one smelled like Zoey. Before he left, he would have to buy a bottle of this for himself. If he couldn't take her with him, he'd take her scent. He read the name on the bottle: *Fleurs dorées*.

In the end, Mr. Finch decided on getting one of each and paid at the front with Zoey's help.

"Lois is going to love this!" Zoey said, packaging it all with a neat bow. "Great choice."

Mr. Finch hooked a thumb in Archer's direction. "He helped. I'm hopeless with this stuff."

Archer and Zoey exchanged a smile, but hers dropped within minutes. He turned and it didn't take long for him to find out why.

Robin had walked inside the shop.

Chapter Twenty-Six

Zoey couldn't believe her eyes. This woman wasted no time. Robin strutted her bad self right past Archer, waving to him in a quick greeting. In the process, she nearly mowed down poor Mr. Finch on his way out.

"Zoey!" Robin said, arms outstretched. "If you could fit me in, I'd appreciate it. I can come back later if this isn't a good time."

"Oh. I didn't realize you were serious."

"Of course I am! The timing is perfect, what with my being here already. We're staying a couple more nights. I'd rather give you the business instead of some random company."

She had a point. Zoey came around from behind the counter and appraised Robin's lean, statuesque form. She could have done well on the Paris runways. It occurred to Zoey that Robin knew that, and instead she'd become a doctor. Not a bad choice for a woman to make. Mami always told Zoey that women should support each other in the choices they made. Childless by choice, mother, businesswoman, homemaker, they were all valid choices.

"Let me see what I can find. You're a size ten?"

"Great guess! Or a nine on a day when I haven't stopped to eat lunch." She chuckled.

Zoey meant to go to the annex alone, to have a minute to get her thoughts and emotions in order, but Robin followed her. She seemed too happy, too joyful, and was totally oblivious to the fact that Zoey was having a hard time with this. At the very least, Robin could be a little more sensitive, considering Zoey was being tasked with finding a wedding dress for her mother's replacement.

Robin gasped when she entered the showroom. "Oh, my! This is *fantastic*."

Now the woman was laying it on a little thick. The room was a work in progress, the racks of dresses not nearly as full as she'd like them to be. The mirror and pedestal in the middle of the room were secondhand, and it showed. But, baby steps. She would get there…eventually.

Zoey focused, putting to mind all of her creativity and fashion insight. She found the vintage dress she'd envisioned on an older woman the moment she'd seen it: a sequined taupe and off-white cocktail-length gown that could be a bridal dress. In fact, it *had* been the bridal dress for the wife of a CEO, who'd worn it for her fifth marriage. Zoey had picked it up at an estate sale not long ago. She also selected a few others—all tea-length dresses—because c'mon, she couldn't see Robin in a long white gown. Zoey had an entire section of white gowns and grew concerned when she saw Robin eyeing the dresses. She couldn't be serious.

"When I saw this one, I thought this would be ideal for a sophisticated woman over fifty." Zoey turned, showing her the sequined dress which, according to the estate sale, was from the 1940s.

"It's not white," Robin said, nibbling on her lower lip.

Zoey was about to explain her thought process when Robin said, "You really *get me*."

"Do I?"

Zoey was trying to be helpful. Mostly because she couldn't stop reliving the look on her father's lovesick face and hearing Archer's voice, reminding her of her faith in love. He'd reminded her that her father deserved a chance to be happy. He did, but with the right woman, and maybe not so soon. If Robin was the right one, surely waiting a little wouldn't hurt. That way they could be sure.

"I worried you'd want something else," Zoey said, handing her the dress. "Something white."

Robin took it in her hands and lifted it up, turning it back and forth, inspecting it with a slow smile on her face.

"I'm not a first-time bride, so this is perfect. Just what I had in mind."

"I feel I should tell you first about the history of the dress," Zoey said. "I got it at the estate sale of a prominent family. She was the wife of a CEO, and it was her fifth and last marriage."

"A dress with history. I love it."

"Want to try it on?" Zoey gestured toward the changing room.

Almost giddy, Robin strolled in the room, carrying the dress. Zoey took the moment to find Archer in the store. He was holding court with a middle-aged woman Zoey had never seen before. She had no fewer than three dresses she was holding up for his approval, one after the other. Archer shook his head, shook his head again, then eventually pointed and nodded to one.

When he saw Zoey watching, he hurried over to join her. "Is everything okay?"

She nodded. "She loves the dress and is trying it on now. I don't know, maybe she'd love anything I chose just to win me over."

Archer narrowed his eyes. "She doesn't look like the kind of woman who would wear something she doesn't love."

"Maybe you're right."

Robin had an easy fashion sense about her, but today she'd come in wearing a black pantsuit. Zoey thought she looked like a politician, but hey, to each her own.

"I know I am." Archer clasped her shoulder reassuringly. "Face it, you have an eye for this."

"Okay, I guess I do." Zoey smiled and went to rejoin Robin, who'd just come out of the dressing room.

She gracefully stepped on the pedestal for a view in the mirror. The dress fit too loosely on her, especially around the hip and waist.

"We could take it in," Robin said. "I have a favorite alteration shop."

Zoey stood behind her and pulled it in at the sides, seeing that with a few minor adjustments, it could fit like a glove. The taupe and off-white complemented Robin's flawless ebony skin beautifully.

"I'll take it!" Robin said. "I could look for weeks and I wouldn't find anything more perfect than this. Sometimes you get lucky the first time."

That made Zoey think of her father and Robin, because they'd met before her parents had. Maybe if things had been different, Robin would have been Zoey's mother. The thought made her heart ache.

"My father was your first love," Zoey said.

"Yes, but we weren't so lucky," Robin said. "Sometimes you can meet someone too soon. We were very young."

Zoey guessed that was true, but she didn't like to think that timing was the only reason her mother and father wound up together. It was love, pure and simple.

"Are you sure about the dress? It's such a big decision. Maybe you should think about it, at least for a day."

Robin surprised Zoey by reaching for her hands. "Honey, when you get to be as old as I am, you recognize when you've found something precious and don't want to lose it by waiting too long."

"I would hold it aside for you. What if it's not the one? What if you change your mind?"

Zoey was referring to much more than the dress. She didn't want her father hurt in case things didn't work out between them. He'd already been through losing the love of his life, and honestly, it took him years to recover. There had been months when he wouldn't even leave the house.

"It's a dress," Robin said. "I'm looking forward to the *marriage*, and while I want to look fly on our day, I have the rest of my life to be with your father."

"It's not about the dress or the day," Mami said. "It's about the rest of your life together. And it won't always be easy, Zoey, but it will be worth it for the right man."

"What did you say?" Zoey said, shaking her head.

"I just said that it's not about the dress for me. Believe me, I'm going to make this work. I—"

"My mother used to say something similar about love," Zoey interrupted.

It put things into perspective. While she loved fashion, she'd told Zoey repeatedly that a wedding shouldn't be about the dress—that the dress was often overpriced. And for the first time Zoey wondered if she'd not meant overpriced so much as *overvalued.* She wished Mami was here now so she could ask her whether there was a better use of her time than putting designer wedding gowns into the hands of women who couldn't really afford them, discounted or not.

"Your mother was a great woman," Robin said, touching her chest. "I am barely qualified to take her place. But honestly? I think we would have been good friends if we'd ever met."

It was a gift, even if Zoey knew it wasn't true. Robin had the confidence to know that she was more than qualified to be her father's new wife. She might not look or behave like her mother, but if she were honest, Zoey thought they might have been friends, too.

When Robin insisted this dress was "the one," apparently with the same degree of certainty that her father was "the one," Zoey knew she had no choice but to ring Robin up.

"Thank you, thank you!" Robin gushed as she reached out to hug Zoey tightly to her. "I'm going to look beautiful thanks to you."

Zoey didn't exactly hug her back, but she also didn't pull away. *Progress.*

She followed her to the door and watched her stride over to her rental car nearby. It wasn't until a minute later that she noticed Archer standing right behind her. He placed his hand on her back.

"You okay?" he asked softly.

"Yes. I'm okay." Zoey turned and tried to flash him her best smile. It felt fake and forced. This still hurt. Right or wrong, it was painful to see another woman taking her mother's place. While it might be the natural order to move forward, it left a pinch in her heart that would not go away. It was a little like having the flu, this feeling of general malaise and discomfort. She would have to get used to this new reality. Given time, she hoped she would be okay with it.

"She's so different than my mother. It's interesting how one man could love two such different women."

Archer didn't say anything, just studied her with those amber eyes.

"Life goes on, right?" she said.

"It does."

Then he just took her into his arms. Those strong arms pulled her close, crushing her to his chest. Hands down, the world's best hug.

"I've got a new assignment for you," Ian said over the phone later that evening.

Time was up. After a few days off, Archer would head on to his next assignment, one he'd share with a team. He'd have to tell Zoey tonight. They'd arrested the stalker and were able to book him on several other criminal charges having nothing to do with Patch. Either way, a win-win. For everybody else, of course. Not so much for Archer.

After discussing details with Ian, he hung up and joined Zoey in the living room to binge-watch whatever show she'd chosen for them. If it was another episode of *Frasier*, he wouldn't complain once.

But he found her wrapped in a yellow blanket, reading.

She glanced up. "Hey."

"You did good today," Archer said. "I'm proud of you for the way you handled Robin. I know how hard that was for you."

"She's a nice person." Zoey lowered her eyes. "Just not my mother."

"Well, no. Your mother can never be replaced. That's how it is when you love someone."

She smiled. "It sounds like you're speaking from experience."

He realized that she'd just spoken his truth out loud. Unfortunately, he'd fallen in love with Zoey, which was crazy.

It had happened so organically and felt as easy as a warm bath. He had no business falling in love with her and even less telling her that he had. If he told her, she'd want him to stay and wouldn't understand when he couldn't. He had to make a living; he had to save money and get established in his career. Zoey deserved nothing less than a man fully in control of his own future. He wasn't there yet.

"Hey." He sat beside her on the couch. "It's time for me to go."

Her shoulders slumped. "What? Tonight?"

"Probably in the morning," Archer said. "They arrested the guy who was making the threats, and he won't be a problem anymore."

"For now," she said. "It seems my daddy always says something on TV that pisses a sports fan off."

Archer snorted. "No doubt. It's too bad people can't agree to disagree more often."

"Tell me about it." Zoey set her book aside and stuck out her lower lip. "I'm going to miss you."

"Yeah? You won't have a helper in the boutique anymore, but you'll do fine without me, just like you did before."

"I'll find out how much foot traffic dies down once you're gone." She crossed her arms.

"Not much, I bet."

"Maybe I could have a cardboard cutout made out of you and put it by the front door. No matter how hard you tried, you still always looked like you were standing guard."

He cocked his head. "Sorry. That was my real job."

Zoey scooted closer. "Yet you got pretty good at giving fashion advice to both men and women."

"Difficult to believe." He lowered his head, biting back a smile.

"Do you know that so many men came in purposely asking for white button-down shirts like yours?"

He suspected as much, since they'd asked him where he bought his shirts. Unfortunately, not at Zoey's boutique, so he pretended not to know. He didn't want people shopping anywhere else but at Zoey's. Then he'd noticed that Zoey had started stocking shirts that looked an awful lot like his.

"Did you start selling white button-downs because of me?" he asked.

She grinned. "I'm ordering more because I don't think the need will die with you."

He rather liked the sound of that: Zoey remembering him, even in some small way, after he was gone. She'd think of him every time she sold a white button-down. People didn't die when they were always in your thoughts; not that he was dying, but he may as well be for all intents and purposes. He'd be out of sight, out of mind. Gone from her life. And Zoey wouldn't be alone for long.

With those words, she lowered her head to his chest and they just stayed there for a long time.

At least he had a chance to say goodbye.

Chapter Twenty-Seven

The first morning Archer was officially free from his duties as Zoey's bodyguard, he went out for coffee while she swam laps. He didn't even bother to set the house alarm when he left. *Living dangerously.*

Archer stood in line at The Green Bean and caught sight of Alec, one of Patch's bodyguards, standing in line.

"Hey," Alec said. "Heard you're between jobs now."

"Yeah, I'm going to check in with my agency. I believe I'm headed to Asia next."

"Whoa! You still travel a lot, do you?"

"Zoey was actually only my second assignment."

"Seriously? You look like you were born to do this work."

He shrugged. "She made it easy."

"Zoey doesn't make anything easy." Alec coughed. "That girl has a mind of her own. And if you tell Patch I said that, I'll deny it."

Archer chuckled. "When I went to work for Ian, I'd just recovered from an accident in the Middle East. I'm basically trying to get my bearings being a civilian again."

"You were over there training their troops?"

"One of the last to leave." Archer nodded, leaving out the part where he'd left his foot behind.

"Let me share something with you. If you ever get tired of traveling and want to settle down and get married or something, people like Patch always need bodyguards. Anyone in the public eye, basically. Athletes, musicians, reality TV stars, any kind of celebrity. It's good, steady work, and the travel is minimal. You wind up getting close to your assignments. I'm sure I'll be invited to Zoey's wedding one day. It's like you become part of the family. A great place to be." The barista passed Alec his coffee and he took a sip.

"It's probably good for me to gain more experience first. Maybe someday that will be a good fit for me," Archer said. "Good to know."

"Keep in touch." With that, Alec slipped Archer his business card and left.

A short while later, Archer let himself back into Zoey's house, carrying her beloved pumpkin spice latte and his own plain coffee.

She rushed out of her bedroom, having changed into jeans and a shirt.

"You're *here*." She looked surprised, her eyes wide.

"You didn't think I would leave without officially saying goodbye." Triumphantly, he plunked both cups down on the kitchen counter. "Pumpkin spice latte, and I asked for the extra pump. Remembered this time."

"You're leaving just when I've got you trained," Zoey said.

Archer snorted. "You have me *trained*?"

"You're the perfect man and now you're leaving me."

"I wish I didn't have to go, but you don't need me anymore."

"Says who?"

Zoey moved closer to him, and he smelled the enticing

scent of her lotion or shampoo or whatever she used from the products she carried at the store. Like flowers and vanilla and sugar.

"The agency. You know the drill."

"I know you don't work for me anymore." She stopped two steps in front of him, and now the flowery scent enveloped him. "Which means, you know, being with me doesn't mean you're violating an oath or crossing a line."

He knew exactly what she meant and where this seemed to be headed, yet he found himself stammering, "W-what do you mean?"

"You can kiss me as many times as you want. You can do a lot *more* than kiss me." Then she reached for him, taking a fistful of his shirt and pulling him the rest of the way to her.

He kissed her then, not expecting this, not prepared for any of it. But he would fall into this place with her, which felt natural and easy. She wasn't wrong; no ethics prevented them from finally following through on this attraction that had been brewing between them for weeks.

"Zoey," he said, cupping her beautiful face in his hands. "Are you sure?"

"One hundred percent," she said with a smile, and took his hand, pulling him toward her bedroom. "Let me show you how much."

"But I can't promise you anything. I can't start a relationship. My next job is going to take me to Asia soon, and I've no idea how long I'll be gone."

"Well, as long as 'soon' doesn't mean 'right now,' we have time."

He eagerly followed her into her bedroom, a place he'd never seen before except from the outside patio area. Double French doors led to her backyard garden, and they were closed now, the blinds drawn.

Archer reached for Zoey, pulled her close, kissing her deeply until they both broke apart for air. He'd never touched softer skin, never felt that he would jump out of his own. All worries of intimacy were gone.

"This is going to be good," she said. Then she pulled off her top and revealed a plunging red satin bra. He nearly swallowed his tongue.

"Oh, you have no idea."

Hours later, Zoey lay wrapped in Archer's strong arms. Being with him was better than she could have ever imagined. While they could be together now, it also meant he would be taking a job sending him far away for God knew how long. Just her luck to find the perfect man for her and have to watch him leave. Love just wasn't in the cards for her.

"Zoey." Behind her, Archer pulled her closer to him and whispered into her neck. "I have an idea."

"You're *not* going to Asia?" She shut her eyes. "That's a great idea. Stupendous."

Make a wish, Zoey. Close your eyes and make a wish.

Not just on birthdays, but anytime Zoey wanted something, her mother had encouraged her to make a wish. But her mami's magical thinking wouldn't work here. This was Adulting 101. Real life. Messy and raw and imperfect. You didn't always get what you wanted because you wished for it. Zoey first learned magical thinking didn't work when Mami's doctors had told them that no further treatment would extend her life.

"I have a few days off before I have to go to Asia," Archer said.

She turned in his arms. "You do?"

"My boss seems to think since I never had a day off on this assignment, I should take a few days for myself. Tie up any loose ends at home since I might be gone for months."

Oh my God. Months?

He was going to meet some beautiful woman over there, get married and bring her home with him. Zoey would be heartbroken, but there would be nothing she could do if he fell in love. She would have to encourage and support it, or be called a hypocrite.

"Am I a loose end?" She winked, trying to make light of this.

"You're not. But I'd like to spend more time with you, you know, and…do some more of this." He rolled on top of her, keeping his weight off, kissing her shoulder.

"Yes, I accept," she said, biting her lower lip. "Let's do this every day and night until you have to go. I want you to remember me and remember me *well*."

"There's absolutely no chance I'm ever going to forget anything about you."

Then he kissed her again, trailing sweet and hot kisses down her neck, her shoulders, her breasts. He worshipped her body and she worshipped his, and it was hours before they thought about anything else.

"I'll be back for dinner," Archer said at the door.

It was difficult to leave, Zoey clinging to him in her silky bathrobe when he knew she wasn't wearing anything else under there. He wished he didn't believe in a damn thing called *ethics*—they could have been doing this all along.

"We only have a few days, so I don't want to waste any time," she said. "I'll close the shop early."

"What are you going to tell them about me?" He'd been in every day, never getting a day off unless she did.

"I'm going to tell them that we had a huge fight, a disagreement over the window display, and I fired you!" She said all this speaking into his neck.

"Okay, sure. Whatever works." With great reluctance, he pulled himself away, because if he didn't, they were going to wind up in bed again.

After one last kiss, he headed out the door and climbed into his sedan. He drove the thirty minutes to his condo in Houston, arriving to find only a few pieces of random advertising scattered outside his door. His mail had been redirected to a post office box.

Archer closed the door and surveyed his apartment with more of a critical eye after having stayed at Zoey's. Hers was a home; his was a station, an in-between place. Half of his stuff was still in boxes, except for the TV and cooking essentials. Packing would be easy. He'd learned to travel light over the years.

It was time to check in with the folks and let them know he'd be gone again, this time farther away and for much longer.

His father picked up in his usual way, now that he had decided to pay for caller ID. *"Bon Giorno, mio."*

"Hey, Pops. How are you?"

"It is my knee this time. The doctor says he has to replace. Is the job over? *Tu Madre* wants to know if you're coming home for Christmas."

Damn. It hadn't occurred to him that he'd likely be in Asia at Christmastime. His parents were going to have a fit.

"I don't know yet," Archer said. "I'm going to Asia now. A diplomat there needs a team of agents. It's a good opportunity and I was given the job."

He never told his parents about the way he'd screwed

up his first assignment. Pride kept him from doing so, but even more than that, he never wanted his folks to worry.

His father groaned. "And I will be the one to have to tell your *madre*."

"I'll tell her," Archer said, not looking forward to it.

He kept thinking about Zoey and how much she would love to have another Christmas with her mother. Archer was going to squander yet another Christmas away from his family for the sake of a job.

His father sighed deeply. "Well, at least you are not in a war zone."

It reminded him of when his father had said, "At least you did not lose your entire leg." Always the optimist, his dad. When he had a headache, he'd say, "At least I don't have a brain tumor." If he got the flu, he'd say, "at least I don't have cancer." Archer figured he'd inherited his father's sense of what counted as doom and what didn't. And whenever you had a breath left in your body, no matter how bad things were, there was hope.

"Right," Archer said. "Look on the bright side."

"How is the foot?"

"Much better. I'm getting used to it. Believe it or not, it's starting to feel like a part of me."

Joey had helped. He'd reminded Archer of how blessed they both were to have the technology available to them. They could both live full lives.

This morning, he'd forgotten he was missing his foot. Amazingly, the lack of his foot did not at all affect his ability to have sex with a beautiful woman. Turned out, he didn't need the foot for that extracurricular activity, and was doing just fine without it. Zoey had been great and accepting of it all, never making a big deal out of it. To think he worried she'd feel sorry for him. Like him, she hadn't missed his foot. She'd been far more concerned about another part of his anatomy.

"Anyway, Pops, I should go. I have to start packing up the apartment. I may as well give up my lease."

"Before you go, here is your mother."

Seconds away from a clean getaway!

"Hey, Mama."

"There is a job here you could do. There are a lot of them. I looked, I asked."

"Here we go again."

"Do not say no until you hear! There is a Christmas tree farm looking for workers."

A Christmas tree farm? Archer sighed. He didn't even own a single flannel shirt.

"Ma, I really like my job."

"But it sound dangerous!"

"It's not."

He talked with his mother for a few minutes and assured her he'd get home to his small town in Connecticut soon, then hung up before she could bring up the subject of Asia. He didn't want to argue with his folks, but this was his life, and he had to live it on his own terms. There was no way he could go home after the adrenaline-fueled life he'd led and be a tree farmer.

Archer took off his prosthesis, hopped in the shower, changed into jeans and a T-shirt, and went through his paperwork to find his lease agreement and the contact information. Before he could dial his landlord, the doorbell rang.

Strange, he never had company.

Maybe the landlord was here, which would make this a whole lot easier.

To his surprise, when he opened the door, Patch Lambert was standing there.

Chapter Twenty-Eight

Zoey had been humming Ed Sheeran love songs all morning. Last night with Archer had been incredible. He was tender, passionate, kissing her and taking her to bed like she was a precious piece of china he couldn't drop. She'd never connected with someone like this, not just physically but a heart connection.

She had a little spring in her step when she opened the door to Glamtique. Pumpkin spice latte in hand, she flipped her sign from Closed to Open and went to work. She had a big day planned. Ophelia would get a new outfit: a bright orange-and-yellow plaid skirt with brown tights and kickass boots. It would scream "Autumn" in the best way. She had brought silk faux leaves with her to scatter on the floor of the window box and near the apple barrel. A tiny detail, but one that mattered. She'd fill some orders that had come in online and unbox items she'd received from an estate sale. By then it would be time to go home.

After, she'd stop by the market and get the ingredients to fix Archer a five-star meal. This time, she was stepping away from the pumpkin-infused theme, because she had the distinct impression it wasn't Archer's favorite. And face it, you could only put pumpkin in so much. It felt like time to pull back a little.

He would arrive around seven, and they were going to have a late dinner and then…whatever materialized. *Five days!* She and Archer had five days together before he had to leave for Asia. They would make use of every spare minute they could be together. If it wasn't her busiest season, Zoey would close the shop, but that would be bananas. She didn't want love to make her irresponsible.

Good thing she was open, too, because Valerie Kinsella came in just before closing time, dragging her two children with her. The little girl was in a stroller, but her two-year-old son, Wade, toddled beside her, holding her hand. He was the image of his father and had that same wicked smile and glint in his eyes that spelled trouble.

"Help," Valerie said. "We have a Halloween party to go to, and I can't find a black dress to save my life. I'm going as a witch. Keeping it simple."

Zoey smothered a laugh. Valerie was the furthest thing from a witch Zoey could imagine. She was a third-grade teacher, and all-around saint in general. But she did appear flustered now, her hair wild and unruly, probably due to the wind that had kicked up outside. Yep, on top of everything else going right in Zoey's life, the weatherman had predicted rain. Tonight, she and Archer would have a fire.

"Mama, me want candy!" Wade wailed, but when he noticed Zoey looking at him, he quieted, bashfully smiled and lowered his head.

"If you're good, we'll stop by the boardwalk after," Valerie said. "Daddy will meet us after he gets off work."

"Daddy!" Wade jumped up and down.

Zoey bent down to tweak Wade's little nose. "Hello, cutie."

"Hewo," he said, then turned and buried his face in his mother's skirt.

"You're in luck," Zoey said. "I believe I have *just* the right dress for you."

"If you do, that makes you a lifesaver. I can't buy anything online anymore because my size is different. I don't even know my size anymore!"

"Say no more." Zoey led her to the dress she had in mind, and she held it up to Valerie.

"Something with a longer hem?" Valerie asked hopefully.

"Let me see." Zoey searched through dresses.

After her third try, she found one that met with Valerie's approval. Just then, a loud crack of thunder sounded, and rain started to fall as if someone had just emptied an Olympic-sized pool on the roof. The water came down in sheets, making it difficult to see outside the clear glass windows.

"Uh-oh. I don't think God likes this dress," Zoey joked, since the timing was nearly perfect.

"That rain wasn't supposed to come until tonight!" Valerie said.

The sudden downpour had folks scurrying into her store, seeking shelter. South Texans weren't always prepared for the rain since it came so infrequently. Zoey would bet no one had an umbrella, except possibly in their car.

"I shouldn't have come today but I was worried you'd run out of inventory. Everyone keeps talking about your new assistant and how he gives the best fashion advice." Valerie's head swiveled around. "Is he here?"

"No, I'm sorry. He actually…um, he quit." She couldn't bring herself to say she'd fired him.

"Oh, that's too bad. I never got a chance to meet him!" Valerie shushed her baby, who'd started to fuss.

"Yeah, it is too bad. He was a great help around here."

"Mama, I wanna go spawsh puddles!" Wade began to jump up and down and tug on Valerie's skirt.

"No, sweetie, it's too wet out there to *find* a puddle," Valerie said. "We need to stay in here until it stops raining buckets. Then we'll scoot on out of here and go get that candy."

Customers, not having anything better to do, wandered around the store, reverse window-shopping. Zoey greeted everyone she knew by name, but she also saw a few new faces.

"Is Archer here?" asked a young woman. "I'd love his advice on a pair of shoes."

"Which ones?" Zoey didn't carry many, so the girl's request had her a little befuddled.

She held up a pair of adorable blue-and-white ankle boots with cutouts. "These. I got them online. I just brought them in so I could get his opinion."

"They're super cute, but I'm sorry, Archer doesn't work here anymore."

"What? Are you kidding me?" She jutted her lip.

"Yeah, I'm sorry. What kind of fashion advice did he usually give you? Maybe I can help?" Now Zoey was truly curious, because she'd never asked.

"Oh, he was just the best. What I liked most was his honesty. I could always tell when he didn't want to hurt my feelings but wasn't going to lie to me, either. Every time I ask my boyfriend for advice, he lies like a rug because he thinks I'll get mad if he tells me the truth. Archer didn't have that problem."

"Mmm," Zoey said, nodding her head. "You know he didn't really have a background in fashion."

The girl laughed. "Yeah, I could tell. But no matter what he said, I felt good about myself after talking to him."

For a moment, Zoey didn't know what to say.

"Well, let me know if I can help you with anything," she finally said. "I think the boots are really cute, by the way."

Before long, word got around the store that Archer no longer worked there. Everyone wanted to know where he'd gone, would he possibly be available to FaceTime with them, and could Zoey give them his number. She said no, obviously. She'd known Archer was a hit with her customers, but she had no idea just how much everyone liked him.

When it continued to rain, and little Wade became more and more agitated, Zoey led Valerie to the bridal annex, where she could sit for a while and nurse her baby. To occupy Wade, she found a large box she hadn't yet broken up. Turning it on its side, she presented it to him as his new fort. He squealed with delight and climbed in.

"Oh, my God, thank you," Valerie said, leaning her head back against the wall. "I need to call Cole. He'll be worried."

Zoey heard Valerie on the phone explaining to Cole that they were hunkering down at Glamtique, and not to worry. Cole told her to stay at the boutique and he'd come and get them.

Even as her shop took on the distinct aroma of damp clothes and wet hair, Zoey couldn't complain because she sold an item every few minutes. When people were bored, they shopped. Her entire stock of scents and lotions sold out, and as luck would have it, so did all the new sweaters and the few windbreakers she had in the store.

"Your shop has the best fall vibes," one of her regulars said to her. "It always feels to me like we go straight from summer into winter."

"Fall is 100 percent my favorite season."

That statement drew assents from a few of the customers, who started mentioning everything they loved about autumn.

"Piles of leaves that my dog loves to jump in."

"Cozy fires and roasted marshmallows."

"Turkey and pumpkin pie!"

"Mashed potatoes."

"Boots and sweater weather."

Zoey glanced around the shop with pride. Sometimes she told herself that her mother wasn't really here—that it was a nice thought, and nothing more. But she'd never felt her presence more than today. Zoey had created something special here, an extended family of sorts.

And while she loved the fashion, decorating the shop and scouring the internet for vintage finds to sell in her store, the people inside were the best part.

"I'm sorry. I'd offer you something to drink but I don't have much," Archer said once he'd invited Patch inside.

Patch held up a palm. "That's okay, I won't be long."

Archer stuck his hands in his pants pockets. "How can I help you?"

"You can't. I'm just here to thank you for everything you've done."

"Ah, well, sir, I was simply doing my job. Zoey is a nice girl and easy to be with."

Patch snorted. "My daughter is a lot of things, but *easy* is not one of them. She's special and beautiful and unique. But…*not* easy. Anyway, I wanted to thank you for last night. I had not realized that you and my daughter became such good friends."

Archer didn't think it his place to tell Mr. Lambert they were far more than friends now. He didn't think any father would want to hear that, so he went with the safe and plausible. It was also true, which helped.

"She mentioned that in her previous experience with bodyguards, they became like part of the family."

"That's true." Patch walked to the window and looked outside. "But you have influence with her, and I have a feeling it had a lot to do with the way she's accepted Robin. At our dinner, you might have noticed things weren't going well."

"Yes." Archer cleared his throat. "I noticed."

"But when Robin went to get her dress the next day, everything had changed. We both expected to get some pushback—it wouldn't have been out of character for Zoey. I think you might have had something to do with how quickly she came around."

"Zoey wants everyone to be happy and find love, and she wants that for you, too. It just happened sooner than she'd expected. Robin took her by surprise."

"She took me by surprise! Happened sooner than I expected!" Patch laughed. "Son, do you know what it's like to lay eyes on a woman and not be able to *speak* for several seconds?"

Archer almost lied and said no, he didn't have any idea, but Patch kept talking.

"That *never* happens to me. Being a football player, naturally I was used to the attention from the ladies. They came after me hard when my wife died, but I had Zoey there, intervening, knowing I wasn't ready. We spent a lot of time together, the two of us, grieving. And after she left, well…" He tugged on his shirt collar. "Let's just say I had some fun for a while. There was no point in getting married again. I'm pushing sixty and not having any more kids. It seemed like all the women after me were too young, anyway. I don't fool myself—I know they're after a lifestyle I can provide. But Robin…she *knows* me, she doesn't need my money, and damn, she's still so beautiful."

"You don't owe anyone an explanation."

"That might be true, but I felt guilty. Like I'm almost too lucky. Twice in a lifetime, when some people don't even get this once."

Again, Archer could understand the feeling. There was something rare about feeling this way. When he and Zoey were together, he felt like they were the only two people in the world. He'd never felt that way before.

"Anyway, I'm not just here to thank you. You were doing your job and doing it well. I have an offer for you."

"Sir?" Archer cocked his head.

"As it turns out, Alec is retiring early. He really likes you. What would you think about coming to work for me and taking old Alec's place?" He turned to Archer. "I will pay you twice what the agency is and you can stay in Texas. I think my daughter might appreciate that."

It was the last thing Archer had ever expected to hear, and it was punctuated by the sound of thunder crackling.

The rain began to fall in sheets, and all Archer could think of was how happy this would make Zoey.

Chapter Twenty-Nine

The storm gradually let up. Cole picked up his little family and one by one, her shop emptied. Did Zoey have an umbrella with her when she closed up shop? Why, yes, she did, because hope sprang eternal. Hers was a yellow, orange and white-striped parasol printed with little smiling pumpkins. She had the matching galoshes, but those were at home.

Despite the rain, she navigated to the grocery store fine and got home in time to start dinner. Although she was by no means a great cook, she found herself wanting to get better. Because good food brought joy, and she wanted to bring joy to those she loved. And yes, she was talking about Archer.

She loved him.

He was strong and kind and, most of all, loyal to her. She could see the loyalty shining through in everything he did and said. His first loyalty had been to her, even when he had obviously liked Robin from the get-go. Point being, he didn't like her on principle, because Zoey didn't like her. She came first with him. It was all she'd ever wanted. A man who would put her first.

The problem was that he would leave soon, and telling him she loved him wouldn't be fair. She'd simply have to accept that he had to go for a while, and he'd be back. It would be similar to the times her daddy would leave for extended periods. Occasionally, he'd be gone for months. Only now they had FaceTime and Zoom and so many ways to stay connected. No, it wouldn't be the same, but they'd get through it. He'd be back in Texas and they'd have a beautiful reunion.

She could almost see it now, through her tears, as she gently added saffron to the rice for flavor. Five days wasn't going to be enough time.

Archer arrived promptly at seven and actually rang the doorbell. Zoey wiped her hands on her apron, untied it and went to greet him.

"Oh, hello! Have we met?" she joked.

He was clutching a bouquet of flowers, and God bless him, they were yellow and orange. It was almost as if he'd been listening all along.

"For you."

"Thank you," Zoey said, then pulled him inside to kiss him thoroughly.

She'd never get over the feel of his lips against hers, his beard stubble rubbing against her cheek, his firm arms tight around her.

"I want you to know," she said, holding his hand and leading him to the kitchen, "everyone asked about you today. A young girl with a streak of pink in her hair wanted you to approve of her shoes—shoes that she bought *online*. They weren't even from the store!"

"Ah, that must have been Alice." He nodded, chuckling. "She needs affirmation for everything."

"She did say something about that."

"She's a good kid."

As Zoey busied herself at the stove, Archer came around

behind her and began kissing her neck while she stirred the rice and chicken.

"Hmm, you smell like tomato sauce."

"Really? I hope you like tomato sauce."

"Are you kidding? I'm Italian. I love tomato sauce."

"We'll eat in a few minutes."

Archer sat on a stool in the same place where he'd watched her so many times before. Always asking if he could help, always getting told "no thank you."

"Where were you when it started pouring?" Archer said, taking an apple and biting into it.

Zoey placed her hand on her chest, reminded of how happy she had felt that afternoon.

"I was showing Valerie Kinsella a black dress."

She then told him about how lovely it had been when the locals poured into her shop to take shelter from the rain. The cozy feel of everyone being together, safe and warm under her roof.

"Even without a fire, huh? Will wonders never cease?"

"I had such a wonderful feeling come over me, just knowing these were my people. That anyone who comes into my store feels like family. What I've created is amazing to me. I never expected this to feel like a second family." She pointed to him. "And you helped with that."

Archer shook his head. "That's all you. The window decorations, Ophelia, the wedding dresses, all the care and effort you take to make people feel like they belong."

"I'm thinking that this is my legacy. This is what I've been trying to find. Not just the clothes or the wedding dresses, I mean, but the shop itself, and the way it connects us all to each other. My mother would have loved this for me."

"I think you're right."

Archer made a fire again, and they ate in front of it, sitting on pillows. After they finished eating, Zoey grabbed a blanket and threw it over both of them. She straddled Archer, wrapping her legs around him. He held her there for several minutes, in the quiet, with the only sound being the crackling fire. If *cozy* had a smell, it would be the scent of burning wood.

"Zoey, there's something I need to tell you."

"Is it serious?" To lighten the mood, she stuck out her tongue and made a goofy face.

Archer laughed. "It could be."

"Don't keep me in suspense." She grabbed him by the shoulders.

"I was offered a job that would keep me in Texas."

She stared at him. "You wouldn't go to Asia at all?"

She couldn't have hoped for such good news. This was the luck that the rain had brought. These were the kinds of blessings that arrived when you had faith in love, took your time and never gave up hope.

"I got an offer today and told him I'd think about it."

"Think about it? What's there to think about? You've got to do it, Archer!"

When the words came flying out, she feared immediately they sounded too presumptuous. Maybe he didn't want to give up Asia for her.

"First, as you know, Texas is a big state. I'd still be far from Charming, all the way up in the Panhandle."

The Panhandle was far, but she could handle it. And her father lived there, too, so she could see him more often.

"It would still be a hell of a lot closer than Asia."

"Yeah, but while Asia would be temporary, this job in Texas would be permanent. I'd have to move everything and make it my home. Houston would no longer be my base. I wouldn't be doing much traveling."

"So what are you going to do?"

"I don't know, baby." Archer took her hand and kissed the inside of her palm. "There's so much to consider."

"Well, who's the client? Are they going to pay you well?"

"Extremely well," Archer said and met her eyes. "And that's the other thing I have to tell you. The client is your father."

At first Zoey thought she'd heard wrong.

"My daddy? Why would he offer you a job?" She froze for a moment. "It isn't to be *Robin's* bodyguard, is it?"

"Not directly, no," Archer said. "It's a family job. He said Alec is retiring and recommended me to take his place."

"So, you'd be working for my father? At his ranch outside Amarillo?"

"And going with him on whatever trips he takes."

Her mind immediately went to all the times she thought a man was actually interested in her but really wanted to get close to her father. And, of course, Peter, who Daddy would have loved for her to marry. Her father didn't see her with Archer, obviously, or he wouldn't be taking him so far away. Or, was he still trying to control her? Trying to get her to move closer to him, where he would always know every move she made.

She'd almost forgotten that the first reason Archer came here was because her father had indirectly hired him.

"He doesn't realize how close we've become," Zoey said. "Or, maybe he does."

"I got the feeling he realizes we're friends, but that's it."

"He's trying to entice me to come home to Amarillo, and this time you're the carrot stick."

She'd worked so hard to find her own way here in

Charming. To create something she could believe in and pass on. She loved her father, but especially with his upcoming marriage to Robin, it was important to establish boundaries.

"I can't deny I was tempted, but I've decided I'm not going to take the job," Archer said, tucking her close. "I need to be clear which Lambert comes first with me. Working for your dad would come with its perks, but I've always made my own way. No shortcuts for me."

It was amazing to hear those words, even if they were not giving her what she wanted. For once, someone was truly choosing her.

"Are you sure?" Zoey framed his face. "Because it would keep you in Texas. I may not like you working for my father, but I like the staying in Texas part."

"I'd much rather have my home base be Houston. That's home. But Zoey, the truth is, right now *you're* home to me. Wherever you are, that's exactly where I want to be."

He couldn't have chosen sweeter words to say to her.

"I love hearing that," Zoey said, and then she kissed him and took him to bed to show him how much.

Chapter Thirty

There was no other way around this. Zoey would have to confront her father. She'd have a long talk with him about boundaries, always a difficult subject for him. The more she considered it, the more she realized that her father had always wanted her to come home. He'd dropped hints over the years, some bigger than others, and anytime he heard of a shop for sale in the small town closest to his ranch, he told her about it. As many times as she told him that she wouldn't love being so far away from everything out in the country, he didn't understand. All he required to be happy was a home with all the amenities and a golf course nearby.

There hadn't been one at the time he'd moved, so he and a few partners had gone in and created one. He'd had his fill of parties and people and relished the quiet comforts of home. So did she, but her home was now in Charming. She loved being near the bay, the gentle Gulf Coast breezes and the people. After a brief, initial adjustment period when she did miss home, Zoey had never wanted to leave again.

Now, with Archer as his bait, Patch thought he could get her to move nearby so he could then try and recreate the life he'd lost—a life with his new wife and his daughter by his side. Not going to happen. It was time to grow up, time to move on, time to accept the new reality. She'd had to, and so would he. He was trying; she'd give him that.

Tonight, after work, she had plans to see Archer, but first a trip to the hotel to see her father before he went back to Amarillo. She worried that Robin would be there and make it difficult for them to have a private conversation, but she had to try. Naturally, he was staying in the penthouse suite, and Zoey took the elevator to the top, knocking once on the double mahogany doors. Harry opened the door.

"Hey, Zoey. How are you, sweetheart?" He waved her inside. "Your father's working out in the gym."

Harry directed her to a room in the back, which was a dedicated weight room. Ever the athlete, it did not surprise her to find her father lifting, Alec spotting him. He waved a greeting.

Daddy groaned and set the barbell down. "Zoey! Didn't expect you. You just missed Robin. She's gone back home a bit early since she got her dress. Her patients needed her."

Zoey was relieved that Robin wouldn't be here to witness this. "I'm glad I had something she liked."

"Liked?" Her father got up, grabbed a towel and wiped his neck. "She *loved* it."

"Obviously, Daddy, I'm not here to talk about the dress." She crossed her arms.

"Let me guess. Archer told you about my offer."

"Yes, he did. What were you thinking?"

"Hey, Alec is retiring, and he likes Archer." He hooked a thumb toward Alec.

Alec put up his hands. "Don't bring me into this. I just suggested it. You're the one who ran with it."

Daddy threw his towel at Alec, and he caught it with a laugh. "You're no help."

"Were you trying to get me to move back to the area?" Zoey said.

"Aha!" Daddy pointed at her. "I *knew* something was going on between you two. Did I call it, Alec? Did I?"

Alec lowered his head, sighed and removed his wallet. He handed a bill to her father. "You win, Patch."

"Oh, my God, y'all are still betting on stuff like this?" She pointed between them. "This is my business. My personal life."

"Sorry, baby girl," her father said. "You're so easy. It's written all over your face when you dig a man."

"You're the one who sent him to me!"

"He was your bodyguard, not someone to date!"

"Okay, okay," Alec said, walking out of the room. "I'm outta here."

Zoey caught her breath, taking a long, deep one to calm herself. "I want you to know, he was always a complete professional. He's got incredibly high ethics and wouldn't violate them. It's the kind of man he is."

"Why do you think I'd like him working for me? I sensed it, too."

"I hope that's the reason and not that you'd like me to find more reasons to visit you or even move back."

"Of course I'd like that. I'm a father. You never visit anymore."

"I was just there in February."

"And it's now *September*."

"Well, I'm sorry. I didn't know how much it meant to you for me to visit." She took a breath. "Honestly? I don't like running into Peter. And it feels like he's always dropping by the house unannounced."

"Is that it? Just say the word and I'll get rid of Peter. I'll fire him. Whatever it takes." He made a slash through the air with his arm.

Zoey was appalled to have that much control over someone's livelihood.

"Don't *fire* him!" She groaned in frustration. "He does a good job for you. Did you ever stop to think that for once in my life I want a man who doesn't work for my father, or who doesn't put my father first?"

"What are you talking about? The only person on my staff who you've dated is Peter."

"You don't understand. It's one thing for someone I date to respect my father, it's quite another for him to idolize him. Do you even realize that over half the men I've ever dated simply wanted to get close to *you*? No sooner did they realize that, yeah, I'm part of 'that' Lambert family, they start in on wanting an introduction to you. You're the star, you've always been the star. Mami and me were simply in your orbit. Oh, we didn't mind. We liked being in the background, supporting you. But everyone deserves that kind of adoration from *one* person in their life. You've got millions. All I need is one."

"I'm so sorry, baby girl. I had no idea you were dealing with this."

"No, you wouldn't. I never told you. It's too embarrassing to think that for some people, I'm not enough. You and Mami always raised me to believe in myself, and I always did. It was tough to realize that my own father was stealing my limelight. Worse, I hate myself for feeling this way. You matter. Your accomplishments and charities matter. I just want to be seen for my own."

"You have every right to be appreciated for what you've done. Don't you know I realize you could be living with me, high on the hog, taking expensive vacations and sitting around the house simply enjoying life? Not contributing to society? I'm very proud of what you've done. You have drive and ambition. That's the one part of you that's most like your old man. The truth is, I relied too much on your mother to be the bridge between us. You were a girlie girl, and I didn't really totally understand you. Your mother was like our translator. And then we lost her, and I honestly felt like I'd lost both of you. I didn't know how to reach you without her, so I just tried to keep you close."

Zoey's heart ached to see her father, such a large man, reduced to such loneliness. With all his adulation, he'd missed the one thing he could never replace: his intact family. It wasn't just her mother, but the picture all *three* of them made together. He'd missed out on so much of it, but he couldn't get it back now.

"Daddy, I'm so sorry." Zoey reached for her father, standing on tiptoes to hold on to his shoulders. "I know you want to recreate the family you once had, but you're going to have to start over with Robin. It's your second chance at love, I'm not going to be a part of that, and neither will Mami. You need to accept that it's just you and Robin going forward."

"God help me, I don't know if I can do it. I made so many mistakes the first time, and your mother forgave every single one. There's no one like her and never will be again. How can Robin compete with that? She's going to leave me, isn't she?"

It had never occurred to Zoey that her strong, famous athlete father worried he might lose someone. But then again, he already had, even if it hadn't been her choice.

"No, I would bet that she's never leaving you."

"Because of the money."

"No, because she *adores* you. She missed having the

first part of her life with you, and now she gets a chance to love you until the day you die. And while I don't have a direct line to her, I'm pretty sure Mami would approve."

"That really means the world to me."

"I'm sorry I gave you a tough time about Robin. Archer made me realize she's a good woman, and that's all that matters. It's your choice, not mine, but if I had to choose someone for you, I think it would be someone exactly like her."

"Thank you. And you'll be glad to know Archer turned me down on the job offer. Oh, he was nice about it. I offered him twice what he currently gets paid. That was the moment he won my respect. He wants to make his own way. That's the kind of man I've always wanted for you."

"Me, too."

Maybe Zoey no longer wanted exactly what her parents had after all. It had looked picture-perfect from the outside, but now with the benefit of her grown-up glasses and a realistic view of the world, she saw how much her mother gave up, being with her father. It had been noble and loving of her, even if a bit old-fashioned. But that was her mother, who'd grown up in an economically disadvantaged family. She'd accepted her role as a tradwife who kept the home fires burning while her superstar husband was away—and she seemed to enjoy it. She and her mami had spent many wonderful years together, with much of that time being just the two of them.

And she was grateful for every minute she had gotten to spend with her mother.

When Zoey reached her car, she saw that she had a message on her phone. It was from Archer, telling her to meet him and giving her an address. She texted him back.

Where are you?

It's a surprise, he replied. I think you'll like it.

A surprise! The idea of being out with him in public appealed to her. It was one thing they hadn't done much of, except within the confines of the shop. They'd certainly been on public display there, trying to hide the connection they had. But she no longer had to be worried about people thinking she had a bodyguard. Now she had a real boyfriend, and she didn't care who knew it.

Zoey plugged the address into her sedan's GPS system and followed the directions, winding up driving to the outskirts of Charming. It was an area she wasn't very familiar with. There were undeveloped plots of land around here, formerly fields of cotton, long gone now. The odd barn dotted the landscape. She pulled up to the address and nearly burst out laughing.

Old-fashioned hayrides! Haunted house! Maze! Corn on the Cob!

Archer stood by his car, one hip leaning against it, a big smile on his face. She walked up to him, smiling.

"How long has this been here, and why didn't I know about it?"

"They just opened this year. I heard about it from Max. You didn't know about this place because you've single-handedly tried to bring fall to Charming, but there are others out here doing the same thing." He held out his hand and she took it.

"I've simply tried to do my part with the shop."

"Well, this is here, and we're going to enjoy it."

"Now that I'm no longer in any danger," Zoey said, "I feel kind of like a bird that's been released from its cage."

"I know you felt trapped," Archer said sadly, pulling her closer as they walked side by side.

"Not so much because of you. I love being stuck with you."

Hand in hand, they walked under an archway marking the entrance. On one side were vendors selling everything from corn to hot dogs to waffle fries. Interestingly, there were no pumpkin spice lattes in sight. Archer stood in line to get tickets for the various activities, and they decided to try all of them. While waiting in line, Zoey took advantage of the opportunity to full-on kiss Archer. She held on to his tie (yes, he was still wearing one) and kissed the stuffing out of him.

Someone behind them nudged them both and Zoey laughed. "Um, guess it's our turn."

"Yeah," Archer said, and reached for his wallet.

While he paid, Zoey turned and caught the eye of someone she hadn't see in a while.

Scott.

Chapter Thirty-One

Scott stood alone in a lineup for food, looking at Zoey as if she'd just slapped him. The idea that she was responsible for causing someone else's pain was not one she'd ever get used to. Swallowing hard, Zoey quickly stepped out of line and went to greet him. She would not hide from him; she had nothing to be ashamed of.

"Hey there," Zoey said. "How are you?"

"Is *that* the guy you were talking about? The Italian dude?" Scott nudged his chin to where Archer stood at the front of the ticket line, paying for their tickets.

"Yes, he's the one. I'm sorry." Then she reconsidered. "You know what? I take that back. I'm *not* sorry."

He scowled. "You could have been honest with me and told me I didn't stand a chance."

"What are you talking about? I *was* honest with you!"

He threw his palms up. "Zoey, you didn't even give us a chance! One month, that's all I got."

Zoey sighed. "One month, and all you talked about was my father."

"That's not how I remember it. Sure, of course, I love football as much as the next Texan. But that doesn't have anything to do with how I felt about *you*."

"Scott, you barely took the time to get to know me.

You might not have noticed, but I don't really care about football."

"How can you not care about *football*?" Scott looked horrified.

"Well, there you have it. I love my father, not football," Zoey said, thinking that she couldn't believe how quickly this conversation had turned to the subject.

"Your father is the greatest of all time! You should be proud."

Zoey straightened. "Well, I am proud of him."

In the next moment, Archer joined them, and when he did, he literally placed his body between Zoey and Scott, forcing Scott to take a step back.

"Everything okay here?" he growled, the tone in his voice announcing that it had better be.

Obviously, he recognized Scott. The look Archer gave him said he should consider running, but Scott stood his ground and didn't move.

"It's fine." Scott shrugged. "Zoey and I were just talking. We used to date until you came along."

"We stopped dating well before that," Zoey interrupted.

"Whatever. Just warning you, dude, don't get too attached to her. Her reputation precedes her. She's had a lot of boyfriends and nobody stuck. I wouldn't want you to get your feelings hurt when she dumps you like yesterday's trash."

Zoey felt her eyes welling up with tears and she fought for control of her lower lip, which always trembled when she was about to cry. Scott had never been mean to her. It wasn't fair of him to describe her failed love life to her current boyfriend, and it also wasn't all true. She was kind to everyone, and look where that had gotten her. She felt her temper simmering.

Archer got right in Scott's face. "Oh, I'm not worried. Guess what? It's not Zoey's job to protect my feelings, no more than it's her job to worry about yours. You got dumped? Too bad. It happens to us all, and it's not her fault if she doesn't want to be with you anymore. She doesn't owe you a thing, not even the kindness I've personally seen her give you. You didn't deserve it."

"But—"

"Here's what you're going to do," Archer said, putting his hand on Scott's shoulder. "You're going to turn around and walk away from Zoey right now."

"Fine!" Scott shook off Archer's arm. "Good riddance."

Zoey could feel her entire body quaking. She wasn't cut out for this. If only everyone in the world could have what they wanted and be happy and content. She wished that even for people she didn't like, because *everyone* deserved to be loved, if nothing else. Someday, Scott would find someone, when he decided to put his partner first.

Archer tipped her chin and she met his gaze. "Tell me you're okay."

"Yes." She wiped away a tear. "I'm good."

"You are not responsible for his feelings, okay?"

She knew that all too well, but life was hard sometimes with a big heart. She nodded. "I know. It's just a shame."

"Yeah, I agree. It's a shame he's a big baby." Archer reached for her hand and brought it to his lips to kiss it. "But I have to admit, losing you *could* make a grown man cry."

Zoey couldn't help but smile at that. He sounded like he meant it, like maybe this thing between them might be able to withstand his trip to Asia. It was all she could hope for at this point, because one way or another, he would be leaving. And though he'd had an offer to stay in Texas, she respected him more for refusing it.

Archer tugged Zoey along, heading toward the activities and rides. "And now I see what you mean. You could definitely take him. Kind of scrawny, isn't he?"

"I tried to tell you!"

"Yes, you did."

She laughed all the way to the hayride.

Prior to this day, Archer would have never considered a visit to the pumpkin patch. But that was what Zoey had done to him. He had the best time in years, riding in the back of a flatbed truck filled with hay and other passengers, as it took them from one end of the park to the other. They stopped to eat sweet and salty kettle corn, huge turkey drumsticks and cotton candy. Zoey refused to go in the haunted house, explaining that she didn't like to be scared—apparently, she was far more of a harvest girl than a fan of Halloween. But they wound up going through the corn maze twice, Archer stealing plenty of kisses every chance he got. They took photos with the fun cutouts of scarecrows and sat on the "king" and "queen" thrones in front of a pile of real pumpkins approximately forty feet high. He banked enough memories of them to take him through the rest of his life.

They ran into many of the folks Zoey knew from town, and even some Archer had met. He waved to Max and his wife, Ava, who was carrying their little one in a sling on her chest. Adam and his wife Stacy were there with their two little girls, as were Cole and Valerie, with their children. It seemed as if every two feet, Zoey would bump into someone she knew, as though the whole town had come out tonight.

"You know everyone in Charming, don't you?" Archer said.

"Because I'm a business owner, I get out there and do community events and try to connect. Twyla was a big help when I first started out. Her family has been doing it for decades."

"Good, then I won't need to worry about you being lonely while I'm gone." Archer pulled her off to the side for some privacy.

"There's plenty to keep me busy, that's true."

She wasn't getting the message. He didn't want to hold her back. Love was so important to Zoey that if she happened to find it with someone else while he was absent, he'd have to let her go. He loved her that much. Yeah, he'd hate it if she found someone else. He'd hate it so much he wouldn't be coming back to Charming to witness it in person. Heartsick didn't begin to describe how he'd feel, but he'd be a man and let Zoey choose who she wanted to be with. He'd be a hypocrite otherwise, given the advice he'd just given Scott. She didn't owe him anything, either.

"What I mean is that if you want to see other people while I'm gone, I will understand. I'm going to be so far away that I can't compete."

"You don't have to compete—"

"That's what you say now, but if you meet someone, if something changes, know that you don't owe me anything. What I said to Scott holds true for me, too. You're not responsible for *my* happiness, either."

"I know, but I—"

"You want everyone to get what they want, but life doesn't work that way. Whatever happens, I'll be okay."

"I want you to be okay," Zoey said, her fingers in his hair, tugging him close, kissing him. "But we just got started."

For the next two days, they rarely left each other's company. Archer packed and made plans, gave up his lease and put things in storage. But every other spare second and night was for Zoey. He drank up her sweetness and kindness, wondering why he couldn't have somehow met her sooner. Wishing for once that he hadn't been trusted with a first-rate assignment and been sidelined for longer. But Ian had been impressed with the way Archer managed to deal with such a low-key assignment without once complaining. If he only knew.

He hadn't been bored since the moment he met Zoey and she tried to sell him some costume jewelry for his nonexistent girlfriend.

On their last night, they were lying outside under the stars in the same sleeping bag, her head on his chest. He'd decided not to tell her that he loved her, not to put that burden on her, but it didn't mean he couldn't tell her how much she meant to him.

"After I lost my foot, I thought I'd never be normal again," Archer said, studying the shimmering sky before him. "I didn't think I'd ever argue with a woman again, much less be comfortable being intimate. But you healed me. The doctors healed me physically but you healed my soul."

He caught a tear in her eye with his thumb and wasn't surprised to see that she was crying.

"I used to think being a soft touch was a bad thing," he said. "That being kind was a weakness. But you taught me otherwise. There's strength in kindness, too, and you have so much of that, more than anyone I've ever met."

"And I was stuck on certain beliefs about love, and you taught me how to let go of traditions that weren't serving me anymore."

"You were still grieving. It's okay to grieve as long as

it takes, even if it's forever. Do you want to know something? My therapist suggested I have a mock funeral for my *lost foot*."

"No way."

"She said it would be symbolic. A way to say goodbye. You did that instinctively, keeping traditions alive."

"Did you have a little ceremony?"

He chuckled. "No. But I did write a note. Then I tore it up. It felt ridiculous, and maybe that was the point. I have more to offer... I'm sure as hell a lot more than just a foot."

"Or a footnote for anyone," Zoey joked. "You're more like a foreword, or the acknowledgments."

He smiled back and tugged her close. "Who knows? Could be I'm the epilogue."

"Don't kid yourself," Zoey said. "You're the whole book."

Chapter Thirty-Two

On a warm September morning, Zoey and Archer parted as friends when she tearfully said goodbye to him at the Houston airport. He texted her to let her know he'd arrived safely in China after an exhausting twenty-two-hour flight and had been set up in a hotel room suite with the rest of the team. She would have liked to text daily, but Archer told her he would be on the move and unavailable a lot of the time. Then there was the twelve-hour time difference. Because of that, they'd decided not to put pressure on each other. They weren't technically in a relationship, because how could they be? Maybe if she'd told him she loved him it would be a different story.

Maybe.

A week later, on Saturday night, Zoey was sitting on the couch watching *Frasier* and eating popcorn when Archer phoned.

"Hey," Archer said. "It's me. I have a moment. We're just waiting outside the embassy to go to our next location."

"Are you having fun?"

"What? I didn't hear that."

"I asked if you're having fun, which is stupid because you're working. You shouldn't be having fun."

On the other hand, they'd certainly had fun.

"It's been interesting. Busy all the time. Mostly, I've missed you. Are you seeing anyone?"

Excuse me? It had been a week!

"Why? Are you?"

"No." He laughed. "No time for that."

Thank God for small favors. Maybe she should enlighten him as to why she wasn't seeing anyone else. She happened to be in love with him, and she needed to tell him that. He might not like it; he might be uncomfortable with the weight of expectations, but screw it. She had to stop worrying so much about other people's feelings. She had to stop thinking they were her responsibility. Archer had told her point blank that she wasn't in charge of his feelings, one way or the other.

Now was the time.

"Archer, listen. There's something I have to tell you and it's important. I love you. What I mean is I'm in love with you. I'm sorry I didn't tell you before, but it all happened so fast. The truth is I'm not going to see anyone else and I don't want you to see anyone else, either." She took a deep breath. "There, I've said it! I don't care if it sounds needy or jealous or possessive. It's the truth. I love you and I don't want anyone else but you. I'll wait. It's all good."

"Hello? *Hello?* Zoey? Are you there? Damn. Zoey, I'm going to have to let you go. I can't hear you. Good night, babe. I'll try calling again."

Oh. My. God. She had just bared her soul and he hadn't even heard her! Or, he had heard her loud and clear and was just trying to let her off the hook. He wasn't ready to jump feetfirst into love after a few dates.

Zoey immediately FaceTimed Twyla. "Archer just phoned from Asia, and I told him I love him!"

Twyla smiled into the camera. She knew how significant this was for Zoey.

"That's amazing, and what did he say to that?"

"Nothing. If he's to be believed, we had a *bad connection* and he didn't hear what I said." Zoey lowered her face to indicate how downtrodden she felt.

"Maybe you really did have a bad connection," Twyla, the voice of reason, said.

"Does this ever get any easier?"

"Telling the man you love that you love him? Why, yes, especially when you can do it *in person*. It's far easier then."

Zoey groaned. She got the message. She should have waited, but the irony of all ironies wasn't lost on her. The lover of love, the champion of *amour*, the giver of hugs, had never uttered those three little words to a man before. And it was about time. The minute he got back, the second she laid eyes on him, she was going to tell him. No more hiding behind the safety of a screen or the phone to reveal her feelings.

Archer called her about once a week after that, rain or shine. It had been mostly rain lately, as September turned into October. Zoey appreciated it, but she'd probably never look at a one-strike fire log in the same way again; she wanted a raging wood fire like the one Archer had made. On the phone, they didn't chat about much, keeping it light, but Archer indicated that there were some political tensions in the city, nothing to worry about. Still, Zoey did watch the news more than she usually did. Tensions were escalating in the region and the press secretary announced a travel restriction.

One afternoon, when Archer had been officially gone for thirty days, the news reported that the Chinese ambassador and his staff had been removed from the embassy and were headed out of the country for safety reasons. Zoey saw the back of Archer's head as he quickly moved through an airport with an entire crew of people, the ambassador in front. Zoey went to work the next day anyway, vowing to stay away from the news. Following that, Archer was radio silent, even after she sent him a flurry of text messages.

Tee came into the boutique later that day, dressed in slacks, a white button-down shirt and tie. He looked like an Archer wannabe.

Zoey burst into tears. Tee might be dressed like Archer, but he didn't do it for her in the slightest. Archer had those amber eyes that were so expressive and tender, and he had a way of listening to her that made her feel like he valued everything she said. Nobody was ever going to be able to take his place.

"Oh, hey, hey." Tee awkwardly held his hands up like this was a holdup and he'd give her everything he had if she would only stop crying. "Please don't cry. What happened?"

Debbie from the Salty Dog had been shopping for a holiday dress, and Mrs. Finch for something she could send Ruby for Christmas. They both surrounded her within seconds, offering tissues and hugs.

"What did you *do* to her?" Debbie asked Tee.

"Nothing!"

Zoey shook her head. "He just reminded me of Archer."

Tee straightened. "Thanks, dude."

Zoey looked up. "Archer is…he might be in trouble."

"Oh, no, honey," Debbie said. "What is it?"

"Don't you watch the news?"

They both shook their heads vehemently. "Oh, heavens, no."

"Well, I'm going to stop, too. But there was some problem at the embassy in Asia and they had the military out in force. They sent the ambassador home. The one Archer was working with."

"Great, honey! Doesn't that mean he's coming home?" Debbie said. "Nothing to worry about then."

"That's right," Mrs. Finch said, patting Zoey's back. "Why, I bet he'll be home lickety-split. Wait and see!"

No talk of how difficult it might be to get out of an airport with violence or dissension. These ladies didn't watch the news and could afford to be positive.

"Did I *really* remind you of Archer?" Tee asked, head cocked, wide grin on his face.

Both ladies gave Tee such a glare that he slowly backed out of the store with his palms in the air. Eventually, after more uplifting talk from the two women, who focused on the positive, Zoey felt a bit better. But the entire ordeal made her realize the awful feeling of worrying that someone you loved could be in real danger. It must have been so difficult for her poor father, worrying about Zoey being so far away, where he couldn't protect her. Love was a funny thing. When you truly loved someone, you didn't want to let them go. But the catch-22 was that you couldn't really love someone *without* letting them go. Because love wasn't possession or fear or control. Love was having confidence and faith.

Zoey glanced at her phone, still seeing no reply from Archer. It was okay. She pictured him in his happy place, under the stars with her, as she went about closing up the shop. She emptied the till, swept the floors and rolled down the blinds. She said good night to Ophelia. Tonight, she'd go home and binge-watch *Frasier* until she laughed so hard she cried. Of course, she'd try not to watch the news, but no guarantees there.

Zoey heard a rap on her shop door and glanced at the

time. It was 9:00 p.m., way past her closing. She peeked through the blinds and there he was, looking worn and exhausted. But he was alive and in one piece.

"Archer."

She rolled up the blinds and hauled open the door, tugging him inside.

"I saw the news! Are you okay?"

He was actually disheveled, his tie loosened, hair mussed, his shirt half untucked at the waist. She'd never seen him like this.

For several seconds, he didn't say anything, just tugged her into his arms and held her tight, his face buried in her neck.

"I came straight from the airport. Actually, I had them drop me off. I'm home," he said. "That's all that matters now."

"Did everyone get back okay?"

"Yes," Archer said. "We made sure of it. It wasn't easy."

"I missed you so much," Zoey said. "I have something to say to you."

"Let me go first," Archer said.

"O-kay but mine really can't wait."

"Neither can mine."

Archer dropped to one knee. "Maybe you think this is too soon, but—"

"No, I don't think it's too soon!"

"Facing life or death has a way of clarifying your priorities. I could take a lot of time to get to the same place, or I could just do what I know is right and cut to the chase. I've known since the moment I laid eyes on you that you would be everything to me, and I love you, and I'm *in love* with you. I never want to be apart again. Zoey, would you marry me?"

"I was going to tell you that I love you!" Zoey said, pulling him up off his bended knee. "That was *my* big news."

"So, is that a yes?" He grinned.

"Yes, yes!" Zoey jumped into his arms.

"Hang on," Archer said, taking her hand and leading her to the jewelry counter. "We need something."

"Aw. This is where we first met," Zoey said, leaning her head on his shoulder.

"Yes, that time I was speechless. I want you to know I've never been speechless—before, or since then." Rummaging through the jewelry, he pulled out the sapphire ring that sparkled with color. It was the same one she'd shown him the night they met.

Zoey held out her finger and he slipped it on. "I've always liked that one. It's gorgeous."

"I will replace it with something real," Archer said, lifting her hand to brush a kiss across the knuckles. "Whatever you want."

She looked down at her finger, then at him, her dark eyes shimmering.

"Well, that's what I like to hear, because what I want is *you*."

Epilogue

One month later

If you would have told Archer Rossi last month that he'd be getting married next September, he would have laughed in your face. Instead, he was attending the wedding of Patch Lambert and taking notes. This was also an autumn wedding, and Zoey's one sticking point for the wedding had been that it take place in the fall. *Shocker!* He reserved the right to veto pumpkins, but had already agreed to a pumpkin spice latte fountain.

"Do you think a seven-piece orchestra is necessary?" Archer asked, eyeing the musicians tuning their instruments.

She shook her head. "Good grief, no."

Patch and Robin's wedding was held two months after they'd announced their engagement to Zoey, at her father's impressive estate outside of Amarillo. Archer and Zoey's wedding, on the other hand, would require quite a bit more planning, *and* a church. Archer's family was so excited to hear their son was getting married that they'd arranged to spend Christmas in Texas and meet his bride-to-be. They claimed to already be able to tell, from speaking to him over the phone, that Zoey had changed him. He sounded calmer, his mother claimed, more centered. Focused. Maybe that was true, but it wasn't all Zoey's doing.

After Archer's injury, he'd wanted to believe that nothing would change. He still wanted an adrenaline-filled lifestyle and the career to match it. Deep pride in his ability to protect and defend others fueled his decision. His natural-born competitiveness did the rest. But then he once again found himself thousands of miles away from home, facing a crisis, and when he'd come out on the other side of it, he was changed. Just because he *could* do something didn't mean he had to. He was a different man than he'd been before the accident, and he could make different choices. It did not make him any less of a man to want to be on the sidelines for once.

When he returned to the agency, he had a long talk with Ian about a desk job. At one time in his life, Archer would have called this decision a failure, but now he saw the opportunity within his reach. He could have a life here with Zoey, and he could still do the work he enjoyed, only on a different level. The timing was perfect, because when an old friend asked for his help, Ian had found himself roped into a special project that took him out in the field, unexpectedly. Now Archer was running the cybersecurity department for Texas EP and enjoying it more than he'd ever thought possible.

He still drove Zoey to work each day, but now he dropped her off and then drove on to Houston, where he currently worked banker's hours. Life was good, and best of all, he was in love. The object of his devotion stared at him now, smiling from under lowered lashes.

"Are we going to dance?"

"We've been practicing for weeks. Of course we are." He held out his arm and led her onto the dance floor.

The seven-piece orchestra played "It's a Beautiful Day." While a celebrity crooner sang. Apparently, Robin was a big fan.

"Who are we getting to sing at our wedding?" Archer joked while he spun Zoey.

He was still getting used to occasionally brushing elbows with actual celebrities. It had started with the job but had worked its way into his life.

"We stand a good chance of an even bigger celebrity, especially if Daddy finds a way to praise the Chiefs this year. I have high hopes."

"And to think his criticism was indirectly the reason we met. It would be full circle."

"Would it be okay if I cut in?"

They were interrupted by Robin. She wore the dress she'd bought from Zoey's boutique, and the best thing about it in Archer's opinion was that there was no train. Zoey nodded, smiled and stepped aside. Her father found her momentarily and spun her away.

"I just wanted to personally say thank you," Robin said. "It's because of you that Zoey accepted me in her father's life as quickly as she did."

"You would have been fine without my help. Zoey has a big heart and she secretly wants everybody to be happy and find love. You'll find out. She would have reached that point with you eventually."

"I'm glad love finally happened for her. Some of us are lucky in love twice, but her father tells me she's never been ready to settle down with anyone before you."

"I'm the lucky one," Archer admitted, stealing a glance at Zoey, who'd thrown her head back to laugh at something her father said. "Maybe I arrived in the nick of time."

The song ended and they switched partners again.

"You're back," Archer said. "I missed you."

Zoey wound her arms around his neck. "I couldn't be gone too long, or you might forget me."

"Forget you? Not a chance, babe. Not a chance."

* * * * *

Get up to 4 Free Books!

We'll send you 2 free books from each series you try
PLUS a free Mystery Gift.

Both the **Harlequin® Special Edition** and **Harlequin® Heartwarming™** series feature compelling novels filled with stories of love and strength where the bonds of friendship, family and community unite.

YES! Please send me 2 FREE novels from the Harlequin Special Edition or Harlequin Heartwarming series and my FREE Gift (gift is worth about $10 retail). I may cancel anytime by emailing ReaderServiceInfo@Harlequin.com or by calling 1-800-873-8635.If I don't cancel, I will receive 6 brand-new Harlequin Special Edition books every month and be billed just $6.39 each in the U.S. or $7.19 each in Canada, or 4 brand-new Harlequin Heartwarming Larger-Print books every month and be billed just $7.19 each in the U.S. or $7.99 each in Canada, a savings of 20% off the cover price. It's quite a bargain! Shipping and handling is just 75¢ per book in the U.S. and $1.75 per book in Canada.* I understand that accepting the free books and gift places me under no obligation to buy anything—they are mine to keep for free no matter what I decide.

Choose one: ☐ **Harlequin Special Edition** (235/335 BPA G3CD) ☐ **Harlequin Heartwarming Larger-Print** (161/361 BPA G3CD) ☐ **Or Try Both!** (235/335 & 161/361 BPA G3CE)

Name (please print)

Address Apt. #

City State/Province Zip/Postal Code

Email: Please check this box ☐ if you would like to receive newsletters and promotional emails from Harlequin Enterprises ULC and its affiliates. You can unsubscribe anytime.

Mail to the **Harlequin Reader Service:**
IN U.S.A.: P.O. Box 1341, Buffalo, NY 14240-8531
IN CANADA: P.O. Box 603, Fort Erie, Ontario L2A 5X3

Want to explore our other series or interested in ebooks? Visit www.ReaderService.com or call 1-800-873-8635.

*Terms and prices subject to change without notice. Prices do not include sales taxes, which will be charged (if applicable) based on your state or country of residence. Canadian residents will be charged applicable taxes. Offer not valid in Quebec. This offer is limited to one order per household. Books received may not be as shown. Not valid for current subscribers to the Harlequin Special Edition or Harlequin Heartwarming series. All orders subject to approval. Credit or debit balances in a customer's account(s) may be offset by any other outstanding balance owed by or to the customer. Please allow 4 to 6 weeks for delivery. Offer available while quantities last.

Your Privacy — Your information is being collected by Harlequin Enterprises ULC, operating as Harlequin Reader Service. For a complete summary of the information we collect, how we use this information and to whom it is disclosed, please visit our privacy notice located at https://corporate.harlequin.com/privacy-notice. Notice to California Residents—Under California law, you have specific rights to control and access your data. For more information on these rights and how to exercise them, visit https://corporate.harlequin.com/california-privacy. For additional information for residents of other U.S. states that provide their residents with certain rights with respect to personal data, visit https://corporate.harlequin.com/other-state-residents-privacy-rights.

HSEHW2603